D0932975

WINGS
in the
SNOW

Also by Jim Oliver
available from Alyson

CLOSING DISTANCE

WINGS
in the
SNOW

BY JIM OLIVER

alyson
books

LOS ANGELES • NEW YORK

MANUFACTURED IN THE UNITED STATES OF AMERICA.
PRINTED ON ACID-FREE PAPER.

THIS TRADE PAPERBACK ORIGINAL IS PUBLISHED BY ALYSON PUBLICATIONS INC.,
P.O. BOX 4371, LOS ANGELES, CALIFORNIA 90078-4371.
DISTRIBUTION IN THE UNITED KINGDOM BY TURNAROUND PUBLISHER SERVICES LTD.,
UNIT 3 OLYMPIA TRADING ESTATE, COBURG ROAD, WOOD GREEN,
LONDON N22 6TZ ENGLAND.

FIRST EDITION: OCTOBER 1998

02 01 00 99 98   10 9 8 7 6 5 4 3 2 1

ISBN 1-55583-462-0

LIBRARY OF CONGRESS CATALOGING-IN-PUBLICATION DATA
    OLIVER, JIM, 1940–
        WINGS IN THE SNOW / BY JIM OLIVER. — 1ST ED.
        ISBN 1-55583-462-0
        I. TITLE.
    PS3565.L475W5 1998
    813'.54—DC21   98-7837 CIP

COVER PHOTOGRAPH BY GREGORY ZABILSKI.

To Klébert, for the best years

Chapter 1

He stood in sweat pants and sneakers at an open drawer of the
bureau in the dim dawn light feeling among balled socks and sex
toys for his wallet. Sure he had placed the billfold there, impatient, he pushed sock balls into a pile on one side, then on the
other. About to turn on a lamp, he saw the wallet on the bureau
top among the framed photographs.

At the center of the arrangement of photos was a black and
white print framed in silver. He looked at himself standing in a
row with his sisters and his father two years before. He and his
father wore tuxedos; his two sisters wore long, dark dresses. They
were all the same height. They had the same pale skin, the same
spaded noses, the same dimples. His father was heavy-set, blocky.
His hair was white. He and his sisters were slender, black-haired,
long of neck as was their mother. Theo stood at one end of the
line, his father at the other. Thalia was next to him, then Cassie,
then his father. It was the occasion of the 30th wedding anniver-
sary of his father's second marriage. Everyone except for Cassie
looked happy; her smile was forced. Rosy was not in the picture.
Sam was not in the picture. Bradley was not in the picture. It was
a photograph of the nuclear family. The only one Theo had.

He slipped the wallet into his gym bag. He turned to the bed.
He watched for a moment the blanket-covered form, watched
the slow rise and fall of breathing. This bedroom, where little but

sleep occurred, was still and silent. He squeezed a foot. There was no response. "Bye," he said. He left.

At his gym, he rowed before a mirror. His face was impassive. The muscles in his arms and legs defined themselves with his pulls and releases. His jet hair, cut longish, blew back in the breeze of the machine's fan wheel. The bandanna around his forehead was sweated through.

Theo saw that he was losing muscle tone under his armpits. Had he passed the age when he could erase the slight sag there? Row longer? Learn to lift weights specific to the effects of gravity just there? The rest looked good for a man who had fallen, without noticing, into middle age. He sighed. He closed his eyes. He rowed.

"Good morning, doctor." Spandex body suit. A former patient. Some orbital repair. Theo did not remember. Whatever the procedure was, her face was symmetrical, attractive. He nodded. He smiled into the mirror. He rowed.

"Dr. Tithonus? Are we having fun yet?" A fat heart surgeon.

"Grab a machine, Bob," Theo said. "It's better than sex."

The heart surgeon waved him off.

He rowed.

Vince, a trainer on the gym staff, settled his Lycra-covered behind onto the seat of the rowing machine beside Theo.

"Hey, doc."

"Hey, Vince."

Vince drew back the handle of his machine. He pushed buttons on its calculator. Vince had no sags where Theo's were. Vince was very packed together.

"How many calories you up to?" Vince asked, sliding back and forth, adjusting himself to the seat.

"A slice and a half of pizza."

"I love pizza," Vince said, beginning a slow row. "I could eat pizza for breakfast…I like broccoli the best."

"Me too," Theo said, though he did not. He hoped this would be a short conversation.

"Say, doc. You're a plastic surgeon, aren't you?"

"I do reconstructive work mostly," Theo said.

"Reconstructive. Like you fix things?"

"Yeah. You could say that," Theo said, glancing over at Vince then back to the mirror.

Vince looked up and down the floor of the gym. "I have a little problem I was wondering if I could ask you about?"

Theo did not like to discuss his work outside its context. He did not like to talk at all during his workouts.

"What?"

"Actually, it's not my problem. Well, it sort of is."

Theo wondered what this man could possibly want fixed.

"It's my wife. I mean, my girlfriend. My fiancée, actually." He glanced side to side again.

"Congratulations. When are you getting married?"

"Well, see, that's the whole thing. It depends."

Vince adjusted his rowing to match Theo's. They moved in tandem.

Vince tilted his head toward Theo. His voice lowered. "See…um…That's the problem."

"What is?"

"She has two kids."

"You don't like kids?"

"No. No…I like 'em. They're great kids. We get along terrific. No problems…It's Maureen."

"Maureen."

"Right."

"You don't love Maureen?"

"No. No. I *do*," Vince replied through the mirror. "She's terrific. She loves my ass. She's the nicest lady I ever met."

"That's wonderful, Vince," Theo said. He looked at the calorie counter. Almost two slices of plain.

Vince rowed. He seemed very ill at ease. Theo wanted to finish this conversation within 20 calories. Forty strokes. A minute and a half, then a quick drink of water, then climb on the Stair-Master machine.

"So. Why wouldn't you marry Maureen?"

"Oh, I would, " Vince said quickly. "She's the one for me. I don't even look at other women anymore…Well, I look at 'em. You know. Around here you can't not look at 'em. Jesus. I mean, this place is a candy store, if you know what I mean."

"Vince?"

"Yeah, doc?"

"Then…" Theo looked at himself in the mirror, at the slightly loose flesh under the armpits of his tank top. Vince rowed. "Then, what's the problem, do you think?"

Vince seemed relieved. He rowed. He glanced right and left. He tipped his head toward Theo and said into the mirror, his voice barely audible above the whir of the fan wheels, "She's not…um, tight, doc."

He should have known. Should have guessed where this was going. It was always the face, or it was always the genitals. "Tight?" Theo repeated.

"Right. Her, uh, you know…Having two kids and all? She's very…um…There's not enough…You know?"

"Right."

"You do that? Can you reconstruct that?"

"No," Theo said. Vince seemed pained. "Have you talked with Maureen about this?"

"No! Jesus."

Two slices.

"You were thinking maybe you could drug her or something?

Take her in for a procedure and take her back, and she'd wake up tight?...You have to have a talk with her, Vince. It's her body."

"But can it be done? Can you tighten her?"

"Sure. It's very common." Theo looked over at the trainer. "But I don't do it."

Vince was deflated. "Well, do you think *you* could just talk to her about it? I mean, Maureen'd like you. You're easy to talk to and all."

"Vince. I don't even know Maureen. How could I tell her she's not tight? You have to talk with her."

"I don't know."

Theo stopped rowing. He placed his hand grips into their holder. He slid back and forth on his rowing seat.

Vince stopped rowing. He looked down at the carpeting.

Theo wiped sweat from his face. "I have a friend. Her name is Dr. Zack. I'll leave her number down at the desk for you."

"A woman? I don't think I can talk to a woman doctor about this."

"No. You have a talk with Maureen first. Then Maureen can talk with Dr. Zack if she wants to...What if she doesn't want to have this procedure? Would you still marry her?"

"I don't know, doc. It's very..." Vince spread his palms apart. "Loose."

"Right."

On the StairMaster, he paged through *Scientific American*. He began an article regarding the migratory instincts of sea turtles and how it is thought that they know where they are in their vast seas of possibilities. He closed the magazine. He considered the building up and the planing away of bone. He created complicated physical anomalies and attempted to resolve them. He earned 200 calories.

He was grateful that the steam room was empty, that he did not need to make conversation. He paced in the hot, saturated air to cool down. He reviewed the tasks of his day as the day had been arranged for him by his office staff, and by the staff at the hospital.

Patients appeared to him. He used his skills and knowledge to correct, to ameliorate at the least. He did not consider that his work was work. Everything came to him: the patients, the complications he hoped they would present, the solutions he offered based upon his accumulated knowledge, the money he could no longer spend enough of—all of that came to him. If he were to think about what motivated him, Theo would say that he searched for that which was truly puzzling. That he sought to solve the surgically insolvable.

When his pulse rate dropped to 65 and his shirt and shorts were wet, he went to the showers.

The locker room was quiet at this early hour. He dressed slowly and with care. His clothing came from the smaller men's stores on Walnut and Locust and Sansom Streets. He was good at mixing and matching. When he shopped, his memory of the colors stored at home in his closets and drawers was unerring.

He stood at the sink mirrors. He adjusted his tie. He ran the fingers of both hands through his hair.

In the mirror, behind him, Dr. Barthe shuffled past. He was of his father's vintage and a man whose talents Theo once respected deeply. Dr. Barthe wore a bathing suit, and the effects of his stroke were apparent. His left arm and wrist were curled. His towel was draped in the crook of his bent arm. His left foot turned in as he led with it. "Theo. Good morning. You finished?"

"Morning, Walter. Yes. You?"

"Christ, no. I wish that I were."

"Keep doing the pool," Theo said into the mirror. "You're improving."

"Thank you, Theo," Dr. Barthe replied, as if he appreciated the observation but did not believe it. He shuffled on toward the door to the swimming pool.

Theo left the gym at 7:17, two minutes behind his schedule.

In the parking garage, he stowed his gym and suit bags in the trunk of his car. He removed a briefcase. He stepped down into his forest-green Jaguar sedan, onto the cold, buff leather seat. He closed the door with a reassuring click. The engine started instantly. The automobile purred onto the ramp and down the spiral exit, tires squealing in the corkscrew turns.

On this 4th day of March, Dr. Theo Tithonus, 46, and his associate, Dr. Susan Zack, 44, had eight surgical patients of their own at the Hospital of the University of Pennsylvania and five cases on which they were consulting. Although they did heads and necks mostly, they were also sought out for their shared expertise in the restoration of burned flesh, for his particular skill with crushed bone, and for her skill in the reconstruction of hands.

By agreement, he did early morning rounds, she afternoon admissions and evening rounds. Over the nine years of their association and practice, they had developed a style of communication which struck observers as intimate. They often touched. They smiled more frequently at each other than seemed appropriate. They looked into each other's eyes when they conversed. It was assumed, and discussed behind their backs, that they slept together. Dr. Tithonus and Dr. Zack fueled these suppositions by arriving together at medical socials and leaving together, usually before anyone else, in one or the other of their cars. If it were known that Dr. Tithonus was the father of Dr. Zack's five-year-old daughter, there would be further speculation.

Theo addressed patients and staff by their first names whenever he thought he could get away with it and encouraged others to reciprocate. Many called him "Dr. Tithonus" in the presence of patients and of other doctors, "Theo" in the halls. Some, confused, called him "doctor" or "Excuse me?" Arguments developed out of his hearing between younger and older staff over the professionalism of his casual manner. He was held in high regard among nurses. His orders were clear, sharp only in crisis. He asked their opinions. Many nurses found him sitting at bedsides, his arm through the bed rails or over the pads, his hand resting on a hand, on a sweat-slicked forehead, cupping a shoulder, watching.

Theo liked to begin his rounds with the most serious cases and finish with patients at or near the end of their hospitalizations. He and Susan had three patients in Surgical Intensive Care. He sat at the nursing station facing the glassed rooms of these patients. He read the first of their records. He always started at the beginning, skimming to refresh his memory. As he neared present time, he read all the words and the numbers.

The patient, a 17-year-old male, was catapulted head first through the windshield of his car. His right hip and his hands were burned when he landed on the flaming hood of the car. The patient writhed before him.

"Is he making any sense?" Theo asked Rebecca, the nurse assigned to the boy.

She leaned on her elbows at the counter next to him. "Yes. He wants to know if it was cut off."

"His nose?"

"His penis."

"Oh. Did you tell him?"

"Sure. He doesn't believe me."

"Did you show him?"

"Well, no. His eyes are swollen shut."

"How insightful of me," Theo said. The pun was lost on Rebecca. "Let's change his dressings," Theo suggested.

As he washed at the lavatory next to his patient's bed, Theo announced his name, that he was the doctor who did the repairs to his wounds, that it would be necessary to change his dressings. He asked Rebecca to remove the boy's arm restraints and began to cut away the wrappings which covered the boy's head. "Not bad," he said, examining the smashed and lacerated face. "Looking good. How do you feel, Tom? Talk to me."

The boy moved his gauze-mittened hands toward his head.

"Don't touch your face. I did some good work there; you don't want to mess it up. Talk to me, Tom. Tell me where you live," he said, peering closely at his stitch work.

The boy mumbled.

"Tell me again. You can talk. Where do you live?"

"N-co," the boy said.

"Wyncote. I know Wyncote. It's hard for you to talk because I've closed your jaw for a little while."

"Hur…"

"Yes. It hurts. You had a car accident, but you're going to be fine."

The boy's hands moved to his groin. Theo held his wrists.

"S'OK," Theo said. "You've got everything you came in with."

The boy shook his head back and forth. Theo told the boy to keep his hands at his sides. He asked Rebecca to raise the head of the bed.

"I'm going to show you that you're all right, Tom. I'm going to lift your eyelid. It'll hurt when I do that. Try to look quickly, OK?"

Theo pulled the hospital gown to one side, exposing the groin. In one move, he lifted the boy's head and pulled back the puffed flesh of one eyelid with a fingertip.

"Down. Down. Look down, Tom. See? You're all there. Nothing is missing. That's just a catheter, so you can pee easily."

He placed the boy's head back on the bed. Something like relief passed across the stitched and bloated face.

He examined the two other cases on the unit: a leg lengthening, an excised malignancy of the neck.

He worked his way back and forth on the fifth and sixth floors, finishing on the pediatric unit with a cranial reconstruction of which he was especially proud. He told the mother that her daughter was being released. He liked to tell people they could go home. It was to Theo the stuff of soap opera. He loved the gratitude of those released from the hospital.

He was at his practice by 9:30, 45 minutes before his first appointment.

He sat for a few minutes with his partner in her office. He reviewed for her his hospital rounds over their mugs of black coffee.

"You look tired," he told her.

"Theo," Susan said wearily. "I am a 44-year-old mother in a nonstop job. I was up with Natalia half the night."

"She sick?"

"Not now. But she was upchucking. For hours. No fever. Just nausea and throwing up until there wasn't anything left, and then she was fine. I kept her home from PlaySchool."

"How's da maid?"

"Da maid's OK. We've reached an accord. I stay out of her shit, and she stays out of mine. We're fine if we both stick to the rules. I think I like her. Natalia does. I hope she stays."

"Do you and Natalia need anything?"

Susan sighed. "A very long vacation."

"Take a few days off," he said. "I'll cover."

" 'A few days,' he says. And I suppose you'll do all my surgeries? You'll take over my classes?"

"You should give up teaching."

"I love teaching. That's my only recreation."

"You want some more money for Natalia?"

Susan rolled her eyes. "Theo. Thanks to you, she's probably the only five-year-old in town with TCDs...We made a mistake, you know. I made a mistake. We have to tell her."

"Tell her?"

"You know, tell her. I should have told her before when she asked me."

"What did she ask you?"

"Sunday she asked me if her daddy divorced her like Billy Bastian's daddy divorced him."

"What did you say?"

"As usual, I chickened out. I changed the subject. We have to tell her, Theo. Together."

"Maybe she won't ask again."

Susan stood. She sighed. "You know, you don't know shit about kids."

He sat at his desk. He dealt with his mail.

His secretary had arranged papers in piles according to their priority. The pile to the far left consisted of forms which required his signature. He began to sign these, tossing each of them into his "out" box. His secretary announced a call from his sister Cassie.

Cassie was fifty, the oldest sibling, the most clever with money. She managed Theo's investments. She charged him a stiff monthly fee.

"Good morning," he began, hoping she would tell him that he had made some profit.

"Theo, have you talked with Daddy?"

"Since when?"

"Since awhile ago."

"No."

"Something is wrong. He sounded very strange. He said Rosy wouldn't let him leave his room."

"Maybe he's been a bad boy."

"This is not funny, Theo."

"What did he say?"

"I told you what he said. He said Rosy won't let him leave his room. Then he said she might be listening on the downstairs phone. Then he hung up."

"Did you call back?"

"No. I called you to see if he called you."

"He didn't call me. Maybe he will. Probably his blood sugar's off. You know how he gets. Rosy knows how to manage that."

"I think you should call him. Then you call me back. Something is wrong, I know it."

"Cassie, you worry too much. Rosy would call me if something were wrong."

"I wouldn't trust her to call the plumber. Now, you call. Then you call me back."

"Cassie."

"Humor me."

"OK. I'll call."

"Then you call me back."

"And then I'll call you back."

"Call now."

"I hear you, Cassie."

"Well? Do it."

"Would you hang up?"

He placed the handset in its cradle. The phone rang.

"Your sister Thalia on four," his secretary said.

He frowned. He sighed. "Hi," he said a little wearily.

"Can you hear me?" Thalia asked. "I'm out in the hall. Classes are changing."

"I hear you."

"I just got the strangest call from Daddy. He told the office it was an emergency. They called me out of my class. He said Rosy was holding him prisoner in their room. He wanted me to come and get him out. It sort of frightened me, Theo."

He heard the raucous noises of junior high students. "Did you talk with Rosy?" he asked.

"I told Daddy to put her on the phone, and he said, 'Talk to her yourself. She's down there listening.' Then he hung up."

"I'll call. It's his insulin."

"Theo? The funny part was, when he hung up, I swear I heard someone else hang up."

"Oh, well," he said. His sisters were always ready to think the worst of their stepmother. "I'll call. You want me to call you back?"

"I better call you. But after 12. I have classes straight through. I have to go," she added and hung up.

In spite of his sisters' obsessive concern for their father, in spite of his sisters' irrational distrust of their father's wife, knowing that he must report back to his sisters or pay the piper, he dialed his father's house at Summit Lake. Rosy answered after three rings.

"Hey, Rosy," he said. "It's Theo."

"I'm not surprised." Rosy's voice was soft, high, girlish for a 56-year-old. "Your father's been on a tear this morning. He admitted he called the girls. Did he call you too? He didn't do his insulin this morning. Well, I did it. I had to practically sit on him, but I did it. That's the second time in a week. You want to talk to him, Theo? You better talk some sense into the old fart before I find him in a coma. Or dead. Here," she said. "Talk to your son, the doctor."

There was the sound of muffling and rustling. His father spoke: "Theo? That you, Theo?"

"Hi, Dad. How're you feeling?"

There was a pause. "I'm feeling fine. How're you feeling?"

"I'm fine, Dad. Listen. You have to have those insulin shots every morning. First thing. It's very, very important. You could die if you don't."

"Might as well," his father replied.

"Dad?"

More rustling. Rosy whispered.

"When are you coming up? You haven't been up. In a long…" his father's voice broke, "in a long…time."

"Soon, Dad. Soon."

His father made a choking sound.

"Dad, put Rosy on for a minute."

"Theo?"

"Rosy, is he all right?"

"No. But he will be in a couple of minutes when the insulin kicks in."

"When did he have his last physical?"

"Right after you were up here at Christmas. First week in January."

"Rosy, can you make sure he takes his insulin as soon as he gets up in the morning? And the finger pricks?"

"Who else…do you *think*…is going to do that?"

"OK. Put him back on a second. You'll call me if you have any problems?"

"Oh, *no*," she said, her voice oozing sarcasm. "I'd call *Cass*ie, first. Or bloody Shop 'n Bag."

"Theo?" his father said. "You coming up?"

"Soon, Dad."

"When?"

"I'll figure something out. I'll call you."

"Good-bye, Theo."

"You OK, Dad?"

His father hung up.

He dialed Cassie's office and was put on hold. While he waited, he played with his ballpoint pen, clicking the button on the top, snapping the tip back in with the clip—over and over.

"Well?" Cassie said after several minutes. "I suppose you're going to tell me I'm overreacting?"

"You're overreacting. He didn't take his insulin this morning. He was a little confused, is all. Rosy gave him his shot. He'll be fine."

"He is fine, or he will be fine?"

"He's fine."

"Something is wrong up there," Cassie said. "I know it."

"What's wrong is that he thinks he can get by without his insulin. Or he's forgetting to take it. Rosy will watch him."

"Something is going on. Mark my words."

"Cassie..."

Theo had office appointments on Wednesdays and on Thursday mornings. He operated other weekdays. On alternate Saturday mornings, after rounds, he handled pro bono cases. He gave two evenings each month to board meetings of a hospice for victims of AIDS, his only community project. On alternate Sundays he and Susan traded off hospital rounds so that one of them had an entire day off.

As he worked through the morning schedule, he forgot about his father and Rosy and his sisters. He examined patients with wide-ranging problems. He also saw patients who thought they had problems which would go away if Theo could change the way they looked. He had no interest in cosmetic work, but he listened. He examined the body parts of concern; he tried to reassure. He pointed out—sometimes using his own large, ridged nose as an example—that physical irregularities were often points of interest to others, points of attraction. Theo referred lifts and tucks to other doctors. He preferred the challenges of serious distortion and disfigurement, the correction of impaired function.

Shortly after 12, he took a call from Thalia. He reviewed for her the problem of the insulin. He soft-pedaled.

"Did you talk to Rosy or to Daddy?" she asked.

"Both."

"And did she sound strange?"

"Strange?"

"You know—evasive?"

"No. She sounded like Rosy."

"That's what I meant," Thalia said.

"And you are beginning to sound like Cassie," he said.

Silence.

"What do you expect from Rosy, Thalia? You and Cassie pick at her like leftover turkey. Hey," he said, pulling back a bit, "We ought to be grateful. Rosy's taking care of Dad. If he didn't have Rosy, he might have to live with one of us."

"I'd certainly have him," Rosy said indignantly. "So would Cassie. And you would too, for that matter, though in your case that wouldn't be so easy…I'd better go. I'm on second lunch—I hate lunch duty. It's like herding gerbils."

When the last of their patients had left, when the last nurse had closed and locked the outside door, at 6:15 they sat at the conference table in Susan's office, she with a glass of wine, Theo with a bottle of Bud Lite.

"What do you think?" Theo said.

"I am beyond thinking," Susan said. She loosened her chestnut hair from its chignon. She shook her head. She lay her cheek on the marble tabletop. "I feel like shit," she said, closing her eyes.

"How about if I go on call tonight instead of you?" Theo said.

"What do I have to give up?" she said to the surface of the table.

"Saturday night."

"No."

"Saturday nights are quiet," he offered.

She grunted. Her eyes remained closed. "I hate it when you lie to me, Theo…What's going on Saturday night that you want off?"

"We're having a dinner."

"Poor planning."

"Yes."

"Mrs. Guth will start bleeding again," Susan said sleepily. "Count on it. Or there'll be a train wreck during the meat course. No, not a train wreck. I'd have to go in myself if there was a train wreck."

"Do you have a date?"

Susan sat up. She nodded. She sipped her wine. "The cute oncologist from Wilmington I've been telling you about."

"The tall drink of water?"

"No. The one with the buns. He asked me out."

"You're overdue for a breast exam."

"God, yes," she said. "And a pelvic. I *need* a pelvic. Bad…I probably shouldn't go out, though. Natalia's been behaving like the Antichrist."

"Besides, you have to go out tomorrow night."

"What's tomorrow night?"

"The Micaris's? Cocktails? Dinner? The Four Seasons?"

Susan's head fell back onto the table. Her hair covered her face. A tuft over her mouth puffed as she spoke. "I can't. I just can't."

"You forgot?"

"I repressed."

"I'll be out of surgery by six. I'll pick you up."

The tuft of hair rose. "I can't."

"You must. I'll pick you up?"

"No."

"We have to, Susan. I'll pick you up?"

"You take a cab. I'll meet you there. I'll drive you home. Plan B."

"We did Plan B with the Micaris last year."

"They won't remember."

"He won't. She will."

"The Iron Cross, then."

"I liked the Iron Cross…It's been a while too. OK, we could. But I'll pick you up." He drained his beer. He cupped her hand on the tabletop and jiggled it. "I'm going home. You won't fall asleep?"

"I am asleep. The cleaning service will wake me."

"Do they come tonight?"

"They come every night. Lucky bastards."

Chapter 2

Cassandra Tithonus Bitler did not sit on nonprofit boards. She did not wear candy stripes. Her money did not improve the minds or the lots of the young or the disenfranchised. Her money had, until recently, grown upon itself.

In her library, a room with few books and many electronic components, Cassie ate her dinner of small, decorative roast beef sandwiches which Mrs. Wimmer left for her. She watched CNN, and, bored by news which was not financial, she considered the issue of her stepmother, Rosy, whom she disliked on the first day she met her.

Cassie did not believe that her father was deluded by his pancreas. She believed that her father was the victim of intentional abuse, both physical and mental, and that Rosy was the perpetrator.

She licked hot mustard from the lettuce at the edge of her sandwich. She inhaled and exhaled. The mustard burned in her adenoids. She would put that woman on the streets. She would see Rosy punished. She would see her penniless. Divine retribution. For having manipulated Cassie's father, for having connived her way through Cassie's father's grief into his bruised heart, Rosy would pay. A younger woman falling, as if it were natural, into a marriage with a man old enough to be her own father. How long, really, could it take before his body would begin to wear; how long before doors could be locked behind him?

At her silver chest, open on the buffet, she counted her service, counted the butter knives, the sweet little fish forks, the dear demitasse spoons, then on to the soups, the oversized dinner forks, the salads, occasionally holding one up to the light to assure herself that Mrs. Wimmer had indeed polished each piece as instructed, to assure herself that a slotted serving spoon or even an entire place setting had not made its way, inadvertently, into the pocket of a dress or into a purse. And you never knew who they brought in during the day. You never knew who wandered through your rooms while you sat with the president of the board of the Pugh Foundation itemizing the value of its trust at yesterday's market closing. That impressed them. That made them sit up and listen. You did not offer the value of the trust as of the 13th of last month. You did not give the value as of last week but the value as of hours ago. She loved to watch the narrowing of eyes above the slightest of smiles around the oval table as she ticked through the stocks and holdings, loved the small nods of approval and of satisfaction, the stirrings in high-backed chairs. When you pay for the best, you expect the best. And Bitler & Morant Associates delivered.

She did not know how she had survived that terrible time. She knew when Warren died the difference between common stock and preferred, and that, as they say, was that. She did not know when Warren died how much he owed on their house or that it was Chase Bank that got the payments. She was left no insurance to speak of—just enough to keep her half a year. Had he expected to live forever? Had he expected, overweight and underactive, to outlive *her*?

And they all say how easy it was in the '80s. How all you had to do was stand under the tree with a basket. Not under her tree. As others stood, she bent and snatched for the drops. She scurried for their leavings. And she learned every working detail of Warren's business, picked at every brain that would stand there long enough, learned at the knees of junior analysts—at the knees, even, of file clerks. "Who's that?" "Oh. That's just Mrs. Bitler." "Oh, that's just Warren's wife, poor thing."

She turned a fluted sugar spoon in the light.

Not any more. The poor thing just refused an offer from Princeton University (oh, graciously) to lecture its School of Business. The poor thing owned a firm which was sought out by some of the largest union investors in the nation. The poor thing burned her mortgage in that very fireplace three years after she buried her husband.

At the desk in her bedroom, in the light of a lamp by Waterford, she drew curly-ended delete lines through the names of certain stocks on the list of holdings of a minor client. The end of the curl led to penciled notations of stock abbreviations, her own recommendations. It was after midnight. She had been up since 6.

Her soft lead pencil made tiny dots on the cover sheet of the portfolio file as she tapped idly.

Her mother had not been dead ten months when Millie Tompkins was sucking up to Rosy like a pig to a trough. Cassie heard her mother's dearest friend—as the woman sat in her mother's house at her mother's kitchen table—saying: "Ah, honey. Alex *wants* ya ta move in. Why *don*cha? Wadya think, people'll talk? Let 'em!"

It would have been better if Rosy had just moved in. But no. She held out for the ring. Held out for the credentials. Made it ironclad legal. Rosy was no fool. She was a diabolical sneak. Well, she may have won the son over, but she would never take in the daughters.

They'd send Theo up there is what they would do. Let him see for himself what was going on up there. Let Daddy tell him face-to-face what was going on in that house.

Theo was always so gullible—sweet as the day was long but dumb, dumb, dumb when it came to reading people. And where did he find that friend he had living with him? They had heard "doctor," and all they saw was big bucks. Well, there would be no joint tenancy on Theo's house so long as she handled his affairs, and that, as they say, was that.

Cassie sighed. She returned to the file before her. She would finish this one and get some sleep and maybe be at the office by 7:15. Or 7:30 at the latest.

She noticed the client's address. A block from her own. On Spruce Street. Almost directly across the alley from her own house. She looked again at the name. Peter Parker. How curious. What a coincidence. Her bathroom window probably over-looked the windows of his own home. Did she know him, per-haps? Had they passed on the street?

She continued down his list of holdings. Mr. Parker should keep Symtac, at least until the new management showed its stuff. And Genticorp was still hot.

"Oh, *Lord!*" she said aloud, casting her eyes up to her ceiling and back to the master list. "Teshigahara!"

She had expressly forbid her staff to trade in Teshigahara. What idiot managed this account? She checked the outside of the folder: "Manager, Stuart Flowers."

Her own vice president?

She slapped the folder closed. She pounded it with her fist.

Chapter 3

T heo pulled in at the back of his house. They had two parking spaces, one behind the other next to a long, brick-paved patio. The Camry was not in the driveway.

"Home again. Home again. Jiggedy-jig," he said.

He removed his gym bag and suit bag from the trunk. He entered the house and dropped his bags on the laundry room floor. He climbed the stairs to the second level, feeling the weight of the day in his legs and in his neck and shoulders. He wanted to lie on the bed and be rubbed, close his eyes and feel knuckles and palms knead deep into his muscles, fall asleep that way. It would not happen.

His mail was stacked on the kitchen work island. There was a note on top. He read the message in the light of the stove hood:

Theo—
I'm on 3 to 11.
Dinner's in the fridge. Zap it.
XX OO

He sorted through the mail, through bills and periodicals. He left the mail in a pile. He loosened his tie. He stood for a moment, the palm of one hand on the island. Pleased to be alone, he listened to the silence of the house. Had he known and forgotten that today was 3 to 11? Knowing, would he have changed the schedule of his evening?

In their room he removed his tie and hung his jacket. He lined up his shoes in his closet in a row with other shoes. He removed his trousers and belt and hung them. He tossed his shirt and socks and underwear into the hamper. He pulled on a sweatshirt and jersey shorts. Lights had been left on for him. The bedroom was dusted, orderly. Their bed was without wrinkles.

At the open medicine cabinet he looked at the neat rows of brown, labeled bottles. He examined a few that did not have his own name pasted to them: Valium, Xanax; dated recently, prescribed by doctors whom he did not know. He brushed his teeth.

He sat alone in the dining room of the quiet house. No sounds of television. No music. He ate the well-rounded meal prepared for him. He read a medical journal, occasionally stopping to enjoy the food, occasionally forgetting the food for the reading, occasionally sitting, staring before him at the papered walls or at the étagère filled with fine china or at the polished tabletop that reflected—repeated deep in the wood, it seemed—the silver candelabra, the rim of his plate, even his pale forearm and the black hairs there.

He was startled by ringing, did not know where he was for some seconds as the telephone rang very near him.

"Dr. Tithonus, please," a man said.

"This is Dr. Tithonus."

"Good. You're there," the man said, low, secretive.

"Yes," Theo said, becoming alert in his den, in his enveloping leather chair. He sat straight. The journal slid to his side.

"Theo," the voice said, breathy.

"Yes?"

"I have to talk fast. I may have to hang up…"

"Dad?"

His father's mouth was very close to the handset. The sound was distorted.

"She is putting…away…the *car*," he said with great care. "The garage door is closing now. She will be coming back in a minute. Theo, you must come here. You must come here as quickly as you can. She locks me in our room. Sometimes she takes the telephone with her. She's coming in the front *door*." He whispered now. "She doesn't bring me my insulin, my medicines sometimes. I've got to go."

Before his father hung up, Theo heard a small click on the line followed by another, stronger one. He pressed the phone to his ear. The line was not dead. He held the phone for half a minute, directing his shallow breaths away from the speaker. He heard a third click. The line was dead.

He stood. He could feel his heartbeats. His armpits were slippery. His hands trembled.

It was 10 o'clock. He thought of calling his father's house. He did not. He thought of calling one, both of his sisters, and did not.

On the first floor he tossed soiled gym clothes into the tub of the washing machine. He gathered the gym bag and the suit bag and, on the way to the second floor, convinced himself that he was behaving like his sisters, being sucked into their dislike, their distrust of his father's wife. He was allowing himself to be dragged into their foolish paranoia. As he turned out lamps and checked to see that others were left lit, he thought of the 33 years over which he had known Rosy, of the difficult years of her stepping in to help after his mother died. Of Rosy's constancy, of her patience in the face of 17-year-old Cassie's bitter resentment spread gleefully like lemon juice upon the wounds of the younger ones. He thought about himself, half an orphan at 13, and skinny Thalia, confused and bereft at seven, and of Rosy's gentle, counteracting balms—her picnics, her day trips to Rocky Glen Park and to Harvey's Lake—and of her sufferance of their funks and sulks in the back seats of several cars; she, the perfect hostess, the friend in waiting. How long had she waited for her *Pax Romana*? Years. And she had lifted, finally, his father's heavy gloom and brought laughter back to a place deep in his father's chest. And smoothed out his sad eyes.

He packed his bags for his morning workout.

He woke to Sam sliding into their bed, to his cool leg extending along his own and then moving away. Sam breathed deep and exhaled several times.

"What time is it?" Theo asked and slid closer.

"One. I woke you."

Sam rolled to his side, his back to Theo.

"S'OK. You go out after work?"

"No…We had a shooting. Then an attempted suicide. Ten of 11. Five of 11. The shot person died. The suicide lived. Shouldn't have."

"Why?"

"You don't want to know…I hate the emergency room."

"Why do you work it?"

"I like the excitement."

"I don't get it."

"I don't either."

Chapter 4

Yes?" Theo said into the phone.

"Sorry," the office manager said. "It's your sister Cassie again."

"You told her I'd call her back?"

"Yes. She insists."

"Clare," he said, frostier than he had intended. "I'm with a patient."

"Don't kill the messenger, doctor. What do you want me to do with your sister?"

He frowned. He cupped the phone. "Mrs. Moranski?" he said to the black-and-blue-faced woman lying on the examination table. "I have a family matter to attend to. It won't take long, I promise."

The woman waved her hand in the air.

"I'll take it in my office, Clare."

He sat at his desk. He sighed. He punched a blinking button. "Cassie, I hope this is important."

"Would I call you if it were not? I've spoken with Thalia. We want you to go up to the lake."

"Why?"

"Daddy called my office a half hour ago and left a message. I was in a meeting."

"You didn't take the call?" he said sarcastically.

"I was in a meeting," she repeated. "He told my secretary that

27

someone had to come and save him. Those were his very words: 'Someone has to come and save me.' Then he hung up."

"And you called him back."

"No, I didn't call him back. What if *she* answered? I called Thalia immediately. We want you to go up there right away."

"Is your car broken or something? Why don't you and Thalia go up there right away?"

"Because he needs a doctor. You are a doctor."

"It is because I am a doctor that I can't just take off. I have surgeries scheduled for this afternoon and for most of tomorrow."

"Then you will have to go up Saturday."

"Cassie, I'm at Children's Hospital Saturday. We have people coming for dinner Saturday night."

"Your friend will just have to handle that."

"This is a dinner party."

"This is our father. As you are fond of pointing out, Thalia and I are not objective. If he needs medical attention, you are the one to assess that, not we."

"I'll see what I can do."

Theo and Susan timed their arrival at the annual, obligatory Dr. and Mrs. Marvin Micari cocktail/dinner party to coincide with the last possible opportunity to have a drink. They had had their receptionist call the Four Seasons to determine the time dinner would be served. They crowded the hour.

Dr. Marvin Micari, chief of surgery, held court near the bar. Sondra Micari circulated among their 60 guests—surgeons and their wives, surgeons and their girlfriends, surgeons and their husbands, their boyfriends.

Susan's outfit defied medical convention. Her sleek, black suit was cut in a very deep V, and she wore no blouse beneath. She knew the limits of the movement of its tailoring and exploited them.

Theo and Susan moved together in the crowd waving, smiling, and sampling conversation. They sailed gracefully away from any topic having to do with the practice and politics of medicine and drifted on to the next couple, the next group, the next clutch discussing illness, anaesthesia, insurance, lawsuit, surgical technique—all in order to accomplish their two pre-dinner goals: the greeting of their host and the greeting of their hostess.

The men focused on Susan's chest and legs, the women on Theo's green eyes and chiseled face. Theo and Susan were aware that they made a striking pair and used their attractiveness as both an entrée and an easy exit from everyone with whom they spoke. They were as superficial and as charming as was necessary. They worked the room in practiced routine and left behind a wake of murmurs.

"*Mrs.* Micari," Susan exclaimed, squeezing her hand. "Wonderful to see you again. That dress is absolutely stunning. No one has your sense of color. You always choose the perfect shade."

"*Thank* you, Susan," Mrs. Micari tittered. "You look pretty stunning yourself," she added with a quick glance at Susan's décolletage and then away to Theo. "And Theo," she said, drawing him close by the arm. "Listen," she whispered conspiratorially with a nod toward her husband at the bar. "Someday after work, I want you to take Marvin clothes shopping. Just look at him. Take him to one of those little Italian shops, why don't you? Now, where did you get that suit, Theo? Marvin needs something like that. Something with pizzazz. Good Lord, but he looks dull."

Theo and Susan edged together toward the bar, smiling, greeting, paying equal attention to mates and to guests as to fellow surgeons. The teamwork was flawless: short, cheerful conversations terminated with grace.

"Dr. Micari," Theo said, stretching out his hand.

"Dr. Micari," Susan said, stretching out her own.

Their host was gray-haired. He wore tiny, round glasses which magnified his pale, watery eyes. He was short, pear-shaped, feared, and respected. Clipped in his speech, he was voluble and kindly only twice each year—at Christmas and at this annual staff dinner in March.

"Susan, Theo, how good to see you both. I think you know everyone," he said, his weepy eyes darting about the group that surrounded him at the bar. "Except Dr. Timothy Garlington," he said, indicating a man standing at the periphery.

Theo started. Susan's head turned slightly at his reaction.

"I was able to lure Dr. Garlington from your alma mater, Theo," Dr. Micari said. "He has agreed to head up pediatric orthopedics after Dr. Winslowe retires next month."

"Ah," Theo said with a curious expression. He shook the new doctor's hand perfunctorily. "My associate, Dr. Susan Zack."

"Of course," said Susan, shaking Garlington's hand. "A pleasure to meet you finally. Dr. Garlington and I conferred by phone once on a case," she told Micari and the others. "He designed several of the tools we're using now."

"He did indeed," Dr. Micari beamed. "Did you know each other at Hopkins, Theo?"

"I think not," said Garlington before Theo could answer.

Theo's expression shifted quickly from distant to puzzled.

"Dr. Micari allowed me to look in on a patient of yours this week," Garlington told Theo. "Little girl with a cranial reconstruction. Released yesterday? Nice piece of work. We'll have to talk about it sometime."

"Yes," Theo said.

"I hate to intrude, Marvin," Mrs. Micari said, taking her husband's hand. "They are ready for us in our dining room. Please. Join us, everybody," she said to the group as she led them toward a doorway.

Theo and Susan held back as the guests disposed of their drinks and moved to follow their hosts from the bar. They trailed behind the crowd.

"That hunk. Garlington. You know him, don't you?" Susan said.

"Yes."

"Well? What's the poop?"

"The poop?"

"Theo. I know you like a book."

"He's a friend of Dorothy's."

"Dorothy. Dorothy Pinnsacardi?"

Theo gave her a withering look.

"Oh, *Doro*thy! Oh, I get it!" Susan squealed.

Theo elbowed her.

"Now *that* is a real disappointment," she whispered. "How do you know?"

"Because for two years we did it together all over Baltimore. Until he started dating a nurse. A girl nurse. I told him to fuck off."

"He goes both ways?"

"He grazes where the grass is greenest. She had a lot more money than I did. He married her."

"Really," Susan said, craning her neck toward Garlington ahead.

There were eight large, round tables. There were place cards. Theo and Susan were seated nearly back to back at separate tables. Theo was surprised to have been seated at Mrs. Micari's right. Mrs. Micari declared that medicine would not be discussed at her table. When her initial foray into politics failed because her table guests were all fearful of offending, she began to talk about babies and small children. This common ground carried them through two courses.

As they ate and talked about babies and small children they

had known, Theo did not bring up his daughter, Natalia. He looked about the room. At each table had been placed the head of a surgical branch. No surgeon of the same branch had been seated at the same table. To Dr. Micari's right was Dr. Margaret Steinhower, a woman who, because of her surgical and administrative skills, was rumored to be Micari's heir apparent. Two tables away and catty-corner from Theo, Dr. Timothy Garlington pretended fascination with the conversation of the woman to his left while leering over at Susan. He did not meet Theo's eye.

Theo noticed that, by the meat course, Mrs. Micari had downed three glasses of chardonnay and was now working on a Medoc with her rack of lamb. He decided he had nothing to lose by being direct with her. When the conversation had centered further down the table, he leaned to her and said, "Mrs. Micari, I am pleased—and surprised—to be seated next to you."

"Please call me Sondra, Theo."

"Thank you," he said.

"What do you think of the lamb?" she asked, taking a swig of her Medoc.

"It's perfect."

She touched her napkin to her lips. She returned the napkin to her lap. She assessed the table. She smiled warmly, socially.

In a low voice, still smiling broadly, she said to him: "The main reason you are seated next to me is that I find you very decorative. But there is another. As you know, Marvin is retiring at the end of December." She leaned toward him now. Her fork was inches from his nose. "Dr. Steinhower will be the next chief of surgery." The fork waved slightly. "She will stay only briefly, then she will leave to teach at Harvard. If you dare repeat that, I shall make sure you fall into very deep ka-ka." Mrs. Micari smiled warmly. "When she leaves, Marvin wants *you* to be chief of surgery. You are also Dr. Steinhower's first choice. All that having been said…," Mrs. Micari stabbed a piece of lamb. She turned to her left. "Mr. Bromly, your wife tells me that you raise…button quail, is it?"

Theo was stunned. His relationship with Dr. Micari was distant. The two of them had often disagreed angrily in large meetings over hospital policy. Their conversations, more often than not, were short and cool.

While Stanley Bromly's surgeon wife prattled on at his right about how much she missed Baton Rouge, Theo tried to imagine himself as chief of surgery. It was a position to which he never aspired, nor one for which he ever thought he might be considered. His politics did not seem to match those of the hospital. He did not see himself as a manager.

A waiter cleared the meat course.

"A penny for your thoughts," Sondra Micari said.

"I…don't know what to say."

"Theo, coyness is not your strongest suit. Do you want the position?" she asked. She finished off the Medoc, touched her napkin to her lips, looked at him and waited.

"I think."

"Good," she said. "Marvin's going to make an announcement after dessert."

"About *me?*" Theo said, suddenly panicked.

"God, no! It's a secret, dear boy. No one knows about Dr. Steinhower going to Harvard. She should never have accepted the position, planning to take off like that. Oh, you'll have some time to consider. But not long….What do you think of the new one? Garlington?"

"I don't know."

"Watch him," she said. "He's a snake in the grass." She turned again to Mr. Bromly on her left.

Theo glanced at his watch. It was five minutes before the Iron Cross. He stood. Susan was several feet away. As he passed her table he leaned and said quietly through her hair: "We've got to abort the plan."

"It's too late," she said, low, through her teeth. "And if we don't get out of here soon…"

"Turn off your beeper."

"No!"

"Susan!"

"No! I have a headache."

"Trust me!"

"Why?"

"Later!" he hissed. "Turn it off!" He smiled sweetly, straightened himself, and walked out of the dining room.

In the men's room Theo turned off his own pager. He washed his hands.

The door opened. Dr. Timothy Garlington entered—tall, good-looking, gray at the temples. Their eyes met in the mirror. Theo nodded. As he took a towel from a stack at the side of the marble sink top, he saw Tim bend slightly to look under the doors of the toilets. Tim stood at a urinal, his back to Theo. He said, "Thanks for earlier."

"For what?" Theo said, drying his hands.

"For not saying anything."

"So," Theo said into the mirror. "We never met at Hopkins, is that it?"

"That would be best, I think."

"We did surgery together. Varsity soccer for two years. Among numerous other things."

"I'm sure you agree that discretion is the best course," Tim said to the wall tiles.

"If I'm asked, I'm going to say that I knew you at school. I suggest you do the same."

Tim nodded.

"You and Jennifer still married?" Theo asked, tossing his towel into a hamper.

"Divorced."

"Well. You're still a shit anyway," Theo said, walking out of the men's room.

There was dessert. There were after-dinner drinks and coffee, during which Dr. Marvin Micari stood and rapped his water glass with a spoon and announced his gratitude to the entire surgical staff for its support, spoke briefly of his impending retirement (appropriate murmurs of disappointment), and the appointment of Dr. Margaret Steinhower as next chief of surgery. Dr. Steinhower bowed, spoke for a moment, and sat. Dr. Micari rose to speak again. Susan smiled wanly at Theo.

"We could have been out of there before dessert," Susan groused, her head against Theo's car window. "Why did you make me stay for that? Fifteen years of hospital history. Gawd!"

"We had to stay."

"Didn't."

"Susan, we have to think about next year."

"They'll be gone next year."

"So will Margaret Steinhower."

She looked over at him. "What are you talking about?"

"She's leaving. To teach at Harvard."

"Then why did she accept the appointment?"

"I don't know. But who do you think she'd want to replace her?"

"I don't know," Susan said, losing interest. "George Fellin. Some ass kisser."

"I resent that."

"You don't like George Fellin any more than I do."

"The 'ass kisser' part. You think I'm an ass kisser?"

"You? Hah!" She looked at him again. "Theo? *You?*"

"Yes! Yes!" He shook her forearm. He pounded the steering column. The horn blew.

"Theo! You are kidding me! Oh, can I have a sabbatical? Can I have a CAT scan of my very own?"

They lay in the dark.

"Sam?" he said.

Sam grunted.

"You awake?"

"Yeah." Sam rolled to face him.

"I have to go up to the lake Saturday."

"For the day?"

"No. For the night."

"We've got eight people coming for dinner," Sam said. A statement.

"Cassie and Thalia want me to go. They're making a stink. They think there's something wrong with Dad."

"Is there?"

"I don't think anything serious. I don't know. Maybe his blood sugar's off. He's been calling them at work. He called me here last night."

"Why not just call Rosy? Tell her to get him to the doctor."

"Dad's got the girls all roiled up."

"So? Let them go."

"They'd make things worse."

They lay in silence for some minutes.

"I'm sorry," Theo said.

Sam rolled over. "It's all right. It's not the first time. It won't be the last."

"Who's coming to dinner?"

"Some people." The conversation had ended.

Chapter 5

Late Saturday afternoon, after performing surgeries on three children for which he would never present a bill, Theo drove resentfully up the northeast extension of the Pennsylvania Turnpike. The day was gray. The mountains were gray. The woods and the pavement were gray. He resented his sisters for sending him on this wild goose chase, resented their resentment of Rosy, resented having to take much of his little free time to make this appearance.

He felt guilt about these resentments.

He drove through the Lehigh Tunnel and out into the zinc-gray, polluted valley of Palmerton, devoid of any sign of spring or of wildlife. The Jaguar's tires blipped across the pavement breaks. He turned on his headlights as he began to climb into the mountains, into the fog into which the mountaintops disappeared.

He left the turnpike at the Pocono exit and headed north, then east. He drove on secondary roads, higher and higher into the Appalachians, into mist and heavier fog. Landmarks loomed before him: lamp-lit inns; small stores standing on orange islands of mercury vapor light; old, familiar trees indistinct until, near the crest of the mountain, he rose above the clouds and drove into clear air, into black sky and stars. The tired road leading into Summit Lake was twisted and potholed. The Tompkins' house was lit. The Reyfords' was not. He pulled into his father's long driveway. He coasted down its slope through the field in back of the house; his lights reflected red in the eyes of deer lifting their heads from grazing to stare. He could see their jaws move.

The Jaguar crackled across the pebbles into the gravel parking area of his father's house. He stopped beside the garage. He turned off the engine and sat. Why should this visit be such a chore? Why this drained feeling before the visit began?

His father's house was a long, high construction of cedar shake siding and windows with white shutters. Low, wind-dwarfed Scotch pines, like bonsai, stood in groves at either end. The beach was close to the front door of his father's house. There was a light above the back door, yellow to deceive flying insects. The gravel path leading to the house was wet, shiny, the color of spoiled mustard.

He sighed. He opened the door of his car. He sighed. He paused briefly in the seat. He stepped out of the car.

The back door opened. The storm door opened. It was Rosy.

"Theo!" she called. "I thought I heard you coming in. Alex! Theo's here!"

She was small, kempt, well-dressed. She wore her graying, brownish hair short. She hugged one arm across her breasts against the cold.

"You need help?" she called in her high, girlish voice.

"No," Theo said. "No. I can get it."

The house was knotty pine paneled, darker, it seemed, each time he visited. There were five rooms on the first floor, four on the Second. There was a high, steeply gabled attic above stacked with bat-dunged magazines and cribs, enameled bed pans and empty picture frames. Rosy reached to hug him. He gave her a good squeeze. His father rounded the kitchen corner in bedroom slippers, smiling broadly, his hands reaching out. He moved very slowly, one hand extended. He walked high, as if by standing his tallest he could take weight from his feet and shins. Theo took his father's hand. He held on to Rosy at her waist. Rosy released herself.

"Get that coat off," she said, reaching for his collar. "Alex keeps the heat at a hundred and ten. I can't even breath."

"How about a drink?" his father asked. "We waited on ours thinking you'd want one. I got some sour mash bourbon Tomkins made that'll about kill you. I don't know how he ever got a brewer's license. The stuff's poison."

"Lay it on me." Theo said as Rosy trotted off with his coat.

His father made his cautious way toward the kitchen cupboards.

"Are your legs hurting you, Dad?"

"Well...some. How're the girls?"

"Fine," Theo said, looking his father over, checking out his color, his skin tone, his slow movements. "You talked with them," Theo added.

His father turned and looked toward the interior of the house. "Well, yes. Silly," he said quietly and arranged glasses on the counter. "And you? What's new with you?"

"They tell me I'm going to be chief of surgery next year."

"Of the whole hospital? Well, I'll be damned. Hear that, Rosy?" his father called. "You hear that? Theo's going to be chief of surgery! I'll be damned!" His father took his hand again. "That does call for a drink!"

They sat at one end of the dining table over coffee following a meal of low-fat, low-salt broiled chicken and steamed vegetables. Healthy. *Bland,* Theo thought, approving. Rosy had measured out his father's portions. She made angel food cake for dessert. "With Equal," she pointed out with both pride and apology.

Throughout dinner his father and Rosy kept up a discourse of news of the neighbors, of Theo's high school classmates, of country politics—all of which Theo had lost track of over many years and found boring now. He noted that his father's appetite was as good as ever, that Rosy was both solicitous of his father and quick to correct him. Little had changed for the pair except for the 22 years which separated them. Rosy's energy seemed boundless; his father's was evaporating.

"Bradley called your father and me last week," Rosy said near the end of coffee.

"He did?" Theo said, surprised. "How is he?"

Rosy deferred to his father.

"He's a mess," his father pronounced.

"He cried," Rosy said.

"He said Thalia won't talk to him," his father said.

"He said Thalia won't allow him in the house to visit the kids," Rosy added.

"She's being bullheaded, if you ask me," his father said.

"Stubborn," Rosy muttered.

"Well, all those affairs," Theo observed.

"Children should not be denied access to their father," said Alex.

"They're very young," Rosy added wistfully. She corralled bread crumbs on the tablecloth. She cuffed them into the saucer of her coffee cup.

There was a silence.

"How old is Bradley Junior?" asked his father.

"Nine."

"Then Martha's 11," Rosy said. "Does he call you?"

"Bradley? No. Not since this started," Theo said, picking at the lace at the table corner. "I see the kids. Sam and I have them over," he said without thinking.

Rosy preoccupied herself with nonexistent bread crumbs. His father's face clouded. Then he examined a wall.

"Look…" Theo said. He waved an arm aimlessly.

"Maybe…" his father began, too loud.

"What?" Theo said.

"Maybe…you'd like to look at stars?"

"Tonight?" Theo said, shifting in his chair.

"Night's when they come out."

"Yes," Rosy said. She stood. She began collecting cups and saucers. "That'll give me a chance to clean up."

"I'd like that, Dad."

His father suppressed a grin.

"You'll do your looking from the beach," Rosy called back as she entered the kitchen. "You're not climbing that mountainside, Alex."

"All right. All right," his father said as he pulled himself to his feet. "But we're taking rammers."

"Go ahead!" Rosy barked from the kitchen. "Go right ahead. Knock your sugar out! Let Theo deal with it."

"What's a rammer?" Theo asked.

"It's like a nightcap. A last, quick drink." His father winked.

Fat in down parkas, scarfed and gloved, Theo and his father walked along the path of the lake with flashlights and plastic cups of Barry Tompkins's sour mash bourbon. Binoculars hung from their necks. His father led the way very slowly, stumbling now and then on the gravel. Theo's hand reached toward his father's shoulder when it seemed that he might fall. His father always regained his balance. They did not need to touch.

They reached a small point jutting out into the lake a hundred yards from the house. Two molded-plastic chairs sat on this spit of land. His father pulled off his scarf and gloves. He threw them on the ground beside a chair. "Too goddamned many clothes," he said. His father dropped, painfully, into one of the chairs. "God!" he said. "Don't get old."

"Do I have a choice?"

His father ignored him. He turned off his flashlight and placed it on the ground. He took a long pull from his bourbon. He set his cup onto the gravel with great care. Theo watched his father and duplicated his movements.

"It's a good night," his father declared, casting about the heavens. "A very good night."

"It's beautiful," Theo said. "So many. You forget in the city."

There was a ghostly island of ice in the center of the lake. Tiny wavelets lapped on the gravel beach.

The nape of his father's neck rested on the molded chair back. Theo leaned back. Together they looked at the clear, cold sky.

"Remember the names?" his father said.

"A few. The major ones."

"You spend too much of your time looking down," his father said. "Ought to look up more."

"All you can see are airplane lights in the city. And the moon. You can always see the moon."

"Moon's hard to miss," observed his father. He adjusted his binoculars.

"How have you been feeling, Dad?"

"Shouldn't have called the girls," his father said. "Gets them to worrying. They get all stirred up, start bad-mouthing Rosy…She's a good woman. *She* took over when we had no one."

"You called me the other night," Theo said, looking straight up.

"I did?" his father said in the direction of Orion. "I don't remember."

"So. How are you feeling? In general."

"At my age you stop feeling in general. You only feel in particular. My feet burn. My legs ache in the night. But it's still ticking…. You remember the names?" his father asked again, pointing toward Orion high in the west.

"Do you?"

"Hell, yes. I can't see them as well as I could, but I can still name 'em…Taurus is going," he said, looking at Aldebaran, the eye of the bull. He grunted. "I was 8 years old when that light left Aldebaran…And that's pretty much the last of Orion too," he said, pointing again across the lake.

"And Rosy?" Theo said. "How is she?"

His father shifted in his chair. "She's all right. Rosy is…Rosy." He lifted his bourbon and sipped. He rested the cup on the gravel again and aimed his binoculars toward Orion. The subject of Rosy was closed.

"Now. What are the names?"

"Well," Theo said. "Betelgeuse."

"Well, Betelgeuse," his father said. "Everybody knows Betelgeuse. Bellatrix?" he began, as if his son might join in. And when he did not: "Alnitak, Alnilam. Mintaka, Saiph, Rigel." He steadied his elbow on the arm of his molded chair and looked again through the glasses. "Son of a bitch," his father said. "I can actually see it. The Great Nebula. Between Orion's legs. Take a look," he said. "That greenish blur…You see it?

"Do you like the house?" his father asked.

"Yes," Theo said, thinking of his own house in Philadelphia. "Very much."

"It goes to you when I die."

"Your house?"

"Yes. It'll be yours. Do you like it? You can sell it. If you want to."

"I assumed it would go to Rosy."

His father made a deprecating sound. "She wouldn't want it. She's never felt it was hers. It's always been your mother's house. She wants no part of it. Oh, it's all right for her now, but she'll move to Boca Raton when I'm gone. It goes to you…Do you like it? Would you use it?"

"I don't know, Dad. I haven't ever thought about it. What about the girls?"

His father rested the glasses against his chest. "They're covered. Everybody's covered. Rosy gets all the insurance. The girls get most of the investments. I didn't think you'd want money. But if you'd rather…Or you could sell this place real easy. Four hundred and 50 acres? A half mile of lake front? You could sell it for a bundle. I get offers all the time…Do you like it? The house?"

"It's only that it's so dark. All that pine."

"Yes," his father said. "Cozy. I like it that way. But you could change it. Paint it white inside. Tear it down and build another one, if you wanted to. Hell, I wouldn't care. I was just thinking you might enjoy it. For a vacation house. You always liked the lake," he said, looking out at its white, icy center. "Cleanest, clearest water in Pennsylvania," he said. "Gravel and sand bottom. Spring fed. When I stand up to my lips in it, I can see my toes. Think about it…If you don't want the house, I'll figure out another way to handle things."

"I'll think about it, Dad. Thank you. I just always assumed it would go to Rosy…. How is Rosy doing?" he asked again.

His father drained his plastic cup. He crumpled the container and put it in the pocket of his parka. He gathered his gloves and scarf from the gravel surface of the spit. "We should go in," he announced. "My feet are numb."

His father heaved himself out of the molded chair. He tottered. Theo grabbed his upper arm to steady him.

"I can make it," said his father.

Theo followed him down the path toward the house.

"I made Cassie executor," his father said over his shoulder. "She manages everything anyway. Thought about making all three of you kids executors, but that seemed too complicated. Cassie's a bitch, but she knows where everything is." He turned back toward Theo, head and torso. "I wrote down that Rosy's to get all the insurance, no matter what…She was here for us after your mother died," his father said ahead of him. "She's always been here for us. No matter what, Theo, I want her to have that insurance. She can live well on it for the rest of her life."

"Dad," Theo said, his face very near his father's down-puffed shoulder. "You're going to be around for a good, long time."

His father plodded along the path; the toes of his shoes skied through the gravel and sand. He walked very slowly.

"You never know, Theo."

They crunched together toward the lights of the house.

"How long can you stay?" his father asked.

"I was thinking I'd leave after lunch. I haven't had much free time," he said, thinking immediately he should not have said it—that his father was probably thinking, *What was this, if not free time?*

"That'll work. We're invited for cards in the afternoon."

When they reached the dooryard, Theo said, "Dad. How about if I schedule a checkup for you this week? See how things are going."

His father turned to him at the front door and smiled. "I know how things are going, Theo."

His father and Rosy went to bed at 9:30. He called home at 10.

"How's the dinner?"

"All right. How are you?"

"All right. Sorry I can't be there to help you."

"Everyone's volunteering. When are you coming back?"

"Tomorrow. In the afternoon."

"What time?"

"Three, about. What do you want to do?"

"I'll think of something." He could hear Sam smile. "I'm dish-

46

ing up dessert. Gotta go. See you at 3. I love you."

"Me too."

" 'Me too?' " Sam said.

Theo spoke low into the handset. "I love you too."

"That's better," Sam said, and hung up.

"Is Daddy all right?" Cassie quizzed him.

"He's fine, Cassie."

"Are you sure?"

"Yes."

"Did you ask him about being locked in his room?"

"He comes and goes as he pleases."

"Of course he does. When *you're* there. She wouldn't dare do anything when you're there. Did you ask him about that? Did you ask him directly about that?"

"No," Theo admitted.

Cassie heaved a great, impatient sigh. "Well, *ask* him, Theo. Take him aside and ask him. First thing in the morning."

As Cassie rang off, Theo heard a second click.

His father, dopey and confused, stood in his pajamas in his bathroom.

"Theo. When did you get here?" his father asked.

"Yesterday, Dad. Do you remember that?" Theo replied, reading the finger prick test. "Christ, your sugar is out of sight, Dad. Do you drink every night after dinner? Look, you can't do that anymore. A glass of wine with dinner. That's it. No more sour mash, OK? Lift up your pajama top. We'll get some insulin in you…Dad? Lift up your pajama top. Dad?"

His father looked through him.

Theo lifted the pajama top and held it against his father's chest with his elbow. He squeezed several inches of stomach fat between the fingers of one hand and injected the insulin with the other.

"You gotta lose some weight. You're 25, 30 pounds overweight, Dad. No wonder you're all out of whack. What are you eating to gain so much weight?"

His father stood impassive, his arms at his side.

"Come on, Dad. Come with me. Sit down in here for a few minutes."

When his father did not move, he took his father's hand in his and led him back into the bedroom. How odd to hold his father's hand. How unsettling this unresisting, cool, and wrinkled hand which, far younger, had held his own, protecting Theo from traffic, unseen and unpredictable dangers. How strange now to guide his father across a room in which there were no dangers or obstacles. He had his father sit.

"Dad. Dad?"

"Theo?" his father said after a moment.

"Dad?"

"You won't close the door."

"No, Dad. I won't close the door."

"OK," his father said, watching the bedroom door.

Theo sat on the bed next to his father, watching him. Below, in the kitchen, Rosy moved metal objects. His father turned to him. He made a small smile.

"Dad," Theo said very gently. "Does Rosy lock you in this room ever?"

His father seemed alarmed and looked toward the doorway.

"Dad," Theo said. He laid his hand on his father's hand. He spoke as if to a child. "Dad, does Rosy ever lock that door? Does she ever lock you inside here?"

His father looked surprised. His eyes did not waver from the doorway. "No?"

As Theo entered the kitchen, Rosy looked up from the bowl she was whisking and smiled. "We don't eat much breakfast as a rule," she said, "but I'm making French toast for you. The way I used to." She poured a dollop of cream into the bowl and whisked again. "With cinnamon? Alex won't mind. Well, he may stare at yours, but he won't mind."

Theo did not tell Rosy that he ate only fruit or toast early in the day.

Rosy dipped a bread slice into her bowl. She shook off excess eggy liquid and held the slice over the bowl to drain.

"You gave him his shot? He's OK?"

"Yes."

She nodded. She dropped the bread slice onto a plate.

"Rosy," he said. "Dad's carrying too much weight. Does he stick to his diet?"

She made a clucking sound. She dipped another slice into her batter. "Well, he does in this house, I can tell you." She wiped her hands. She pulled a sheaf of stapled papers from the top of the bread box.

"Eighteen-hundred calories a day," she said, thrusting the papers in Theo's direction. "No more. No less. No more unless he dips into that damned bootleg bourbon when I don't see him. I wouldn't have let him have that drink when you went outside last night either if you hadn't of been here, Theo. I don't approve of it. It's bad for him. How was he when you gave him his shot upstairs? I bet he was a zombie. I'm throwing that stuff out, is what I'm doing. Every bit of it. You better talk some sense into him, Theo. I can pretty much control him here around the house, but not when he's up to the Inn with his buddies, playing gin in the afternoons." Her hands went to her hips. Her jaw jutted. "And I hate to tell you what I find tucked down in the car seats and what I shake out of his shirt pockets. Reese's peanut butter cup wrappers and peppermint patty foils and potato chip crumbs—

enough for a start on a cocktail party. And don't think I haven't told him," she said, flipping the diet regimen onto the counter.

She retrieved the soaked bread slice from the batter bowl. She scowled as she wiped it front side and back on the bowl edge.

"I can't watch him every minute of his life," she said in frustration.

Theo nodded. He said, "When Dad called the girls he told them he was being held prisoner in the bedroom. That he was locked in. What did he mean by that, do you suppose?"

Rosy rolled her eyes. She looked toward the ceiling. She slapped the wet bread slice onto the plate. She pursed her lips. She said, "Theo, in the 30-some years I have lived with your father, there has only been one boss in this house, and it's him. The only time *I* held him prisoner—if you could call it that—was last week when I had to sit on his legs, hold his neck down with one hand, and inject his insulin with the other." Her eyes filled. She said quietly, "It's not easy here sometimes. *They* don't have to deal with what *I* deal with."

Rosy turned to the stove and adjusted dials. She wiped her eyes with her wrists. "See if he's able to have a bite to eat. Or I will," she said.

"I'll go," said Theo.

When he entered the bedroom, his father was tucking his shirt tails into his trousers.

"How're you feeling, Dad?"

"Good. How're you feeling?" he father asked, smiling. "Nice to have you up."

"Nice to be had. You've gained some weight," Theo observed as his father hauled fabric from one side then the other to cinch his pants.

"Maybe a little," his father said sheepishly. "I don't know how. On boiled chicken? She doesn't even let me eat the skin."

"Dad, I'm going to talk to Bob Carmitchell about a checkup and a couple of tests."

"Probably a good idea," his father agreed, buttoning his shirt. "You're not getting any younger."

"For you, Dad."

"Had mine."

"When?"

"Three weeks ago." His father walked out of the room.

Chapter 6

When Theo returned to the city, he drove to Children's Hospital. He examined the previous 24 hours of records of each of the children on whom he operated the day before. He visited the rooms of these children. He adjusted pain medications of the two on whom he had done skin grafts; he supervised the changing of dressings of one and spoke for some time with the child's parents. He sat with the third, who had no parents. He was 8 years old and a ward of the state. Theo had been creating a face for the child over some years. He sat in a chair where the child could see him and read yet again the little boy's favorite book, *The Velveteen Rabbit.* As always, Theo's voice broke at the part about being loved for being worn.

He returned home at 6. The driveway was empty. He pulled all the way in.

The house was silent. Lights had been left on for him. There was no evidence of a dinner party. The counter surfaces were bare.

There was a note for him on the work island, held down by a fork. The note had the time at the top: 5:30 p.m. It told him that his dinner was in the refrigerator, that he was to heat it in the microwave using its plastic dome cover, and that, when it was hot enough, he was to shove it up his ass.

He called Thalia. He told her that he believed their father fantasized about being locked in his room, that their father's diabetes was not in control, that he would talk with their father's doctor in the morning. When Thalia accused Rosy of not being vigilant, he told her to tell Rosy, if that was what she believed, and terminated the conversation.

He called Cassie. He repeated the assessment he had given Thalia.

"Something is going on up there, I'm sure of it," Cassie said.

"Well, why don't you just drive up there and check it out?" Theo asked curtly.

"You're the doctor," Cassie pointed out.

"And I am telling you what I think."

"You don't just invent being locked in your bedroom."

Irritated by Sam's note and with himself for having been late, he snarled, "Cassie, why don't you go get a second opinion?"

"Maybe you better take a cold shower," she said. "Why are you being so nasty?"

"Because I have had no time to myself this weekend. Because my father is not well. Because my sisters are being bitchy. Because Sam is annoyed with me."

"Well? That's not my problem, is it?"

"Cassie, why don't you take a cold shower?"

He packed his gym bag and his suit bag for Monday morning.

His laundered shirts had been stacked by color on the shelves of his closet. His suits and jackets had been arranged by weight and by color. His slacks had been removed from their dry cleaner bags and hung by color on wooden hangers. His underwear had been folded and stored in a bureau drawer. His gym clothes had been washed and folded and laid in their places. Everything was where it should be. He had touched none of these items in that process.

He stood at his sink holding his toothbrush and toothpaste. The bowl of his sink had been washed and dried. Sam's sink had been washed and dried. There were no water marks in the sinks or on the chrome faucets or on the handles or on the countertop.

"You are a selfish pig," Theo said to the mirror.

He stood at his bureau. He looked at the framed photographs before him on the bureau top. Fifteen of them, maybe. No dust.

He lifted a photograph of Sam from its position at one side. He moved the photograph of himself and his father and his sisters to one side and placed the photograph of Sam in the center.

Sam had a self-deprecating, embarrassed grin. He sat on the railing of a ship on which they once traveled, a cruise ship. Sam was wearing a T-shirt and shorts. His skin was red. (He did not tan.) One hand was held up as if to ward off the photographer. The other hand supported him on the railing.

Theo regarded the long, strong face, the surprise-crinkled eyes, the red-buff hair blowing. Sam was pigeon-toed, a condition which Theo found oddly appealing.

When they had first been introduced at a cocktail party, they had spoken politely for several minutes and moved on to greener pastures.

When they met again on the dance floor of an AIDS benefit, Theo wheeled about with Susan at the center of the ballroom, and the three of them circled—evaluating each other, smiling tentatively—and danced on to greener pastures.

When they saw each other again across a long bin piled with kale, cabbages, and collards in a Korean vegetable store, they had smiled and spoken. They feigned interest in vegetables in which they had no interest and moved on to stand elbow to elbow, finally, at a table of lettuces. There were no greener pastures.

One told it that they went directly to his house; the other told it that they went to his. This was one of their favorite stories.

He watched television. He read in bed. He watched the clock. He fell asleep.

He was awakened to Sam slipping into his side of the bed. Sam's leg did not slide down the length of his own. His arm did not settle on his shoulder or his back. Sam was careful not to touch.

"Hi," Theo said in the dark.

Silence.

Theo sighed. After a minute he slid toward Sam. He laid his palm on the middle of Sam's back. "I'm sorry," he said.

Silence.

As Theo was about to say "Sam?" Sam vaulted from the bed and stalked from the room. The hall light snapped on. The linen closet door opened. There were sounds of rustling fabric. The closet door slammed shut.

"Sam?"

The hall light went out.

"Where're you going?"

Sam passed the guest room and descended the stairs.

Theo sat on the edge of the bed in the dark. He weighed the moment. For Sam to pass up the guest room bed for the living room couch was a very bad sign. He thought that if he were to follow Sam downstairs and attempt to speak with him, he would be ignored. He thought that if he did not go downstairs, he would pay yet a higher price.

He sighed. He stood. He padded down the stairs and through the long dining room. The living room, at the front of the house, was lit by a street lamp. He could make out Sam wrapped in a sheet, bent to fit into the length of the couch, which was a convertible. He had not bothered to pull out the mattress. Another bad sign. Sam liked his comfort.

Theo approached. He sat cross-legged on the floor before the couch. He touched Sam's shoulder. Sam did not shrug him off. There was no response.

"I am truly sorry. I should have called. I stopped at the hospital."

Silence.

"Sam?"

"I've heard it before," Sam said. A good sign.

Encouraged, Theo rubbed Sam's shoulder in little circles.

"I didn't think. I mean, I thought I wouldn't be there long enough for it to matter—that we'd spend the evening together. I was looking forward to that."

"You never think," Sam replied coolly. A statement of fact. "You do what suits you."

Theo removed his hand from Sam's shoulder.

"Yes, I do. And I apologize. I want to change that."

Sam was silent for a moment. He sat up. He pulled the sheet around his chest. His face was stern in the streetlight. He said calmly, matter-of-factly, "I'd like to believe you want to change things, Theo. I've believed it before. But here is what is going to happen; this is the way it will be: I'm moving to the guest room tomorrow. For four weeks. That's the only change I'll make for the moment. In four weeks—by four weeks from tomorrow, which will be the ninth of April—if I'm not convinced that you are really committed to this relationship, I'm moving out."

Sam waited.

Theo said nothing.

"You think I'm not serious, Theo. That's what you're thinking. Good old Sam is upset. He'll come around. You're thinking that all you'll have to do are a few considerate things to calm old Sam down, to pacify me. Show up at the time you said you would for a few days. Have a special meal delivered, even clean up. Buy some concert tickets. That I'll get over this. That I'll settle back to the way it was.

"No, Theo," Sam said evenly, pale in the lamplight. "This is different. I called in tonight and took tomorrow off. I'm going to begin to look at apartments. I'll go around and look. Whenever I have free time. And if I find one I really like, I'll put a down payment on it—to hold it. Just in case. Now go to bed. Think about what you want. I've already thought about what I want. Good night."

Sam settled himself back on the couch, facing the back of it now.

"Sam?" Theo said, not knowing what he would say next.

"There's one more thing," Sam said into the couch back. "I said that the only thing that will change is that I'm moving to the guest room. There's something else. I will not be initiating sex during the next four weeks. That will be on you."

Theo thought about this for a moment. "OK," he said.

"Good night."

"Good night."

He lay on his side of their bed in the dark, his hands pillowing his head on the pillow.

He felt sorry for himself. He felt offended. He was a doctor. His days were used up by the needs of others. He was at the beck and call of people with scheduled needs and with needs for him which happened suddenly in the crushing of metal, in fire that flashed without warning, in the speed of a baseball hitting an eye socket. He could not live the predictable life of a normal person. When he was needed, he was needed.

It was impossible for him to say no to the lacerated people

rushed through pneumatic hospital doors on bloody gurneys, to the children born with the faces of trolls or with no faces, to the bone plates which have not coalesced, to the yawning holes in palates, the misplaced eyes. It would always be the same: they, the victims; he, the healer.

His life and Sam's seemed to him a fair division of labor and of resources. Sam, the efficient organizer of their home, repaid with a comfortable life: the commodious town house in a stylish neighborhood of other well-kept town houses, the new cars—the Jaguar due to be replaced, the Toyota Camry which replaced the Olds Ciera. They lacked for no appliance, no state-of-the-art sound or video device. Their closets were full. Their refrigerator and freezer were full.

Yet, Theo admitted, Sam had never been on a free ride. He had never asked to be. His checks appeared on the work island three days before the first of the month, one for his share of the house payment, another for the average half of utilities. He maintained the Camry, an unsolicited gift. He had never asked for a dime.

It was true that Theo was careless of time. It was true that he forgot to call or that he thought it not necessary to call. Sam worked in the medical field. He was a nurse. He knew as well as anyone the demands placed upon doctors whose time was not their own. Shit happened. What could he do, not go to his father? Not follow up on the Saturday surgeries? Leave those kids in the lurch?

This was not the first crisis nor the first ultimatum. But maybe the last. Sam was not just blowing smoke. Theo had heard the finality. Sam had thought this out.

Maybe let him leave, Theo thought, *if that was what he wanted.*

After five years, maybe it was time. If Sam was not happy with things the way they were, maybe let him leave. Maybe do that. Maybe even suggest that living separately might be a positive thing. For both of them. Certainly they were happy living separately the first year. Maybe use a time of separation to reevaluate things. A time for renewal. Go back to the time when they dated. Maybe use the space as space for them both to cast about in new directions. Take a tentative stroll into the world? Flirt a bit with risk?

Theo rolled onto his side. He extended an arm and a leg out into the cold, empty side of the bed and retreated immediately to his area of warmth. He pulled the down comforter around the back of his neck.

How willing was he, really, to step back into the free and fickle world of risk hidden beneath every appealing face and torso? They were at least safe, the two of them. How long would it take to find another man whose fidelity he need never question? One who used his own spare time to augment the quality of Theo's? One who could still make him stiffen at a touch? One who kept in his jewelry box a discolored certification from the testing center when it was still on 12th Street?

He was a fool, he thought, to be so cavalier about an issue that took so little attention. If all Sam wanted was for him to call when he had to be late, he should call. Just pay a little more attention and they could settle back to normal. Maybe hire a cleaning service. Hire a cook.

He just wanted his life to be easy. That was all that he wanted. He wanted his life arranged and ordered. He deserved this. He spent great amounts of money on the town house. He employed eight people at his office. His malpractice insurance alone cost $47,000 last year. How much would it cost this year? All he wanted was some peace and some pleasure after a day of repairing horrific abnormalities, after a day of performing miracles on teensy smashed and severed nerves, after a day of intricate and perfect stitching of flesh and of skin so that no one would know in some months that anything terrible had ever happened. All he wanted at the end of such a day was the warm comfort of touching, the warm comfort of knowing that he was loved with no conditions. Was that too much to ask?

He rolled into the cold side of the sheets. He retreated to the hollow of warmth he had left. A doctor's life was not his own.

Even a doctor could not call all the shots.

"I hate this," he whispered in the dark.

Chapter 7

Sam Meacham crossed Broad Street at Chestnut against the light. His plastic shopping bags—from Strawbridge's, from a poultry stand at Reading Terminal Market, from Fischer's Lamp and Electric—flapped and rattled in the March wind into which he hurried. He bit the leather of his jacket at his forearm and pulled up the sleeve to reveal his wristwatch. He calculated the time required to stop at the hardware store for the hinge screws and a new phone cord. Better to go on to the restaurant and double back after lunch. But what to do with the chicken? No time to drop it off at the house.

Take it to lunch. Hope that the waiter was someone he knew.

He hung his coat in the restaurant hallway. He stuffed his scarf into a sleeve. Where were his gloves? He checked the pockets of his jacket. He looked through his packages. Gone. Left on a counter. Dropped in the street. Lined. Leather. Forty-two fifty.

The hostess of Carolina's, young, limp-haired, and languid, had been watching him from her tiny entrance table.

"One?" she said when he turned to her.

"No. A reservation. Zack? Or Meacham?" Sam stood with his shopping bags and his plastic sack of chicken while she checked her book.

"Zack," she said flatly. "This way."

Sam hesitated, looking at his bags.

The girl indicated the coat rack behind him with a glance. "You could leave those there," she said doubtfully.

Sam swung a white plastic bag in her direction. "Um. This is a chicken?" His face assumed the puzzled, helpless expression which he knew women found irresistible. "Do you think maybe you could put it in a refrigerator while we have lunch?"

"They might cook it back there."

"Cacciatore, if they do," Sam said. "I was going to make that."

She took the bag. She did not smile. She held the bag out from her skirt and gestured toward the dining room entrance. "Side window," she said. She glanced in. "Classy lady. Great hair," she added enviously.

"I'll tell her."

When Sam and Susan Zack met in the doorways of their homes, in the lobbies of banks, on sidewalks outside shoe stores, there were kisses and boisterous carrying on. In the tin-ceilinged dining room of Carolina's, between tiny, tight tables, amid the confusion and rattle of plastic shopping bags, they were heard above the din.

"My goddess!"

"Oh, I've *missed* you!"

Red flannel embraced violet tweed in a clutch which attracted the attention of diners. Who were these demonstrative people? Long-separated lovers? Was there a movie being filmed in Philadelphia?

They were the same height. Susan's skin, pale as a fiberglass manikin's, was pressed against Sam's flushed cheeks. Her gleaming chestnut hair slid on his own, the color of a rusted hull.

"Ha *ha!*" and "How *are* you?"

When they had settled in their chairs, when their napkins had been spread in their laps, when the noise of the restaurant had returned to its normal, hollow, and unpleasant pitch, Susan said, "So!"

"So."

"How *are* you?"

"I'm terrible."

"Uh, oh," she said, leaning forward, concerned.

"I didn't call you for a fun lunch," Sam told her. "I needed to whine."

"You should have invited my kid. That's all she does."

"I needed a mature reaction."

"To what?"

A waiter appeared.

Susan ordered coffee; Sam, a vodka martini.

Sam played with the salt and pepper shakers.

When Sam did not speak, Susan placed fingertips to her temples. She looked at the tin ceiling. "I'm getting something," she said. "Definitely something…'Theo.' I'm getting 'Theo.' Does that name have any meaning for you?"

Sam shrugged his shoulders.

"Wait," she said. She pressed her palm flat against her forehead. " 'Jeff' something. Jefferson Hospital…job issues. It's not real clear. Maybe if I held your sock?"

"Maybe go back to 'Theo.' "

"There was a resonance?"

"A small one."

"So what's the poop?"

"You get right to the point."

"Life's short."

Sam tinkered with his utensils. Susan waited.

"Well, at least Theo's not seeing someone else," she offered. And when Sam did not reply she said, "So what, then? He's having a midlife crisis? Acting moody? Snapping at you for no reason?"

"No. He's always the same." Sam ran his fingers along the hem of his napkin.

Susan crossed her legs and sat back. She folded her arms.

"OK," she said after a moment. "I'm on strike. You've got three minutes to choke this up, then we're going to talk about me."

"Five years in three minutes?"

Their drinks arrived.

"You want to gulp that one down while the waiter's still close?" Susan asked.

"Am I boring you?"

"I'm getting a little edgy," she said. "This is like pulling teeth."

Sam sighed. "It all seems so stupid now that we're here."

"Oh, go ahead, Sam. Whine away."

"It's just that I'm getting no help…He never remembers to do anything. It's like *I* have to do everything. He can't even remember to take clothes to the cleaners. When he remembers to go to the cleaners, he takes his own clothes, and when I go pick them up, mine aren't there.

"And I do all the housework. Hey," Sam said, rising to his occasion, "I have a job! I work 60 hours a week some weeks. You think I like split shifting? I do 18 hours on when somebody gets sick or goes on vacation or the paramedics keep driving people in even when the emergency room is full up, and guess what? I manage to do the shopping after work, and I dust, and I clean bathrooms and change the sheets and entertain all our friends. And then he doesn't even show up for dinner?"

Susan nodded.

"I get five, six hours of sleep if I'm lucky, but I manage to make meals ahead for us. I sweep the leaves out of the driveway. I change the lightbulbs. If a lightbulb goes out? Theo goes into another room. And *I* call the plumber when a sink stops up. He just goes to another sink. And shopping. I do all the grocery shopping. All of it. He doesn't *do* grocery shopping. What's he think?

Ivory soap and Bounty towels get delivered by UPS? What's he think? I have a truck farm out there along the driveway?

"I shop every day. Every day. Every day I leave for work with a list in my wallet. Theo does not cook. Ever notice that? You know what Theo's idea of a home-cooked meal is? Calling Towne Pizza and choosing the toppings."

Susan nodded.

"And we don't talk anymore. Oh, *I* talk. I rattle on about my work and our friends and what I read in the paper, and he just lets me go on. If I ask him about his work, he changes the subject."

Susan's gaze began to wander.

"And I'm sick and tired of *al*ways being the one to start sex. Always, always it's me. It's never him. I am always the one who gets things started."

"Don't hold back, Sweetie."

"I'm sorry," Sam said.

"So why do you do all this?"

Sam squirmed in his seat. He looked incredulous. "Jesus Christ! Who *else* is going to do it?"

"What would happen if you just stopped?"

Sam picked up his drink. "What would happen? What would happen? Well, *noth*ing would happen, Susan. Except the house would fall apart around us. Nobody would buy lightbulbs, and we'd be sitting on folding chairs in whatever closet that had the last bulb burning. And eventually we'd run out of sinks, and instead of calling a plumber, Theo'd be knocking at the next door neighbors with a towel over his shoulder!" He sighed. He sipped.

"Have you talked to Theo about all this?"

" 'Talk?' What is 'talk?' I told him I'm looking for an apartment. He's got one month."

"Sam, would you do that? Leave Theo over housework?"

"We're not just talking housework here, Susan."

"Lightbulbs? Leaves? Groceries?"

"There's more involved here than housework."

"Fixing meals? Clogged sinks...?"

"Hey, I feel taken for granted."

"Welcome," she said.

Sam looked away.

"Theo does things," Susan said in her friend's defense. "When I come over for dinner, he helps serve. He cleans up after."

"Yeah. But he never gets the counters clean."

"How about laundry? Does he do laundry?"

"Sure. When he needs gym clothes or something. He throws in everything in sight. White things with blue jeans. Hot's the only button he knows. I'm wearing puce underwear today."

"Maybe you could cut a deal? I mean, have him do all the shopping? You do the laundry?"

"He doesn't know how to shop, Susan. He doesn't look at prices. He doesn't read labels. He forgets half the things he went out to get."

"Maybe get a housekeeper. You guys can afford one."

"That's throwing away money."

"Because you do it all so well?"

"Ah. So this is all *my* problem," Sam said, rolling his eyes at the ceiling.

"Sam, I think I'm with Theo on this one, the way you describe it. You don't like the way he does the work so you do it all yourself and then complain that you do it all."

Sam frowned. He had come to this lunch for vindication.

"Well, Sam? I don't understand. What's different now from the way it's always been?"

Sam turned the stem of his martini glass. What *was* different? He had always run the house. Everything was done much as it had been done for years. It was just that he had somehow lost, along the way, the point. He reached for a menu. "We should decide what we're having," he said.

Susan's hand covered the menus. "What is it you want?" she asked.

"A Reuben sandwich, maybe," he replied.

"They're sold out." Her hand remained on the menus.

Sam sat back. He folded his arms across his chest.

"Really. What is it you want?"

He regarded a wall.

Susan leaned forward. "What? A pat on the back when he gets home because all the *lightbulbs* work? Congratulations on the folded fitted sheets? A blow job because the sinks all drain? What?"

"You're being simplistic."

"What then?"

"I want...his attention."

Susan handed Sam a menu. "What did Theo say when you told him you were going to look for an apartment?"

"Nothing."

"Nothing at all?"

"He said, 'Good night.' "

"He thinks you wouldn't move out."

"What am I supposed to do? Move out to prove I would?"

"Why not? Sometimes you have to hit 'em with a crowbar...Look, it was the same for me when I was married, Sam. We were both residents in hospitals. We were both run ragged. But I'd come home and do what you're doing because I knew how and he didn't. One day I said to myself, I said, 'Susan, wake up and smell the dirty laundry. This is not the marriage you said *I do* to.' So I threatened to leave."

"And did you?"

"No. He did. He told me he'd rather find himself a new apartment. A clean one."

"I'm sorry."

"What's to be sorry? I got out of a lousy marriage."

"With a kid to raise."

"No," she said, looking at Sam curiously. "I didn't have Natalia then…I guess the point I'm trying to make is that ultimatums do get attention, but when you make one you better be damned ready to carry through."

"I looked at an apartment. This morning."

"Did you like it?"

"No."

"Sam, I understand your frustration. You and I need to hear appreciation. We're unable to assume it. But Theo feels more comfortable showing he cares than coming right out and saying so. Next to you, I think I'm his best friend. He has never, ever told me that I am. He'd be mortified to say that to me. Hey, *I* don't know why—he just would. But he'll go out and buy me a bracelet he knows I wouldn't buy myself. And when I haven't had a date in two months, he'll take me to some gorgeous place for dinner."

"What you're saying is, he trades money for affection, Susan."

"No, I'm not saying that. Well, maybe I am…No, I'm not. What I'm saying is, the man doesn't know how to give affection. He knows how to give things."

"But I don't want *things*. I can buy my own things!"

Susan was growing impatient. "Sam, I know exactly what you're talking about; I feel the same way you do sometimes. But I also feel the same way *he* does!

"You know, we really should have invited Natalia to lunch. You two have a lot in common. She's pissed at me right now because I'm not spending time with her. I don't *have* time to spend with her. It's not easy being on demand, believe me. Look. This is going to sound terrible to you and it's not that I don't love you, because I do. But Sam, I almost called this restaurant an hour ago to cancel. I don't have *time* to have lunch with you. Sam, you made a terrible mistake, but live with it: You married a doctor. We *don't* always have time for you, Sam. We don't have time for our*selves!*" Her cheeks flushed. She lowered her head in embarrassment.

"All right, Susan," Sam said. "So what do I do?"

Susan opened her menu. "Sam, *I* don't know. *Shoot* the fucker. Shoot *me!*"

Chapter 8

After his surgeries, at the desk of the head surgical nurse, Theo called his father's doctor, who was once his own doctor.

Carmitchell's accent, somewhat more clipped after thirty years in upstate Pennsylvania, reverted to the tidal basins of South Carolina when he discussed his favorite subjects, "dee-uh" and "bay-uh." He would rather hunt than eat. He would rather hunt than be with his wife. He would rather hunt than practice medicine. During their small talk Theo avoided mention of wild animals.

"I was up to see Dad yesterday," Theo told Carmitchell. "He told me he saw you three weeks ago."

"He did," Carmitchell replied, offering nothing.

"Did you do blood work, Bob?"

"Certainly."

"And his insulin was off?"

"It was totally fucked up."

"What did you suggest?"

Carmitchell paused. "Well, you saw he's overweight. I gave him a diet to follow, but I can't follow him around all day to see he stays on it. Neither can Rosy. She says he goes up to the Inn and pigs out. I haven't seen that. I play gin with him every Wednesday afternoon, and all I see him eat is stuff off the relish plate—carrots, celery, not even the gherkins. Maybe he stops off at the SuperFresh on the way home, I don't know.

"He complains about his legs. He's starting to get resting pain, and he won't go in for tests. He says if he's going to have a heart attack, he'd rather have a natural one." Carmitchell grunted. "He thinks the dye test's dangerous. I've been trying to get him to go down to you for a few days. You could get him set up with good people, but he won't consider it.

"And he won't exercise because he says it hurts, and if he won't exercise, the feet are just going to break down sooner. Of course, you know where all this is going, Theo."

"Yes."

"Well, maybe you can talk some sense into him. I can't. He's a very stubborn man, your father…. You hear my Ellie got a dee-uh last month?"

"No."

"Eight pointer; 210 pounds," Bob said proudly. "With her new BMW. Whole front of it's gone. Must've been doing 90 when she hit it."

Theo and Sam sat at the dining table at a meal which Sam prepared. Theo had made a point of arriving home before he was expected.

Sam's conversation was not stilted; there was no indication in his voice or manner that anything was different. Sam seemed perfectly normal, perfectly comfortable. It was Theo who was ill at ease.

"We're invited to dinner with Roger and Kenny Saturday," Sam said.

"I'm on call, you know."

"We could tell them. You want to go?"

"No problem, so long as they know I'm on call."

Sam paused. "The Melinowski-Mellos are coming."

"Oh, shit."

"I know."

"You want to go?" Theo asked.

"No. Do you?"

"No…Can we get out of it?"

"We're not in it yet. I told them I had to check with you."

"I don't like them."

"I don't either," Sam said.

"I thought you did."

"No. I thought you did."

"No."

"Really," Sam said, folding his arms on the table. "Why don't you like them?"

"They're so…self-absorbed or something, you know? If I said, 'My grandmother was born in Greece,' one of them would say, 'I had a grandmother once. She was born in Chicago.' Then the other one would say, 'I had a grandmother once. She was born in Lake Charles. She was the sweetest, kindest grandmother in the world.' Let's not go."

"OK."

"What would you like to do instead?"

Sam ran a fingertip through the sweat of his wine glass. "I don't know. What would you like to do?"

"I don't know. Can I think about it?"

"Sure…I'm on a 12-hour shift tomorrow," Sam said. "You remember?"

"Right," Theo said, not remembering. "You want me to get dinner?"

"That'd be nice."

"We'll have to move the cars, then. I have you blocked in."

They were in their separate bedrooms. Sam had moved all his clothes, his toiletries, his medicines, his shoes, and some of their framed photographs into the guest room down the hall.

Theo lay on his side of their bed, still surprised at the change of rooms, at the thoroughness of the move. As he prepared for sleep in their bedroom and Sam prepared in the guest room, Theo was disappointed to find that no object owned solely by Sam remained in any drawer or on any bathroom shelf. Sam's shelves had been washed. It was a clean sweep.

He lay on his side of their bed in the dark. The hall was dark. There were no sounds from the guest room. It was very awkward. He felt alone, surprised, even shocked. He had thought that after their dinner with no rough edges, after coffee with easy talk about their work, after cleaning up the kitchen together to light banter and talk of Sam's mom and dad, and after an amusing hour of television together—they might go to bed together. Not touch, maybe, but that Sam might have relented. He was bothered by the emptiness of Sam's closet, by the vacuum cleaner tracks on the carpet on its floor, by the absence of the glow of the digital readout of the clock radio that belonged to Sam. How would he wake up?

He lay on his side of their bed in the dark.

He said, his voice sounding odd to him in the room now so empty, "Sam?"

There was no answer.

"Hey, Sam?" he said louder, his voice sounding more curious still.

"What."

"Good night, Sam."

"Good night, Theo."

Chapter 9

Theo stood as Susan wended her way toward him among the tables of the White Dog Café. Men's eyes followed her—some surreptitiously, some with clear interest—as she approached Theo in a sleek, green dress showing much leg.

"What a knockout," he said, pulling her chair out for her at their window table.

"Music to *these* tired ears," she said. "God! Sunshine!" She extended her arms, palms up, in the window light. "This has been the longest, dreariest winter I have ever endured. I had a call last week from a clinic in Palm Beach. They wanted me to fly down for a few days to look them over. I almost took them up on it."

"You didn't tell me about that," Theo said.

"What's to tell?" Susan said offhandedly. She smiled and waved across the room. "Your friend's here."

"Who?"

"The new hunk, Garlington."

"Fuck him. You didn't tell me about Palm Beach, Susan," he said.

"Theo, you get calls like that all the time. You don't always tell me about them. Sometimes they call us both. We're talented. We're good catches...Doesn't mean I'd ever do it," she added with slight irritation.

"You said you almost did."

"Theo, I could use a vacation. So what if they'd want to pay me for a few days off?"

They picked up their menus.

"You having a drink?" Theo asked.

"No. I'm operating at 2," she said. "You?"

"I don't know. I have nothing till 4:30. I'm assisting Millard Roberts on a jaw job."

"The Hummer?"

"None other."

"I scrubbed with him once and had 'Blue Moon' running through my brain for the rest of the week. He's coming over here," she said to her menu.

"The Hummer?"

"Garlington."

"Don't ask him to sit down," Theo snarled.

"Maybe I will. He's very cute, Theo."

"Dr. Zack? Dr. Tithonus. How're you doing?" Garlington extended his hand to Susan, then to Theo who squeezed it for the briefest acceptable time and made no attempt to rise.

Garlington stood at the end of their table. He directed himself to Susan, only glancing at Theo, including him because he was there. He leaned his knuckles on their tabletop.

"I'm having some people over tomorrow night," he said. "Sort of a house warming. I just got moved in and I'd like you both to come if you can."

"Well, congratulations, Dr. Garlington!" Susan said with more enthusiasm than Theo felt necessary.

"Tim," Garlington corrected her, smiling more than warmly.

"Tim," she repeated. "Please call me Susan. So where did you move?"

"Eighteen thirty Rittenhouse Square. It's temporary. A friend of mine is spending a year in Paris and rented it to me while I look around."

"Eighteen thirty," Susan said. "On the south side? With the old marquee?"

"Right," Garlington said, pleased that she recognized the tony address. He raked the fingers of one hand through his sandy hair and leaned the hand, knuckles down, close to one of hers on the tabletop.

"Nice digs," she said.

"On the 14th floor," he said. "Incredible view from my bedroom."

"Co-ops?" Theo asked disinterestedly.

"Condos," Garlington replied with a small, slightly superior smile. Then back to Susan: "I hope you can come. Six o'clock. Just give your names to the doorman. I'll see that you're on the list." Garlington's hands left the table and disappeared into his trouser pockets where they pulled the fabric of his slacks tautly at his crotch to display the bulge there. He faced Susan. "Well, have a nice lunch. The salmon's delicious," he told her. "See you then?" He turned and ambled comfortably to the other side of the restaurant.

Theo retrieved his menu. " 'Please call me Susan,' " he mewed.

"Don't start," she said.

" 'Incredible view from my bedroom.' "

Susan took up her menu. "You were barely civil."

"He's an asshole, Susan. Who's he with?"

She looked to Garlington's side of the restaurant. "Micari. And Steinhower."

"Terrific. That's why he came over. He just wanted to be sure I saw who he's with."

"You're still bitter because he married the nurse," she said behind her menu.

Theo was annoyed. Their waiter approached. "You know what you're having?"

"Iced tea…and salmon."

Theo smirked. "Bloody Mary, extra lemon. The Belgian endive. Oil and vinegar." He handed his menu to the waiter.

"No," he said, looking across at Susan. "I am not bitter about the nurse. That was 20 years ago. I was a naive kid then. He's an opportunist; she was rich."

"What happened between the two of you just happened. A lot of men have some kind of homosexual experience between puberty and maturity, Theo. That was probably just a phase for him."

Theo grunted. "When I met Tim Garlington, he already knew more about sex with men than I've learned since. Besides, after he married the nurse he still did it with guys. Go to the party. Be my guest. Be *his* guest."

Theo looked out the window. Susan reached across the table. She laid her hand on the sleeve of his jacket. "Theo, he's an attractive man, is all. Now tell me he isn't easy to look at. What's with you today? Lighten up."

"Sorry. I'm in a mood."

When their drinks had been placed she asked: "How are things? You OK?"

"I guess," he said, pleased to have her ask, relieved to have her draw him out. "Except my Dad isn't well, and my sisters are no help. Thalia's in the middle of one of those deadly divorces and they both hate our stepmother. And Sam has moved into the guest room. He's looking at apartments."

"Oh, Theo," Susan frowned, hoping she looked surprised. Her hand went back to his sleeve. "What's happening? Sam adores you. You two are an institution or something."

"Or something." Theo poked his celery stalk up and down in his drink. "He's pissed. It's my fault. I'm always late. I don't call. I like my work. He doesn't understand. I forget things—like his birthday? Little things like that. I forget when we're having people in or when we're going out. I forget to do stuff. You know, read the papers and see when Yanni's coming to town and get tickets. He loves Yanni."

"Me too. Don't you?"

"No. And I forget to do the dishes and to call the electrician when he asks me to, and then Sam makes the call and gets snarly because he's *my* electrician and Sam thinks he's a con artist. Well, maybe he is, but where are you going to get an electrician in this city? And I keep putting off setting aside a long weekend to have his parents down. They're nice people. They're really sweet. When they send Sam a present, they send me one too. But when am I going to have a long weekend off to have his parents down? And if I did, I wouldn't want to have his parents down. I'd want to go to New York or fly to Texas or something."

"With Sam."

"Sure. Maybe. I don't know."

"Do you love Sam, Theo?"

"That is a very good question."

Theo looked out the window, then back. "Enough of that. How's it with you?"

"Theo, I know this isn't a good time, but we do have to talk about some things."

"It isn't," he sighed. "But what the hell?"

Susan leaned across her forearms. "Theo, I have to change the way I'm living."

"Jesus, *you* do!" he said to the backs of his hands.

"I'm losing it," she said. "I'm putting in too many hours, and I'm not getting enough time for myself. I'm raising a little Attila. I'm starting to get complaints about Natalia's behavior at school. She's begun to bite other children. Our daughter is biting people, Theo."

"It must come from your side. We're not biters. Not even Cassie."

"She's impossible at home. She avoids me. We used to talk all

78

the time. Now, when I get home she goes to another room and watches television. She loves Mrs. Cristobel more than she loves me. I have to do something. Very soon."

Their lunches arrived. Theo began to work on his salad. Susan ignored her plate.

"Maybe you should get her a therapist," Theo said, slicing through a leaf of endive.

Susan frowned. "She doesn't need a therapist, Theo. She needs a mother." Susan's forefinger tapped the tabletop near Theo's water glass. "And she needs a father."

Theo looked up, his knife and fork poised. "What does that mean?"

Susan hesitated. "The deal we made is no longer realistic," she said. "It isn't that I want to renege on that exactly. I guess what I want to do is renegotiate."

"Renegotiate," Theo repeated.

"Yes."

Theo placed his knife and fork on the salad plate. He felt uneasy about the trend of this conversation. Susan looked very serious.

"Renegotiate what?"

"When we agreed to do this—me wanting to be a mother while I still could and you being the sperm donor, period—I didn't know what I was getting into. I didn't know how very complicated parenthood gets, Theo. I really believed, I think, that because I make a very comfortable living, being a mother would also be comfortable. Because I can afford all the help I need, I'd be able to be a good mother and a good doctor—that I'd have it made." She glanced out the window. She looked back at Theo. Her hands reached toward him. "But I can't," she said, shaking her head. "I can't. I cannot do this alone. Even with the help. It's not working. At all. Natalia is a very unhappy little girl. And I'm unhappy. All I do is work. And worry," she said.

Theo took a swig from his drink. "So...?" he said.

Susan made a small sound of irritation.

"So, I want to write a new contract. I want to write two new contracts. The first one is about our partnership. I'd like to limit the number of new patients I take on and the number on whom I consult. I want to reduce the number of operations I perform, at least until Natalia's a little older. Naturally, I'd expect my compensation from the partnership to be reduced proportionally. Also, I think we should consider taking on a new associate. We'll need one if you become chief of surgery next year."

"That won't interfere," Theo said.

"You're kidding yourself if you think it won't. Micari's so busy he hardly even operates any more."

"Micari is old. You're not eating."

"This is more important. What do you think about hiring on a new associate?"

"I'll think about it," Theo said as if he probably would not.

"The second contract I want to talk about is the one about your being Natalia's father."

"Ah."

"The one we have isn't working."

Theo nodded. He sliced salad.

"When I asked you if you would parent a child with no strings, it seemed very straightforward and sensible to me. I wanted a baby. There were no potential husbands on the horizon. We are friends, and you have acceptable genes."

"You said I had great genes."

"I might have said you look great *in* jeans. The point was that I didn't want an anonymous donor. I didn't want my kid to grow up wondering if every black-haired man she met was her father. And we agreed we would tell her that you're her father. We agreed to that."

"When she's 40."

Susan was not amused. "And that your only obligation was to be the donor."

"Right. And I think I've done more than that. I never wanted kids, Susan."

"You've been very generous, Theo. She has enough socked away for college already."

"It's the least I could do."

"Yes, it is," Susan agreed. "I'm not complaining. But I need to know how you would feel about getting more involved. I mean in the day-to-day things of raising her. That was not a part of our contract...I really thought I'd have found someone by now. You know? Six years?" She sighed.

"What were you thinking?" Theo said. He propped his chin in one palm. She was so beautiful, he thought. And a truly fine person. Men ought to be fighting each other with swords over her.

"Please understand, there are no wrong answers, Theo, but I was wondering how you would feel about coming out. I mean as her father. I mean *being* her father. Because you are. I don't mean that. That sounds like blackmail or something. What I mean is, how would you feel about helping me raise her a little more?" Susan's cheeks flushed. She shifted about in her chair. He had never seen her so nervous.

"There are no wrong answers here, Theo. I want to make that clear. That is not the deal we made originally, and the last thing I want to do is rope you into something you'd resent."

"Right," Theo said. He pointed at her plate. "You should eat, you know. Your food's getting cold. And you have to operate this afternoon."

Susan picked up her fork. "I will," she said, poking at the salmon. "First I need to know how you feel about this. Do you understand what I'm asking, Theo?"

"Yes," he said. "You want me to be Natalia's father. You want me to *be* her father. And help you with her." He speared a chunk of Roquefort cheese.

"Yes. Sort of." Susan returned her fork to the table. "She needs some direction, is what she needs. She needs to know that she has people who are there for her. As it is, all she has is Mrs. Cristobel. I roll in at 7 or 7:30, and I'm exhausted. She goes to bed at 8. This is not good for a little kid, Theo. If you could just be there some. If you could maybe come around every now and then and get to know her?"

It was not that this request came as a surprise to him. It was not that he didn't expect to have this conversation someday. When he had handed over containers of semen to the sensitive, polite lab technician with the small, pasted smile, he knew that his involvement would someday be more than biological, more than doing a friend a favor. It was not that he did not consider the consequences of handing over part of himself. He knew when he did so that the day would come when the debt he was incurring would have to be paid.

He had thought that the due date would arrive years in the future—years, even, from this lunch at the White Dog Café—when the child was an adolescent or grown up. As he wrote them, he even thought that the checks he sent quarterly might somehow serve to satisfy the debt.

However, the timing of this discussion was off. His own family was in chaos. He was not meeting Sam's needs or his father's needs; and what were his sisters' needs anyway?

"You know I'll do what I can," he said. Because he should say this to his friend. Because he saw himself as a responsible person.

"I know you will."

"What do you want me to do?"

"What would you like to do?"

Theo glanced across the dining room to the Micari-Steinhower-Garlington table. They were all laughing. Too happily. Garlington wanted to be chief of surgery. There was no question in Theo's mind that Garlington was positioning himself for the job.

"Susan, are you going to eat or no?"

"I *will.*" She lifted her fork again and held it. "Theo, this is really my problem. You don't have to do anything if you don't want to, you know."

"Have to do what?" he said to his salad.

"Help me with Natalia. Theo, are you listening to me?"

"Of course. Susan, we can't have her biting people…Did you bite people? Your father, maybe?"

"Theo. Please be serious. You don't have to do *any*thing. You're under no obligation, you know."

"I know."

"Maybe you need some time to think about this."

"Maybe I need some time to think about this." Theo looked across the room again and back. "Susan, I don't even *know* what to do. What *do* I do? Come over to your house one night with a teddy bear and say, 'Hi, kid, I'm your father? OK, let's play?' "

"That is a little abrupt, Theo."

"So, how was your date with the oncologist?"

Susan looked up. Her fork clanked to her plate. Her forehead creased. She looked genuinely angry with him. "Theo—on what plane do you exist? I had to *can*cel my date with the oncologist. *You* had to go to the mountains!"

"Excuse me. I forgot."

Chapter 10

Theo and his sister Thalia sat in their sister Cassie's living room.

"You want a drink?" Thalia asked.

"No. You?"

"Yes. But I'll wait."

Thalia sat across from him on the edge of her chair. She looked sleepless and chic. Long earrings of silver snake chain swung at her neck. Until recently she had spent much of her income from teaching on clothing and accessories. She looked at her watch.

"She's late," Thalia pronounced. "She's always late." Thalia examined Cassie's crown moldings.

"Where are Bradley Junior and Martha?"

"My neighbor's," she said.

"Ah," Theo said. He shifted on the couch. "So, how are they?"

Thalia sighed. She adjusted the silver chain at her neck. Her black eyes flashed.

"Terrible. How should they be? Bradley's being ridiculous. One day he calls and leaves a message on the machine that he wants to get back together. The next day he sends me a letter saying it is his intention to take the children away from me." She stood. She paced. "The very idea!"

"Can he do that?"

"*No,* he can't do that!"

"Maybe you both could try again?"

"Try *again?*" she snapped, a little hysterically. "Try *again!* Sure. Everything peachy and lovey-dovey for a month until the next slut comes along? Not on your life." She stalked to Cassie's bar cart. "I think I will have a drink."

She poured a couple of fingers of Cassie's Glen Livet into a cut crystal glass. She lifted the lid of the ice bucket and replaced it.

"You want one?" she asked.

"No."

She returned to her chair.

"You want some ice? I'll get it," Theo offered.

"No...You know what fries me? Really fries me? He has no discretion. I mean, Bradley can't just go off on a business trip and get his ashes hauled; he has to pick a bimbo from our own neighborhood and brag about it to his buddies. Who tell their wives. Who tell me. Well, he did his little dance last time with that Shelly or Sheila person for a couple of months apparently, until I got wind of it, but at least he paid the bills all the while."

Thalia's eyes darted across the ceiling and back to Theo.

"Well, I put a stop to that...I called that one to a screeching halt. But this...this is different. This time he has really lost his mind." Her forefinger jabbed at one of her thin shoulders. Her eyes narrowed. "He *knows* what I make as a teacher. The whole *world* knows what I make as a teacher. This is public knowledge. And he knows that I could no more pay the upkeep on that house *and* keep the kids in private school *and* feed and clothe them *and* make our credit card payments than I could..." her arms flew out, "keep up *this* chateau. Now, he knows this, and he has not sent me a single dime since he moved in with that slut seven weeks ago. Not a *dime!*" She crossed her long legs. One stylish lizard pump bounced nervously.

"Thalia? Do you need some money? I can give you some."

"No. You're very sweet to offer, but we are not out on the street yet." Thalia smoothed her skirt.

"Why are we having this meeting?" Theo asked to change the subject.

"We have some things to discuss. About Daddy."

Theo nodded, learning nothing.

"You know what he did, the son of a bitch? Did I tell you?"

"Dad?" Theo said.

"Bradley!" she jabbed. "Two weeks ago last Saturday? He asked to take the children to the Franklin Institute. Well, OK. I said OK. *No* problem. Let them be together for an afternoon. Children need fathers, I said to myself. And so I got them ready and he picked them up, all polite and sheepish and contrite, and off they go to the Franklin Institute. The children were thrilled. And what do they tell me when they get home? About this nice lady 'Betsy' who sat with them at the movie they have over there and how this nice 'Betsy' went *all* through the museum with them and explained *every*thing. 'She's so smart, Mom.' And then they *all* drove down to Penn's Landing, and they *all* went on this neat ship, and Betsy even knew the captain. Jesus!" Thalia flipped her raven hair back and stalked with her drink into the back of the house.

Theo heard the rattle of ice cubes.

"You want any ice?" she yelled from the kitchen.

"No."

"Yes?"

"No!"

Thalia swept back into the living room with her clinking drink and a bowl of ice cubes. She dumped the cubes into Cassie's ice bucket, banged Cassie's ice bowl to the surface of the bar cart, and sailed toward her chair saying: "I bet that whore knows the whole crew of the ship. As well has half the men in this city— and I've got pictures to prove it. *I* had her followed," Thalia said smugly. "I hired a detective. Found him in the Yellow Pages.

86

Thirteen-hundred bucks for a week, including developing and enlargements. A couple of *real* good ones with Bradley's tongue down her throat in a car. And the best ones? They may have stripes all over them from the venetian blinds, but it's old Bradley putting it to Betsy in the No-Tell Motel. No question about it." She swallowed some scotch. "And the detective didn't cost me a nickel. You know what I did? I sold Bradley's mother's ruby ring. I got $2,100 for it. I'll give him the change," she said with satisfaction.

"Wow," Theo said.

"It's a nightmare, the whole goddamned thing," Thalia said, sad now. "Well, so, how are things with you?"

"Oh? You know. I work. And I work."

"Life's a bitch," Thalia said. She looked at her watch.

Theo raised an eyebrow at Thalia, expecting more.

She stood. She swiped at wrinkles in her skirt. She crossed the room and adjusted the frame of a small still life. "Trucks," she said, standing back from the wall. "They shake the house. You ever notice?"

"No."

Thalia perched again on the edge of her chair. She examined the backs of her hands. Within months Theo had seen her change from happy-go-lucky to bitter. She hated being 40. She hated having to scrimp when she had been able to spend. She hated living in the ruins of her marriage. Her beautiful face had begun to reflect her new, hard edges.

A key clicked. The front door opened.

"Good. You're here," Cassie said, placing her purse and her coat on the hall table.

"Where else would we be?" Thalia muttered.

"What?"

"I said, 'You're late.' "

"My meeting ran over," Cassie said. She was, like her brother and sister, tall and thin. Her short, black hair was cut like Thalia's but included silver strands Theo had not noticed before. He rose and hugged Cassie, feeling her shoulder blades and ribs through the fabric of her pinstriped suit. Thalia kept her seat.

"How are we all?" Cassie asked. She gave Thalia's shoulder a squeeze. She allowed her palm to rest there for a moment. "Did you get drinks? Did you find the hors d'oeuvres? No? Mrs. Wimmer left a plate in the refrigerator, I hope. A drink? Anyone? Theo, I haven't seen you in a month."

Cassie walked through her dining room, into her pantry and kitchen.

Thalia looked at her watch and at the ceiling and at the walls. "Bradley's always late too," she said to the arm of her chair. "He and Cassie ought to get together. God, maybe they have."

Theo paid her no attention. He concentrated on the light reflected in the polished wood of Cassie's antiques, on the designs of her rugs, and on the fresh flowers she kept about the house in honor of no occasion. The house was complete. She had no need or space for acquisition. When appliances wore out, she replaced them. When china or glassware broke, she ordered new pieces by phone from her jeweler. Her possessions were always in the same places. Only the flowers changed. She was satisfied—a well-adjusted widow.

Cassie returned to the living room with a tray of canapés, linen napkins, a cloudy ouzo for her drink, and a file folder tucked under her arm. She sat next to Theo on the couch. She opened her folder.

"Cheers," she said. She sipped ouzo. "Theo, you don't have a drink. What would you like?"

"I'm fine," he said, looking at the papers in her folder which appeared to be lists, then at the mole on her eyelid which seemed to him to have changed color since the time he first saw it. She ought to have that mole examined. She ought to have that mole taken off.

"We have to talk about Daddy's finances," Cassie began. She slid the temples of her gold reading glasses over her ears. She patted her hair on one side.

"How come?" Theo said.

"Well, we just do," Cassie said. "He's getting on. Recently, he hasn't been...himself."

Thalia nodded, her lips pressed forward. She leaned toward the folder.

Theo crossed his arms.

"I want to review his holdings with you and tell you some things I think should be done."

"Excuse me," Theo said, "you handle his finances. He pays you a fee to do that. I think his holdings are between you and him. Why are we all discussing this?"

"We're his children, Theo, for crying out loud," Thalia said. "We have a vested interest."

"Theo, he's getting older," Cassie said quietly. "Things change. It's my job to manage his assets and to anticipate changes."

"Well," Theo said. "I think you should manage them. With him."

"Theo, let her talk," Thalia said. She waved impatiently at Cassie. "Just go on."

"I do think this is important," Cassie said, lifting a page of typed script. "Daddy's estate falls into four primary areas—"

"Just a minute," Theo interrupted. "His 'estate?' What are we doing here, reading the will?"

"Theo, honestly!" Thalia said. "Stop being negative and let her get through this."

"Yes, Theo. Just let me continue," Cassie said in a firm business tone. "The largest area is stock, of course," she said, addressing herself to Thalia now. "Some years ago I encouraged him to consolidate a lot of his paper holdings into two mutual funds, which have done very well, I must say. Beyond the mutuals, I've got him invested in drug and communication stocks. By far, if you look at it over time anyway, Mother's little cable television shares have done the best. For purposes of discussion today, I've broken out the shares the three of us also own in Pro-Media, but try to keep in mind that with Daddy's quarter of those shares, we now jointly own 12% of the corporation. The money I earn as board member—" she looked briefly in Theo's direction, "is reinvested for Daddy. Less travel expenses," Cassie added. "In all, his stock holdings, including mutuals, are worth $1,671,000."

"God!" Thalia said. "We're *million*aires?"

"Well, Daddy is."

"How did he *get* all that?" Thalia squealed.

"By dint of perseverance and because he has a very clever investment counselor," Cassie said, looking over the tops of her half-lenses. "He bought and sold land. And he bought and sold a few houses. Daddy has a very good eye for real estate, Thalia. I took that nest egg, and I hatched it for him. Now," she said, returning to her papers. "The second area is life insurance. His policies total $850,000."

"Jesus H. Christ!" Thalia exclaimed, slack-jawed now.

"Well, the premiums have been a little steep, but I have made it possible for him to afford them. The policies themselves are pretty straightforward," Cassie continued. "As is the third area, bank accounts. I allow him a ceiling of $6,000 in checking, which is entirely too much, if you ask me, but that's the way he wants it. Twelve thousand in savings at 2.58%, which is nothing," she said, disgruntled, "And three TCDs totaling $60,000, which he absolutely refuses to roll into other investments." Cassie looked over the rim of her glasses at Thalia again. "Dumb, if you ask me, considering what he's making on the certificates, but he insists on supporting that stupid little Bank of the Poconos. I admit they lent him a lot of money over the years, but business is business.

"And the last area," she said, returning to her folder, "real estate. The house at the lake has an assessed tax value of $84,500. Add in the car and all that dreadful furniture, which, frankly, I haven't even put a value on, and that's pretty much the story. About 2.6 million," she said, allowing her reading glasses to fall on their chain to her chest.

"I don't know if you are aware of it, but years ago Daddy made it possible for me to…manipulate his financial affairs."

"You have power of attorney?" Theo asked.

"Let us say that I'm able to make decisions for him when they have to be made. That's the way he wanted it; and because I have certain…freedom, I've been able to make some very fast money for him."

Theo shifted on the couch. Cassie looked at Thalia. Thalia seemed transfixed.

"First and foremost," Cassie continued, patting her folder with the flat of her hand, "it is my job as executor to protect Daddy's estate."

"From what?" Theo said.

Cassie looked at him as if he had lost his senses.

"From being eaten up by taxes, for one thing," she replied, "And certainly you, as a doctor, have seen many families lose everything they have when a major illness strikes."

"Theo," Thalia said, "I don't know if you've noticed, but health care is *out* of control. I mean, I'm glad you're a doctor and all and that you get a piece of the action, but what about the rest of us? We're sitting ducks." She inclined her head again toward Cassie.

"There are several things we can do, Thalia," Cassie continued. "First, I am going to arrange for Daddy to give each of us an annual gift of $10,000."

"Ten thousand dollars!" Thalia exclaimed. "We're talking *millions* here, Cassie. Why not just have the bulk of it assigned to us? We could put the money in some kind of trust fund or something and see to his needs." She crossed her arms. "Of course, we'd give him whatever he wanted."

"Thalia, are you serious?" Theo said, taken aback.

"Theo is right, Thalia," Cassie said amiably. "The government doesn't let you do that. They do, but you wouldn't like paying the price."

Theo was appalled. "This has nothing to do with the goddamned *gov*ernment, Cassie! What's going on here? We shouldn't even be discussing this!"

Thalia leaned out from the edge of her chair. "Well, why the hell not, Theo? We're his children, for God's sake!"

Theo stood. His hands waved about.

"I don't believe this. You girls are acting like Dad's in a coma or something. On a respirator, for Christ's sake, gasping at death's door." Theo began to pace. "The man is perfectly capable of handling his own affairs."

"He clearly is not, Theo," Cassie said. She outlined the edge of her manila folder with a fingertip.

"Cassie, he talks to you on the phone when his insulin is off, and you decide he's a basket case. Well, go up there and have a look, is my advice. The two of you."

Cassie patted the cushion beside her. "Theo, sit down, dear."

"Yes," Thalia said. "Relax. We're looking after Daddy's best interests."

"Just hear me out, Theo," Cassie said. "Come on."

"I'm listening," he growled. He did not sit.

"I know this is unpleasant for you," Cassie said, addressing him now. "It's unpleasant for all of us. We don't like to face these truths."

"Absolutely," Thalia said to the folder.

"I'm simply trying to protect Daddy's assets, is all I'm doing," Cassie declared. "There are things you are permitted to do by the government, and there are things which are not allowed. We want to avoid any…implication that what we're setting out to do is done 'in anticipation of death.'" Cassie waved the notion away. "Certainly Daddy is going to have many healthy and happy years ahead of him. We all know that. The purpose of this discussion is to protect his money from…outside interests. Everyone should do this. I do this for you, Theo, with your own assets. I arrange your money so that there will be more for you. Were you happy with your tax return this year? You were very happy. Have you ever been audited? No, you have not. I am proposing here that we take a few perfectly legal steps to protect what Daddy has worked so hard to accumulate, and that is all.

"Now, it is perfectly legal for Daddy to make an annual gift of $10,000 to each of us. It would be ours to do with as we please. I would hope that we would all invest it wisely, rather than squander it," shortest of glances in Thalia's direction.

"Like buying *food?*" Thalia exclaimed. "You know, if I didn't have an income from teaching, the kids and I would *starve!* We would. You know what that son of a bitch gives me for child support? Zip! You know what the son of a bitch made last year? Eighty-three thousand dollars! It isn't that he can't af*ford* to feed his children. No. He for*got* to feed his children. Give me a break!"

"Thalia," Cassie said patiently, "That will change—when you two stop assaulting each other. But back to Daddy. The law allows everyone to set aside funds for burial."

"Peanuts!" Thalia said. Her nails raked her hair.

"Well, I guess it is," Cassie continued. "But everything adds up. Now, the house at the lake. We must take steps to protect Daddy's home."

Theo stopped pacing. "Protect it from what?"

"If Daddy were to be stricken with some catastrophic illness with a half a million in hospital bills, that property could be attached. A lien could be placed against it."

"God!" Thalia said. "A *lien?* On Summit Lake? They couldn't do that. Take the house you live in? No way. NO way!"

"Well, they can," Cassie said. "They can do about anything they please."

"And what is your solution to this lien which has been slapped on our father's house?" Theo asked sarcastically.

"We'll buy the house," Cassie replied, sitting back.

"*Buy* it?" Thalia chortled. "Oh, Cassie! Really!"

"Why not?"

Thalia's back stiffened. " 'Why not?' 'Why not!' My *hus*band has abandoned me, Cassie. I would remind you that I no longer have a pot to piss in! I can't even afford my *own* mortgage!"

"Thalia," Cassie said as if to a child, "I appreciate your circumstances, but they are not the issue just now."

"Well, of *course* they are!" Thalia said shrilly. "How could I buy another house? You're as crazy as Bradley is, Cassie! Bradley has canceled my Macy's card. Sunoco! I can't even buy *gas* on credit!" Thalia's eyes filled. Her lips skewed.

"Thalia," Cassie said gently. "We will lend you the money." She smiled toward Theo.

"Hold it!" Theo said, stopping in his tracks. "Who is this 'we,' white woman?"

"You and I, Theo. Theo and I will lend you the money, Thalia. We give Daddy $100,000 for the house, a little more if he wants it—then we own the place. Summit Lake cannot be attached. Daddy lives there for the rest of his life. Thalia, you can pay back our loan to you when you get your divorce settlement."

"*What* divorce settlement?" Thalia said, aghast. "I never said I was going to divorce Bradley!"

Cassie regarded Thalia, eyebrows raised. "And what *will* you do, Thalia? Be Bradley's doormat for the rest of your life? Child, after what he has done to you, you have no other option."

"Hold on," Theo said, standing over Cassie now. "Just hold on. You're the executor, right?"

"Correct," Cassie said. Her fingers tapped the folder.

"Then you know that Dad is leaving Summit Lake to me."

"No," Cassie said, astonished. "According to the will, Rosy has the use of the house for her lifetime, then Summit Lake goes to the three of us. And we share equally in the assets of the remaining estate. It's all written down, Theo," she said, dismissing him.

"Which brings up another problem," Thalia said, recovering.

"God, another problem," Theo muttered.

"The problem of Rosy," Thalia said. *"She* shouldn't get anything. Locking our father in his bedroom. The very idea. She should be excommunicated. Or whatever it is."

"Disinherited," Cassie said.

"And excommunicated!" Thalia declared.

"You don't know that Rosy did that," Theo said.

"Daddy told me himself," Thalia said. "And he told Cassie. And he told Cassie that he called you. What more do you need, Theo?"

"I was up there last weekend. I asked him straight out if Rosy ever locked him in. He said no."

"And was *she* in the room when you asked him?" Thalia said, chin out.

"No. We were alone. But I asked her too."

Thalia's chin thrust farther forward. "Then how do you explain all the phone calls he's been making to us, Theo?"

"Blood chemistry. When your insulin level is too low, you become confused. It's as simple as that. You can imagine all kinds of things."

"Could we back up here for a minute," Cassie interrupted. "I know nothing about the Summit Lake house going to you. I hold the 1983 original of Daddy's will."

"Obviously, Cassie, there's a will you don't know about," Theo said.

"There couldn't be!" Cassie snapped.

"Dad told me last Saturday night that he wanted you girls to have the money and he wants me to have the house."

"Well, what does *Rosy* get, then?" Thalia sneered.

"Rosy gets the insurance," Theo said.

"Eight *hun*dred and fifty thousand *do*llars?" Thalia thundered, losing her delicate balance. "Over my dead body!"

"Like it or not, Thalia, it's what Dad wants," Theo said. "And what do you care? Half of 1.6 million will certainly keep you in gas money."

"And on that happy note," Theo said, bending to kiss the top of Thalia's head, "I'm leaving you two to sort out the lien and all those massive hospital bills of Dad's.

"Cassie," He kissed his surprised sister's cheek, "maybe you better take a little drive up to the mountains. Have a heart-to-heart with Dad? See if anything's new since 1983? Bye, ladies. I'm sure we'll be talking soon."

Theo walked into the hall. He put on his topcoat. The front door opened and closed.

Thalia raked her hair. "Some executor *you* turn out to be, Cassandra. *You* aren't even working from the right *will!*"

Chapter 11

After seeing Thalia out, Cassie walked through her living room, collecting as she went the glasses, the napkins, the untouched canapés of her unsuccessful meeting.

As she crossed her dining room, she thought she should have handled things differently. She should have called Theo, invited him to lunch or to dinner—just the two of them—and after chit-chat about their businesses, which she would lead around to a discussion of Theo's own portfolio, lead then to their father's finances, to the importance of preplanning. She should have finessed him. Forget democracy. Forget the open forum. This was not your ordinary family. No, sirree.

And Thalia with her two-track mind that flipped from Bradley to money and back. Had she managed her own finances all these years instead of being such a spendthrift, she'd have the independence to handle her jerk of a husband.

Cassie tore a sheet of plastic wrap and sealed the plate of canapés. She placed the plate in the freezer on top of the ice cube trays. She opened the refrigerator and removed the casserole of lamb and eggplant Mrs. Wimmer had made at her instruction. She spooned a portion into a bowl, programmed her microwave oven, and while her dinner heated, she set a place for herself at the dining table: sterling silver, linen napkin, her good salt and pepper shakers. She poured a 1983 French burgundy from a Waterford decanter into a leaded crystal glass. 1983. The year her father wrote his will. The year her Warren died. A fine year for burgundies. The worst year of her life. Oh, well.

Alone in her silent house, at her dining table lit with candles, Cassie ate slowly, savoring her lamb redolent of rosemary. Now and then the quiet was broken by her silver fork striking a Havilland plate. Now and then her wine glass clinked when she returned it to the waxed tabletop. Linen rustled at her lips.

The casserole was perfect. She would tell Mrs. Wimmer.

When she had finished her meal, she remained at the table. She sipped the inch of burgundy remaining in her glass. She rolled the liquid over her tongue, breathing out through her nose so as to increase the effect of its molecules. How many bottles did she have left? Five? Six? And when they were gone, was Warren gone? And how long would the scent of him remain in the suits that hung still in his closets upstairs?

In her bed, in an oyster-colored lace and satin nightgown, with the gold chain of her gold reading glasses pooled above her clavicle, Cassie read financial magazines. Yellow Post-its stuck up above pages she would have copied for her staff's required reading. She made brackets in the margins of certain passages. Sometimes she wrote the names of certain clients before those brackets which applied to them. She was familiar with the holdings of most of the major clients of her firm. Her staff had to hustle to keep up with her.

Her phone rang. Annoyed, she looked at the clock at her bedside.

"I called Theo a little while ago," Thalia said. "Bradley Junior has a fever. Theo was as sweet as pie."

"What were you expecting? An axe in your forehead?"

"I don't know. I expected him to be surly. Or sulking."

"That's not Theo's style. He'll wait for just the right moment, and then he'll put his foot down. Surly and sulking seem to have become *your* style, Thalia."

"Since when? I'm not surly."

Cassie pushed herself up in her bed. "Thalia, you had better sit down and have a conversation with yourself about your situation. And I mean that. You're a mess."

"Listen," Thalia snapped. "Real easy for you to say that, clipping coupons over there on Delancey Place in your piss-elegant house. Come over here to Spring Garden and my mail with red stickers stamped all over everything and a kitchen full of plaster dust and appliances in boxes that haven't even been paid for and a car that sounds like a goddamned motorcycle and two unruly kids getting brattier by the minute. You just come over here for a week and tell *me* I'm surly. You'd be surly too, Cassie Bitler!"

"Thalia, I know, dear," Cassie said soothingly. "It's not easy for you." Cassie opened a magazine. She paged through it. "Suddenly your whole life has changed." She allowed some slight sarcasm here. "And you are taken by surprise."

"Yes," Thalia said wistfully, "I was taken by surprise. I was...but I shouldn't have been." She gained momentum. "I should have known. I should have expected this. I shouldn't have taken the son of a bitch back the last time." Thalia exhaled into the mouthpiece. "But what are you going to do?"

"So, Theo was pleasant."

"Oh, you'd never know he was pissed at us."

"Don't say 'pissed,' dear."

"Everyone says 'pissed.' "

"Well, it doesn't become you."

"All the kids say 'pissed.' The whole faculty says 'pissed.' I even hear it on the news. You'd blow an aneurysm if you heard what I hear around school every day."

"We've never used harsh language in our family, Thalia. Daddy never even said 'damn' around us."

"Well, times change. Shit happens, as Bradley Junior says." Thalia sighed. "I never expected to be cuckolded...Can women be cuckolded? I don't know. That's what it comes down to, whatever they call it. You know, I hate that little slut. I could choke her with my own hands. I could watch her turn blue, with dispassion. I could, Cassie...*She* ought to be making my mortgage payments."

"Thalia, if you need money..."

"Oh, no. I'm just *fine*. It's just Strawbridge's and Macy's and Bloomingdale's and Sunoco and Sears that need money. They're not fine. And my muffler that fell off right in the middle of the art museum circle? It's not fine. And Green Tree School? They're not very fine. One of these days that school bus is going to go whizzing right down our block blowing exhaust in my children's faces. But we'll handle that. I'll just enroll them at Gratz. Time they learned about drugs and metal detectors anyway, don't you think...?" Thalia began to sniffle.

"Thalia, dear. Listen," Cassie said. She wound the phone cord around her forefinger. "I have some money I could let you have for a little while. What do you need, a few thousand to tide you over?"

Thalia gurgled. "Oh, Cassie. That is so sweet. That is such a generous, *dear* thing for you to offer...but I couldn't accept your money. I couldn't possibly. No." Cassie heard Thalia blow her nose. "But what we were talking about this afternoon? If Daddy gave us each $10,000? That would be a big help. That would be acceptable...How soon could you arrange to make that happen?"

"Oh," Cassie said, pushing a pillow behind her head. "That wouldn't happen for awhile. No. I'll have to discuss that with Daddy. And have another little talk with Theo. No. That's a ways off. But I could give that much to you now and then you pay me back when you get yours from Daddy?"

"No," Thalia said. "It would be taking your money. I am not accepting charity."

"It's not charity I'm offering. Call it a business deal, if it'll make you feel more comfortable. This is not a gift, dear. Also, I'd expect you to pay me interest."

"No. I couldn't take it. I don't think I'd feel right."

"Well, all right, Thalia. We'll say no more…Would you like to bring the children over for dinner Friday night? This is probably the last week I'll have free before the tax rush starts. I could have Mrs. Wimmer make something special the kids like."

"Well, maybe just $10,000. To get us through. For the children. But with interest, Cassie."

"Fine."

"When could you do that?"

"When would you need it?"

"Tomorrow?"

"Uh, certainly. Stop by my office after lunch. I'll have a check ready."

"I'll go right to the garage and get that damned muffler fixed. It's so embarrassing. Everyone stares at me when I'm driving. My students call me 'Mrs. Ba-room.' I get off at 3. I'll come by then."

"I'll be in conference at 3. I'll leave a check with my secretary. And a promissory note."

"What are we going to do about Daddy?"

"I don't know, Thalia."

"Well, I'll see you at 3."

"I'll be in conference."

"Right. You said that. I don't know where my head is these days. Well, I do know where my head is these days…. What kind of father would do something like this to his children? What kind of father would leave his home and his family for a common *slut,* Cassie? Now, you tell me."

Cassie pressed the "1" key on her telephone pad. "Thalia, dear, I have a call on the other line. Do you mind? It may be a client."

"All right. But don't forget. I'll be at your office at 3."

"Fine." Cassie dropped the receiver into the cradle.

"You don't know where your head is. Or your manners, either," she muttered. " 'Thank you, Cassie. I really appreciate this.' 'Thank you—this money means so much to me.' "

Cassie sighed. She picked up her magazine. She paged idly. Her hands and the magazine dropped to her lap.

Thalia was such a mess.

Thalia…was Thalia.

Well, she chose Bradley. She made her own bed. Of all the men she could have had, Thalia had to pick Bradley.

But he was a charmer. And who *wouldn't* be taken in by him? Who could be blamed for a few, fast minutes of tipsy indiscretion in a car with Bradley? And nothing happened, really.

Nothing worth mentioning. Or making a fuss over. A few careless minutes in the back seat of a car?

Well, she had been lonely then. Before she learned to live alone and to prefer it, Warren having broken her heart by dying unannounced.

Dear, fat, self-effacing Warren. The only weed in her own garden of Bradleys. So Warren had no charisma. So he was a bit naive. So he slew no women in any crowded room they ever entered. He slew Cassie over and over during 23 years, until he dropped dead on the kitchen floor without so much as a fare-thee-well.

She sighed. She gathered her magazines and lay them on the night table. She pulled the chain of her reading glasses over her head. She turned off her bed lamp.

Thalia's hand rested for a time on the telephone as she made a rapid assessment of her cash flow.

With $104 in the checking account and the eight $100 bills left over from the ruby ring, hidden on the lintel of her closet door, and her paycheck Friday and the $10,000 from Cassie, she will have something over $11,500.

She would strip the joint account, close it, open a new one—in a new bank, in her own name. The ruby ring was a gift to her from Bradley's mother, wasn't it? Never mind the understanding that the ring was to be passed to her first daughter. She would buy Martha another ruby ring. A finer, larger one. There were difficult times not counted on, not expected. Things changed. Shit happened. When Mary Markham gave her the ring, she did not expect that her perfect Bradley would take up with the most conniving bitch in the city of Philadelphia and betray the trust of his wife and his children. Leave them with a hundred and four dollars in the bank and cancel all the charge cards. That ring was Thalia's insurance policy.

Tomorrow she would get the car fixed. It would cost maybe a hundred. Say, a hundred and four. So much for the bank account. And then the bills.

"Bradley! Bradley *Junior!* Bradley!"

A door opened at the top of the stairs. Rock music reverberated in the stairwell.

"Turn that *off!* You're sick. You have a fever! It is 10:05. You know the rules. Turn that *off!*"

The door closed. The sound dropped a step.

"Brad-ley Jun-ior!"

The sound dropped another step.

"*Off!*" she shrieked.

The music dropped to base vibrations.

"Listen to you," she mumbled to herself crossing the hall to the den. "You've become a screamer. One of those out-of-control,

screaming mothers. A goddamned harpy."

She crossed the den and, standing at the desk, stared at the matching photographs of herself and of her husband at the back of its envelope-strewn surface. She sat. She snatched up the photograph of her husband and placed it face down on the desktop. She stared at the back of the frame. She took the frame up again. She pried its little staples out with her letter opener. She stripped the photograph from the frame. She held the loose photograph of Bradley in her hands. Handsome. So very handsome. Could be a movie star. Sexy, smiling like that—slightly at one side of his slightly parted lips.

Thalia tore the photograph in half, then in half, and in half again until she could no longer tear the parts. She threw Bradley into the wastebasket. The frame followed with a crash.

"Lying son of a bitch!"

Thalia gathered bills from the desktop. Her long, thin fingers ticked through the envelopes; they tweezed out folded contents. Envelopes followed the photograph and the frame into the wastebasket. She was interested in original bills. She lay one envelope with a green warrior logo at the side of the desk and on top of it an envelope with a green tree in the corner. She discarded statements and dunning notices. She made a pile of original, itemized bills and sorted these by issuing bank, by department store. She placed utility bills in a separate pile.

She examined charges from Visa and MasterCard and from department stores. When she found "mens furnishings" and "underwear, men's" and "United Airlines" she struggled with herself, but put these bills in the payable pile. She ticked amounts on her legal pad. She included utilities. She added the long column then, disbelieving, added it again. She underlined the total at the end. Over $7,000. Her shoulders slumped. She sighed. She reached for the envelope with the green tree on it. She slit it open. She read. She added the children's tuition to her list.

Her total was now $13,600. She fell back in her chair. Her fingers drummed on her thighs. Rock music tumbled down the stair steps.

"*Brad-leeeey!*"

The music was unabated.

Why should she have to pay the tuition out of her $10,000? The tuition was Bradley's responsibility. The mortgage and the tuition payments. A roof over his children's heads and their schooling. Little enough. And if he paid the tuition, she would have some left over. Something ahead. And why, come to think of it, should she pay for his underwear and shirts? She sorted again through her pile of itemized bills, searching for charges for men's items. She began a new column. And why pay United Airlines? Why pay American? His paychecks did not come to her. Flying was a cost of his doing business. If she were the one making $83,000 a year, she would pay. But she was not. She was the one making $34,000.

She added the cost of socks to his list. She found charges for ties and shoes and belts and amorphous charges which she knew were his—men's this and men's that. And when she had been through all the department stores and the Visa and the Master-Card, she began on the oil company credit cards. She wrote down each charge which listed the license plate of his car, the Cadillac Coupe de Ville—the good car, the car that started each time you turned the key, the one that slid away from a curb and did not sound like a land mover. And when she had finished with the oil companies, she snatched up the other green-logo envelope, the American Express bill. And to the beat of heavy metal that now rattled the glass bric-a-brac and porcelain figurines on the wall shelves above her, she began a third column: "AX," under which she wrote $45.50 and in parentheses, "Stems 'n Petals." She looked at the date of the charge: the week before her wedding anniversary. But no petals had arrived at her door.

"Animal!" she exclaimed, throwing down her pen.

She read on.

More weekly charges from "Stems 'n Petals." And hotel charges. Dinners. And rooms. At the Four Seasons. At the Sheraton Society Hill. At the Hotel Atop-the-Bellevue. The bill in her hand trembled. Nearly $2,000 in a single month. This was not business entertainment.

As she had calculated how she would finance her weekly trip to ShopRite, *he* showered his hinge-legged slut with Stems 'n Petals and dined in the Fountain Room.

Her daughter's voice was shrill in the hall above. "Brad-*leeey!*"

"*Brad-leeeey!*" Thalia shrieked. "*Brad-leeeey, you turn that off now!*"

The music stopped. Martha's door slammed.

Thalia snatched up the department store bills, the oil company and credit card and utility bills, the tuition bills from the Green Tree School. She slapped the American Express bill on top of the pile. She wrapped her own totaled list around the bundle, snapped on a rubber band, and threw the pack onto the middle of the desk.

"That's *it!*" she cried, breathing heavily. "That is *it!*"

She would get sick at lunch hour. No—before lunch hour. She would find herself the sleaziest divorce lawyer in this city of lawyers. She would impound her husband's car. She would swear liens against his suits and ties and Jockey shorts. She would garnish his wages into perpetuity. She would fix it so he and his whore would be spending their nights in a homeless shelter. She would emasculate the bastard legally and hang his balls under the portecochere of the Four Seasons Hotel.

Chapter 12

Sam washed pots and pans. Soap bubbles adhered to the reddish hairs of his hands and wrists. On the few occasions when Theo cooked, he did not clean up after each step. He would not wash a pan to reuse it. He would take up another and work his way down to each new, clean space along the length of the counters until sometimes there were no clean spaces left. The cost of Theo's cooking a meal. A cost Sam would pay without complaint to have Theo cook a meal.

He would give Theo an hour in his den, more time if he needed it, with his medical journals and his sketch pads of flayed-open faces and skulls, his precisely drawn plans for reconstruction. He would give him as much time as he needed. Up to a point. Up to some intuitive point, after which Sam would feel disappointed. After which he would feel taken for granted again. A point after which something would be lost again and not found this day.

Day five of 30. Thirty-one, maybe, depending on how you chose to count a month, depending on the level of your patience or your generosity. Or your desperation.

Five days of no touching of special significance. Oh, touching as you passed behind or leaned across—"excuse me" kinds of touching. But no hand laid at the center of a back or looped over the biceps and allowed to rest there longer than would be socially acceptable in an elevator or some public place. No coming up behind you while you washed dishes, no wrapping of arms around your waist. No insinuations at your ear.

Sam was dealing with a cripple. He needed to remind himself of that daily. He was dealing with a man who had been socialized as most men were, a man who, having received little touching, had been taught not to touch. A man who had been taught to get along without touching because it was not done.

How curious that Theo would become a doctor, that he chose a profession that was performed through touching, a profession that required that hands be placed on people's bodies. All over them. He chose a profession which made the touching of any body part appropriate if it were a part of treatment or examination or simple comfort. Yet Theo could not reach out to Sam without effort, without his learned prohibitions rising, without lingering anxiety. This had been a puzzle to Sam for nearly five years. He understood the public affection part, understood the discomfort that public affection aroused among the public. But not the other. Not the private reluctance, the hesitation behind closed doors. Theo could not fear rejection, could he? Sam could not remember a time when he had rejected any kind of touch from Theo, when he did not give it back in kind. And with enthusiasm. He never complained to Theo that the vast majority of their comings together in sex were at his own initiation. He thought about bringing that up, but he did not. He might bring it up to Susan, but he did not harp at Theo. What difference did it make who started sex, anyway? Who cared who reached out first? Who cared who looked at the other and gave that unmistakable message, so long as the message was delivered and accepted.

Until there was a point to be made. Until initiation became a symbol of intent, of commitment. Until the point had to be made, or there would be no point.

Theo was trying. He arrived home at about the time he said he would. He had called from the office twice since Sunday. For no reason. At the emergency room where Sam worked. At the house. Their nights were more or less normal. It was only that they slept in separate beds. In separate rooms. And had no touching.

Sam wiped the pots dry. He hung them on hooks over the stove. He sponged the countertop, carrying with him a can of Comet which he sprinkled here and there on discolored scratches in the Formica.

Sam lay on the couch in the living room. His ankles rested, elevated, on one of the couch's arms. He listened to a recording of Bach cantatas and fugues.

He thought of Theo upstairs in his den making anatomical drawings at his desk, planning his next manipulation. Theo spent hours with himself, getting up to examine the back-lit X-ray panel he had had installed on a wall of his den, sitting again to finish the next panel of the surgical storyboard he would review with his surgical team prior to touching the patient. These drawings were so precise.

Theo was a doctor; Sam was a nurse.

Theo was 46; Sam was 37. Theo liked to be by himself; Sam preferred company. Theo burned calories; Sam counted them. Theo avoided confrontation; Sam was a provocateur. Theo lived in the closet; Sam was out to the world. Theo smiled; he guffawed.

They did not travel well together. Theo liked to be on the move, to take off in planes, to board trains to new cities; Sam liked to stay in one place and enjoy. Theo was a clothes horse; Sam lived in blue jeans and T-shirts, shorts in the summer. Theo read medical journals; Sam read biographies. Theo played elevator music; he, Bach and Saint-Saëns.

What, after all, was the glue of this relationship? Their same tastes in furniture?

And was he wrong to have precipitated a crisis? To threaten to move out? One couldn't have everything. If his life with Theo were without bumps and hitches, he'd have tired of Theo within the first months, the first weeks. Was it essential for him to have bumps and hitches? If there were none, was he compelled to create them? Was he, in fact, his own saboteur?

"Sam. Sam?" Theo said, nudging his shoulder.

Theo leaned over the back of the couch cushions. "Hey. Hi."

"I fell asleep."

"Yes, you did." Theo prodded Sam up and sat behind him on the couch. He stretched a leg out along each side of Sam. He pulled the couch pillows away and dropped them to the floor. Sam lay back into Theo's lap and chest. One of Theo's hands rested on the side of Sam's chest, the other arm wrapped across. Sam could not see Theo's face.

"You're done with your work?" Sam asked.

"Yes. I'm going to do something wonderful tomorrow. That is, I'm going to start something wonderful tomorrow. I'm going to build a nose out of some new stuff I've been playing with. It's from DuPont. This chemist down there developed it, and we've been playing with it together. He's figured out a way to make it solidify with light, like they do with tooth fillings? Except the stuff remains pliable. It feels just like cartilage when it's set. The problem was in anchoring it. Before, I could build a nose out of it, but if Bob Calhoon got hit in the face with a volleyball a year from now, his nose would sort of slide into one of his cheeks. Not a pretty sight. Now it'll stay where it belongs."

"You're a genius."

110

"No, the guy at DuPont is the genius. I'm a real good mechanic. It's 'Better living through chemistry.' Susan and I are going to put that on our shingle."

"How is she?"

"I don't know. She says she's doing too much."

"How's her kid?"

"OK, I guess." He had never told Sam about Natalia.

They remained on the couch, Sam in the crotch of Theo's legs. Sam looked about the room. Sam waited and breathed.

"You horny?" Sam said after a moment.

The hand at Sam's shoulder slid across his chest and paused, then moved down and slowly tugged Sam's shirttail out. Theo's palm moved under the fabric of Sam's shirt and across the side of his chest at waist level, the location of one of Sam's many misplaced erogenous zones. This was an old move. And they were off and running.

"You're sleeping in the guest room?" Theo said as Sam turned into its doorway.

"I told you," Sam said over his shoulder. "Until April 9th."

"But, I thought…"

Sam turned. He smiled. His hand was on the door frame. "That was very, very nice," he said. "I loved it. Thank you. Good night, Theo."

In the guest room Sam sat on the edge of the bed. Was he correct in this stance he had taken? Why not give it up and turn out this light and walk in there? Slide into bed where he belonged and resume life as it was?

Alone in their bed Theo squirmed to find a comfortable position. Outside, the March winds vibrated the lamp lit, bare branches. Theo curled into himself for warmth. He stretched a leg out across the bed; he pulled it back from the cold of the sheets there.

"Stubborn," he said into his pillow. "Fucking mule stubborn."

He pulled Sam's pillow to his chest.

He turned onto his back.

What was the block he felt in his life? Why the sense that he must hold back in his relationships when his impulse was to charge ahead?

In his work he did not hesitate to take a body part from one place and use it in another. In his work he had taken toes and made thumbs of them. Tomorrow he would shape a nose out of plastic goo and cement it where there had been no nose and give a man his life back. Given enough time, he could create a face where there had been none, yet at 46 he watched his own life unfold as if on television.

What could he fear?

If he could remove a chunk of a boy's hip and form that bone into jaw, if he could re-form skull into cheekbone, why could he not say to another, This is not acceptable to me?

"Sam?" he said in the dark.

There was no answer.

"Hey, Sam?"

"What?" came the muffled voice down the hall.

"Can I come in *there?*"

"No."

Chapter 13

Susan Zack found herself in the throes of beddy-bye catch 22. It was 11:10 p.m. She had to operate at 7 a.m. She had to be at the hospital by 6. She had to awake at 5:15. In order to feel rested, she needed six hours of sleep. In order to get her sleep, she had to be asleep within five minutes. She could not sleep for worrying that she would not. If she did not sleep within five minutes, she would not feel rested. If she thought about not sleeping, she would not sleep. And so on and so on.

As much as she planned her life—as much as she scheduled the events of each hour of her too-full days—she could not seem to catch up, could not accommodate the small intrusions which scattered her organization.

And what was going on with her daughter Natalia? So obstreperous after years of being docile and agreeable. The perfect baby; the delightful child. No terrible twos. No ferocious fours. But five with a vengeance.

Susan was beginning to feel out of control of her daughter. She was beginning to feel out of control of her own life. She needed to cut back. She needed to begin to say "no" in order to make space. In order to create some living space. Just a few blank slots in her maniacal schedule would make all the difference.

It was her being away from Natalia during much of the day that was causing this rebelliousness, this behavior that was verging on rude. Natalia resented the gradual disappearance of her mother. She resented that Susan did not pick her up from PlaySchool at 3—that it was Mrs. Cristobel who picked her up and Mrs. Cristobel who entertained until dinner and Mrs. Cristobel who prepared the dinner more often than not. And Mrs. Cristobel readied Natalia for bed and Mommy's draggy arrival in time for the golden half hour of quality time with her little precious at jammy time.

Natalia was no fool. She saw through her mommy's thin smiles at Mommy's little sleeper bunny's bedside. Natalia saw her mommy gaze longingly at sleeper bunny's little pillow over the top of the open book, knew that her Mommy could not care less about the saga in which Piglet is entirely surrounded by water. Knew that her Mommy coveted her little sleeper bunny's own pillow.

Go play in the street for awhile, sweetheart. Your mommy needs your bed for 20 minutes. Just 20 minutes. Go visit your sperm donor daddy. Spend the night. Spend a week. Get to know him. A great guy. Sends you certificates of deposit birthdays and Christmas? Enough there for four years of college—no matter what the cost 12 years from now.

Natalia's mommy felt that she was entirely surrounded by water. Her mommy had no Christopher Robin to come to rescue her in a boat named *The Brain of Pooh.*

Though Mommy had received a call from a potential Christopher Robin, a.k.a. Dr. Timothy Garlington. He of the sleepy, half-mast eyelids and the tight, tucked heinie and the silver tongue; he who would probably take your breath away in bed and then leave you breathless.

And why not? Why not go out to dinner? Get gussied up for a leisurely tête-à-tête at Le Bec Fin, followed by the forbidden dessert cart and a B&B or two, followed by a leisurely walk uptown to 1830 Rittenhouse and a long-overdue pelvic in the bedroom with the incredible view? Why not?

Mommy had needs too.

Susan rolled over yet again. She looked at the clock yet again. It was 11:20.

Now she was into sleep debt. Now she had to sleep. She must count sheep. Or count tight, tucked buns. Or surgical tools. Or tools—no, not them.

Clear the mind. Recreate the *tabula rasa*. Pound in the welcome sign for the sandman.

She would never get to sleep. She would fall, exhausted, from her bed at 5:15. She would gather herself up and drag herself in to the operating room, her eyes bruised during her sleepless night, her mind scattered with fantasy, and her hands shaky above the draped neck of the sleeping hopeful whose carcinoma Susan was expected to excise. A slip of a shaky hand followed by a bloodbath.

She should call Theo. She should wake Theo from snugly bear dreams. Call in her chits, have him report to the OR in her stead. Let Theo, sleep-washed and steady-fingered, remove the tumor while she—oblivious, dreamed-out, unconscious—recovered a sense of her disordered life.

She should appear at Theo's door after work, the astonished Natalia at her side, to demand that he assume responsibility for his recalcitrant daughter. That he take her in for some days. That he explain to the puzzled child that her mommy had made a deal with him. That her mommy, concerned that her hormones might run out before her luck did, admiring both his gift of friendship and his tall, dark, handsome, and intelligent genes, asked if he might consider arranging to put a few milky vials in her possession to use as she wished. To have them squirted in and there combined with a few fine genes of her own. To create something very wonderful.

Well, here she is, Theo. And isn't she wonderful? Don't her

own gray eyes cloud with anger just as yours do? And doesn't her jaw square in frustration just as yours does? And is her hair not as thick and black as yours; and does her smile not twist—unlearned—just as yours to show the space where her gleaming Tithonus molars will grow in?

And is she not as bright and as clever as both her mommy and her daddy? And does her laughter not lift and fall just like her daddy's? Is she not her aunts in miniature? Is she not magnificent? Can't you just take her up and raise her for a few days while her mommy takes some days off to get her act back together, so her mommy can come home to blessedly empty rooms? To fall asleep in her trench coat on the couch? To fall asleep in her white lab coat upon the kitchen floor?

Well, she had asked for fluid, not commitment. She had asked only for seed and said that she would do the rest, not knowing how much her days would conspire to drain her and her nights to exhaust her into deep sleep debt.

Now the clock read 11:33. Eighteen minutes into debt. Her jammy land account overdrawn.

And where was the warm arm of her own Christopher Robin? The arm that began at rest over her shoulder and fell to rest in sleep at the curve of her kidney? Where the reassuring and even breathing beside her?

Why not call the suave and famous Dr. Garlington and say, Yes, dinner would be nice? Forget dinner. Bag dinner. Slather the diaphragm with Nonoxynol-9 and insert it before she dressed and met him at 1830. Take the tube of Nonoxynol-9 along and insist he use it in a condom, and go for the gold. Who knew whom he'd been with? Who cared with eyes and shoulders like that? She had not been looked at with such undisguised lust in ten years. She had not been so turned on since she did it with the phone man in 1989 on her living room floor, looking up through her glass-topped cocktail table at a cigarette ad on the back of a magazine. The cheapest thing she had ever done—and the most exhilarating.

Where did you want me to put that jack, ma'am?

Put it right there, big boy!

She would never get to sleep.

Erase the phone man. Erase Timothy Garlington. Erase the looming operating room. Create the *tabula rasa*.

Eleven thirty-nine.

Chapter 14

Nice work," Timothy Garlington admitted, feeling the boy's skull.

"Thank you," Theo said perfunctorily. He smiled at his patient. "Larry and I go back a long way, don't we, buddy? How old were you when you first came to the hospital?"

"Four," the boy said.

"We've done nine procedures over 11 years," Theo explained. "Tomorrow's operation, except for his new teeth, makes it two to go. And then you'll never have to come back here again, Larry. Unless you just want to visit," he added. Theo stood to bring this brief examination to an end.

"I'd like to look at the patient's records," Garlington said, stepping back from the boy.

"Help yourself," Theo said. "In fact, Larry can take you down and show them to you. He's been through them all and knows almost as much about what we've done as I do. I bet you could even assist in an operation, couldn't you, Larry?"

"I don't know about that," Larry said, blushing with pleasure.

"It is the patient's X-rays which interest me, rather than the records," Garlington said, ignoring Larry.

"Fine," Theo said. He squeezed Larry's shoulder. "I'll come by later, sport. We're going to start at 7 tomorrow."

"Which operating room do we have?" Larry asked.

"What, you got a favorite?"

"Four has the best sound system. I brought some new compact disks."

"Satan's Revenge?"

"Nah. That's kid stuff. Now I'm into girl singers."

"I work just fine to girl singers," Theo said. "Give the disks to Dr. Branstetter. He's your sandman. He'll be up to see you later."

Theo and Garlington walked the long hall from Larry's room on the pediatric surgical floor.

"Not a pretty picture," Garlington observed.

"He will be when I'm finished with him," Theo replied curtly and did not engage Garlington further in small talk.

At X-ray records, Theo asked for several of Larry's early operations. He paged through a ratty magazine in which he had no interest while they waited for the plates and still photographs to be brought out. Garlington, impatient and uneasy, stood with crossed arms, shifting his weight from leg to leg.

In a small X-ray reading room, Theo clipped negatives from Larry's thick folders to the backlit wall. He handed Garlington several glossy photos of Larry's head prior to his first operation. "This is why they call him 'the boy with no face,' " Theo began.

"There *was* no left eye?"

"There was. But it was completely concealed under the skin of the cheek."

"Looks like a fucking cyclops," Garlington said with undisguised disgust. "How did he eat? How did he breath? There's just a little hole there."

Theo ignored the comment. "His corrected vision is 20/24. I didn't think we'd get anywhere near that. He wears only one contact lens. The nasal passages were only partially formed. We built new channels and a temporary nose."

"Goddamned ugly," Garlington muttered.

Theo clenched a fist and relaxed it. He sorted through photographs and handed one to Garlington. "Great lips," Theo said. "Maybe the best lips I ever made from scratch. The teeth will all be implants of course. We have a decent bone base. All Dicors," Theo added proudly. "The hospital screamed bloody murder, but they finally approved them."

"I never saw an uglier human being in my life."

"That's what his mother thought, Garlington. She gave him to the Sisters of Mercy—drove him into Misericordia College when he was a month old, handed him to the first nun she saw, and was gone in a cloud of dust. The sisters were wonderful. They found him adoptive parents. Very sweet people."

"Christ," Garlington said, still staring at the first photograph. "Who'd adopt that?"

Theo grimaced. He would endure this. "He has 40% hearing in the left ear. Excellent eye-hand coordination. He plays southpaw baseball. He tells me he has one friend who doesn't care what he looks like."

Garlington seemed repulsed.

"Larry may never be a movie star. Or a swan. But when he's twenty-two or -three or -four, he's going to be a very interesting looking man. He will turns heads—for all the right reasons. Come around when I've given him a new nose. Now, if you'll excuse me, I've got an office to run."

"You'll be using my compression plates and screws tomorrow?"

"Yes," Theo said. "Six screws at $92 apiece. I forget what you rooked us for the plate—$1,800? What's an ounce of titanium go for these days?"

"I don't get involved in all that," Dr. Garlington said, dismissing the question. "What will you be using for the mandible?"

"Rib," Theo replied.

"Why rib?"

"Because it works," Theo said. "That is, if the Garlington plate and the Garlington screws hold."

"You'll incorporate my plate-bending forceps?"

"What else?" Theo said sarcastically.

"I'm going to scrub tomorrow," Garlington said.

"Ah," Theo said. "You have an operation too?"

"No. I am going to observe the placement of my plate and screws on the new mandible."

Theo hesitated a beat. He looked at the center of one of Garlington's eyes. "When I was at Hopkins," he said, "we asked the surgeon in charge for permission to scrub. Has the system changed?"

"It's my equipment. I designed it," Garlington said, pulling his shoulders back, his arms still crossed.

Theo glanced toward the doorway. He said in a low and even tone, "It was your equipment before we paid a small fortune for the 'kit,' as you call it. And if you would like to scrub to watch the placement, you will do what everyone else does: You will ask the surgeon in charge of the procedure. I am the surgeon in charge."

"I would like to scrub, Dr. Tithonus. Is there a problem?"

"With the scrubbing, no," Theo said. "But I want you to know something. When we were young and foolish and doing each other at Hopkins, I used to like you."

Garlington flushed. He glanced toward the doorway.

"I spend my days around surgeons with fat egos, but yours is the fattest. You're a user. You used your wife; you'd fuck your mother if somebody held her down. You're the worst kind of opportunist, Garlington. You are, as I have already pointed out, a shit.

"If you would like to scrub with me tomorrow and observe my patient's jaw repair, we'll begin at 7 a.m. And don't worry, I'll be a very gracious host. No one will have the slightest suspicion that I'd rather be eating fried lard with Hitler." Theo smiled pleasantly.

Tim Garlington stood perfectly still for a moment. His expression was smug. "Dr. Tithonus, Midge was telling me that there's a rumor going around that you won't be accepting the appointment as surgical chief when she leaves. Anything to that?"

" 'Midge?' "

"Margaret Steinhower. Micari's replacement?"

"Ah," Theo said. "That Midge. Rubbing up against her now, are you? No, absolutely no truth to that. Maybe I should do lunch with old Midge myself…Find out where that nasty rumor came from. How do you suppose a thing like that got started?"

"Beats me," Garlington said. "By the way, Susan and I have a dinner date Saturday night…" he smirked. "Just so you know."

"Use a condom, Garlington," Theo snarled. "Use two."

Theo walked out and turned down the hall. He was fuming. His hands shook. He stalked to the elevator intersection. He pressed "up" instead of "down." On the way up he thought that Susan must have lost her mind. On the way down he thought he must have lost his own. What could have attracted him to that asshole in the first place? Never mind the flash of even teeth. Never mind the sun-burned cheeks on the soccer field and the eyes that pierced right through you. And the intimate smile only for you when you shot the ball between the goalie's legs. And never mind the lean and sweaty body on the sweat-damp sheets. Never mind.

If it was political kick ball Garlington wanted to play now, Theo would brush up on the rules.

The forest-green Jaguar laid rubber on South Street.

Chapter 15

Dr. Timothy Garlington did not appear in OR 4 at 7 a.m. to observe. Or at 7:30. As he moved farther into Larry's operation, Theo forgot about Garlington.

He taught as he worked. Remembering his own fears as a surgical intern, being thrown into procedures by experienced surgeons whose attitude was "sink or swim," he explained everything to his team including, sometimes, the obvious.

Theo loved directing. He loved to watch his staff perform at high, efficient speed, loved that they anticipated the moves and that their hands moved with each other like a school of fish. Fingers and thread and forceps and suction tubes appeared and disappeared. The team spliced and cauterized; instruments passed to hands at the ready. Theo placed the new bone prosthesis and held it while Barry Boldini—his green-eyed, half-black assistant cemented—and while they waited for the bonding to set they hummed along to their patient's recording of girl singers. Eubeeda Jones, the lithe, black head of surgical nurses, and her two assistants, Maria deJesus and Dorothy Pinnsacardi, camped a refrain after which Eubeeda said, "You know, I *always* wanted to have *me* a back up group. Follow me everywhere I go, just singin' away. I say, 'Count your sponges,' with my back up group singin' and pointin' their fingers, 'Count 'em! Count 'em!' "

A pneumatic door hissed. Dr. Timothy Garlington crossed the

floor and stepped up to the operating table crisp, fresh, no perspiration. His eyes were narrowed with authority above his surgical mask. The younger team members stopped humming.

"Dr. Tithonus?" he intoned above the music. "I'm here to place the plate and screws. Could we begin, please?"

Theo tilted his head toward Garlington above Larry's draped and splayed jaw. He thought of Garlington having watched the television monitor in the scrub room in his immaculately clean scrub clothes, gloved hands held out from his chest and waiting for the precise moment of the attachment of titanium to bone and bonder.

Theo indicated his surgical resident, Dr. Boldini, with a nod. "Barry will make the attachment," he said.

"I will be placing the plate. *And* the screws," Garlington said, insinuating himself into position at Boldini's left.

Theo could not believe what he was hearing. He turned back to the open jaw, ignoring Garlington across the surgical table.

"And turn off that *noise,*" Garlington said very loud toward the observation window in the surgical supervisor's office.

"Leave it on," Theo snapped just as loud near the boy's draped head.

Garlington paused. He said to Eubeeda Jones, "I am ready for the plate."

"Mrs. Jones," Theo said evenly, "pass the plate to Dr. Boldini."

Eubeeda Jones's thin eyebrows arched. She placed the small metal plate in Barry Boldini's open palm.

Theo said, "I find it easiest to insert the center screws first, Barry. Then the side screws'll slip right in. Go ahead. I'll hold the mandible. The bonding's set." Theo looked up. "Some of you may not have met Dr. Garlington. He also comes to us from Johns Hopkins. In fact," Theo said, "we played soccer there together. He designed this titanium plate, as well as the Garlington retractor, the Garlington bone plane, the Garlington bearing, and other instruments…" he paused a sarcastic beat, "too numerous to mention at this time."

Garlington ignored the team. He glared at the small piece of metal in Boldini's hand.

Barry asked for the first of the six screws that would secure the lath of rib into Larry's jawbone. He inserted the screw. He called for the driver.

"I should point out," Theo announced to the team, "that Dr. Boldini is employing the *Garlington* driver to set the *Garlington* screws. As some of you might be aware, these screw heads have been designed to accept no other driver."

Garlington expelled air. "I will talk with you at the completion of this procedure, Dr. Tithonus," he hissed, turning on his cloth-bootied heels toward the pneumatic door.

"Later," Theo said, "they tell me I've got a severed ear on ice in OR 3. Guy's girlfriend bit it off. You can watch that one too, if you want. Maybe Dr. Boldini will employ the Garlington head brace."

The air-driven door slid open then closed.

"Needs a good spankin', if you ask me," Eubeeda muttered.

"Needs a wheelbarrow for those balls," countered Wiley Branstetter, the anesthesiologist.

"OK, gang," Theo said. "Let's get back to the Garlington erector set."

As Theo left OR 4 to change quickly and scrub again for the bitten-off ear that awaited him, the embarrassed OR supervisor handed him a plain envelope.

"Dr. Garlington told me to give you this."

He carried the envelope with him as he walked to the surgical waiting room. He signaled, smiling, to Larry's long-suffering parents who hurried to join him in the hallway. He explained to them that everything went well, that their son would be taken to the recovery room in a half hour or so, and that his jaw would remain closed for six weeks. He apologized that he had to hurry on because of an emergency.

As he walked back down the hall toward the surgical locker room, he tore open the envelope. The scrawled message was terse:

Dr. Tithonus—Meet me immediately in my office. TMG

Theo threw the middle finger of one hand above his head. "Meet *this,* TMG!"

Having assured himself that Barry Boldini was proceeding comfortably with the reattachment of the severed ear, Theo hurried back to the surgical locker room, showered for the third time that day, and dressed in street clothes.

His black hair still wet on his collar, he picked up the locker-room wall phone and had Garlington paged. The page echoed through the dressing room and in the hospital hallways. After a few minutes a voice in the handset said: "Dr. Garlington."

"Where are you?" Theo demanded.

"I am having my lunch. I will be in my office in 25 minutes."

"Stay where you are," Theo said and hung up. He realized that he did not know where in this vast hospital Garlington was having his lunch. He would seek out every food source in the complex.

In the elevator, moving down two floors, Theo did a breathing exercise to calm himself. He did not think about Timothy Garlington or what he would say when he found him. He thought about the slowing of heartbeats, about the relaxation of muscle in shoulders.

Assuming that Garlington would not deign to eat with com-

126

moners, Theo avoided the public commissary and headed instead to the dining room reserved for staff.

He pushed open its steel, swinging door. He stood just inside, scanning the cafeteria line and the white Formica tables that nearly filled the place. Garlington sat with another man at a small table in a corner of the room.

As he approached, Theo saw that the other man was Millard Roberts, The Hummer. Roberts was not humming. Roberts was giggling.

Theo walked to the table. Roberts looked up. Garlington looked up.

"I told you I would see you in my office, Dr. Tithonus," Garlington said.

"You arrogant sack of shit!" Theo spat.

Millard Roberts moved to stand. "I'll just leave you two for a moment," he said nervously.

"Sit!" Theo commanded.

Millard Roberts slouched into his chair. He looked to Garlington, who now regarded Theo as if he were a garden pest.

Theo's forefinger jabbed the air before Garlington's face. "If you *ever* pull a stunt like that in *any*body's surgery…if you ever so much as *enter* another doctor's operating room again to borrow a *gauze* pad—"

"Fellows—" Millard Roberts said, squirming. He glanced about the dining room.

"Shut up, Roberts!" Theo snapped, turning his attention back to Timothy Garlington. "You won't be cutting lettuce in the kitchen—you will *have* no surgical privileges in this hospital, sir."

Timothy Garlington stood, dislodging the table with his thighs. His blue eyes sparkled then narrowed. "Are you threatening *me,* doctor?"

Theo glared at Garlington. "You don't hear well. I made you a promise."

"Excuse me," Roberts said, attempting again to leave.

Theo's open palm blocked the way.

Garlington's hand darted out. He grabbed the fabric of Theo's jacket and pulled him forward.

"Push your luck," Theo said evenly. "I'll have you hauled out of here on assault charges."

The hand squeezed the tweed coat. And loosened.

"And never approach another of my patients," Theo added. He nodded at Roberts, turned, and walked from the table.

"Faggot," he heard Garlington mutter behind him.

Theo breathed in; he breathed out. He continued toward the door. "How many years for justifiable homicide?" he growled at the ductwork.

Chapter 16

Sam dropped a pizza crust to his plate. "Scrumptious. I wonder what the Cinco de Mayos are being served tonight?"

"Sorry. Really," Theo said. "I forgot about the pizza thing."

"I could've cooked."

"I know. I forgot."

"Theo, you didn't forget. You love pizza…They're having a baby, by the way."

"Who?"

"Leo and Darlene."

"Who're Leo and Darlene?"

"The pizza delivery guy and his girlfriend. Her birth control failed."

"Sam, how the hell would you know that?"

"Leo told me. We've become very close friends this year. I mean, he's here all the time…. She wants to keep the kid. He doesn't."

"OK, I'm sorry. I'll never order pizza again. You want another beer? Have another beer."

"No."

"I did rent a movie," Theo said. "At least I got something right."

"What?"

"*Riders of the Purple Sage.*"

"Huh?"

"Tom Mix. Beatrice Burnham."

"Are you serious?"

"Beatrice Burnham plays his sister. She gets abducted by an unscrupulous person. Tom Mix saves her. I loved it when I was a little kid."

Sam sat, incredulous.

"Just kidding. I got *Day of Thanks on Walton's Mountain*. Ralph Waite. Ellen Corby. It's Thalia's all-time favorite. The one where you think the family won't all get together for Thanksgiving this year?"

"Who'd give a shit?"

"Actually, I got *Eating Raoul*. Buck Henry and I-don't-remember. They invite perverts to their house and eat them?"

"Ed Begley," Sam said ruefully.

"They eat Ed Begley?"

"You didn't rent that, did you?"

"No."

Theo's beeper sounded in the kitchen.

"Well," Sam sighed, "at least we got through dinner."

"Maybe it's something I can handle on the phone," Theo said, rising. "You *will* like my movie: *Man Rammers*."

"Whoopie. You'll probably fall asleep."

In the kitchen Sam heard Theo say, "No, we're here...No, it's just us...Sure...It's OK."

Theo walked into the dining room frowning. "Susan's coming over," he said.

"I thought she had a date."

"She did. She sounded weird."

"She bringing him over?"

"She wouldn't do that."

Susan dropped a suitcase to the laundry room floor. "She's outside. In the car."

"Who?"

"I know you think I'm doing this to force your hand, Theo. I'm not," Susan said.

"What?"

"You're the only one I trust. Except Mrs. Cristobel, and she can't take her. Now..." Susan plunged a hand into her trench coat pocket. She pulled out an envelope.

"Kind of late to be going on a date, isn't it?"

"That's a long story, and I haven't got time. I have to be at the airport by 10."

"He's taking you to dinner at the Sandwich Shoppe?" Theo smirked.

"I'm leaving," Susan said with a swipe at her chestnut hair.

"What are you talking about?"

"It's all there," she said of the envelope. She thrust it toward him. "The number where I'll be and Mrs. Cristobel's number. She'll be here Monday morning at 7."

"Who's Mrs. Cristobel?"

"My *house*keeper. Theo, would you just listen, please?"

"I'm listening, Susan, but you're not explaining."

"I haven't got *time!* I'll call you tomorrow."

"But where are you going?"

"San Diego. Theo, it's *all* written down. Mrs. Cristobel will take her to school. Mrs. Cristobel will pick her up. Tomorrow you have to go to my house and pick up the cat. Call Mrs. Cristobel first. She'll explain the alarm."

"What cat?"

"Oh, Christ, Theo, will you just listen? I have a plane to catch! Explain to Clare at the office that I had to leave town. She'll sort through the patients. 'Johnston.' Remember that. I wrote him down. You'll have to do him. Blastema. Can't be postponed. It's all in his records." She waved at the suitcase on the laundry room floor. "I've packed enough of her clothes for a week. If you need more, have Mrs. Cristobel go get them." She pulled a key ring from another pocket. "My house keys. I'll get Natalia," she said, whirling about in the hallway.

"Wait! Why?"

"Haven't you been *listening?* She's staying with you!"

"Wait! *Wait!* Susan, *I* can't keep her. Why can't you leave her with a friend or something?"

"I thought *you* were my friend."

"I am, but—"

"And you're her father," Susan declared simply.

"But where are you going?"

"San Diego," she said in the doorway. "It's all written *down!*"

"Is somebody sick? Your mother?"

"I *need* to get *away!*" The laundry room door slammed behind her.

Theo opened it and looked out. Susan was at the open car door. She leaned inside. She beckoned. She hauled, lifted a small child into her arms. "Oh, sweetie," she said to the child. "Goodbye, my precious. Mommy will call you tomorrow from her vacation," she whispered to the child as she handed her over. She shook Natalia's arm. "You be good, now."

Susan hurried to her idling car. A window rolled down. "She hasn't had her *bath* yet!" she shouted. The window rolled up. She backed out into the alley and sped toward 24th.

Theo stood stunned in the driveway. Natalia clung to his neck. Exhaust plumes evaporated above the paving bricks.

"I'm *cold,*" the child complained in his ear.

"She's gone already?" Sam asked from the laundry room door.

"Yes."

"Where'd she go?"

"San Diego."

132

"Why'd she leave Natalia?"

"I don't know."

"When's she coming back for her?"

"I don't know."

Sam sat on a stool in the kitchen. Natalia stood barefoot in a red, faded T-shirt which said BOSTON MEDICAL COLLEGE. The neck was stretched. Her shoulders barely supported the fabric. She stared straight ahead.

Theo opened Susan's envelope. Inside were prescription forms. The first had a scribbled name—"Edie," a California address and phone number, and "Mrs. Cristobel" and a number. The second was a list. The first item, "cancel hair, Tues." had been scratched out. Below, the list continued:

> pick up cat
> check refrigerator
> Harold Johnston—blastema
> Natalia—No shrimp!

"No" had been underlined four times.

"Are you allergic to shrimp?" Theo asked the child.

"Yes," she said, looking about the strange house.

"What happens if you eat shrimp?"

"My tongue gets all fat and my eyes close up."

"Sam, I don't know. All I know is what I told you. She just left her and took off."

"But how long, do you think?"

"I don't know. She said she packed her enough clothes for a week."

"A *week?*"

"Hey, what do I know?"

"Where's she going to sleep?"

"The guest room?" Theo asked.

Theo inventoried the spread contents of Natalia's suitcase on the stripped guest room bed.

Seven pairs of socks. Seven tiny panties. Several cotton trousers with crimped, elastic waists too narrow for any human Theo had ever encountered. Teeny-weeny spandex tops in various colors, each no larger than his spread palm. Pajamas. A toothbrush. A tube of toothpaste decorated with dinosaurs.

Theo held up one of Natalia's spandex tops. He stretched the fabric. How could this possibly cover her? How could her head go through this little hole? He laid the tiny thing among the other tiny things.

"I want Roger," announced a small voice behind him.

"Who's Roger?"

"He's in there," Natalia said, pointing at the suitcase. She walked around Theo. She rooted in a side pocket and extracted a stuffed animal.

"What is he?"

She didn't answer.

"Where's Sam?"

"Making cocoa."

Should she have her bath now or after the cocoa? After the cocoa.

He needed to figure this out. How would he get her bathed? Did five-year-olds bathe themselves? Did one just instruct them to take their baths? Did one say, Natalia, it's time for your bath? And she, demurring, would turn obediently with a smile and disappear for 15 minutes to reappear transformed: a neat, clean, perfectly-groomed television kid?

He thought not. Nor did he think that any five-year-old little girl in her right mind was going to acquiesce to being bathed by a 46-year-old man. Offer her a piece of candy?

He would make up her bed, give her time for the cocoa. Then he would stroll confidently down to the kitchen, hands deep in the pockets of his khakis, and say, Natalia, it's time for your bath. He would say this in a kindly but no-nonsense way, then he would go somewhere and do something. As if having announced the way it would be, when he emerged from doing something, a fully-bathed and fresh-pajamaed little girl would appear on the stairs.

He removed a set of clean sheets from the linen closet in the hall. He flapped a fitted sheet in the air.

Susan must have gone crazy.

Susan must have gone bananas to have packed up her kid and dumped her here without waiting for so much as a Simon Says.

Susan must have gone nuts, he thought, circling the bed, tucking. And what had set her off? All right, they had a busy practice, but wasn't that to be expected? After all, you didn't take home 275 grand a year without assuming there'd be a little work involved.

He had the same lousy hours as she every day. He had the same number of patients. He operated. He did rounds handling pre-op and post-op. Was *he* dropping everything and leaving? No, he was not.

Maybe it was the teaching part, Theo considered, a pillow under his chin. Hadn't he always told her she was foolish to take that on with everything else she had to do? Certainly she didn't need the money she got from teaching or the aggravation.

So she had a kid? She also had a housekeeper. And if something broke in the house, all she had to do was call to get it fixed. Or buy a new thing, Theo thought as the blanket settled across the bed. And who did she think *he* was to just drop Natalia off and fly to the farthest place you could go without falling into the Pacific? Probably she'd been fed up for months. Probably she'd been looking for a better practice all along. On the sly. Probably got a cellular call right in the middle of that asshole planking her and squealed, *"What* percentage? Never mind getting it off, Garlington; I am outta here!"* He smacked the pillows. He tugged a wrinkle.

And now the bath. And should her hair be washed? And then do you just comb it, or do you have to brush it out? He looked at his watch. Too late to call Mrs. whatever-her-name-was with a litany of questions about the bathing and grooming of children.

Theo descended the stairs.

Natalia embraced a mug at the kitchen work island. Sam got off a stool. "I'll move my things," he said without enthusiasm.

"Where to?"

"Where else?" Sam left the kitchen.

"Natalia?" Theo began.

She looked through him, past him.

With his hands thrust into the pockets of his khakis he said: "Natalia, it's time for your bath." He said this, he thought, with authority and sounded quite in charge. He shifted his weight from leg to leg.

"My bath's in the morning," she informed the refrigerator.

"Your mother said you didn't have a bath today."

The child ignored him.

"Natalia?"

"What?"

"Did you have your bath today?"

"Where's Mrs. Cristobel?"

"I don't know. Home."

"Mrs. Cristobel always gives me by bath. Or my mommy does."

Theo's hands were pressing the bottoms of his pockets. "They're not here…"

Natalia's mouth twisted sideways. If they were not here, there was no further purpose in discussing the issue.

"And you have to have a bath."

"Tomorrow."

"No. Tonight," Theo said hoping that she understood determination when she heard it.

Natalia waited.

"What does Mrs. Cristobel do to get you your bath?"

The bony shoulders slumped in the face of this incompetence. "She *fills* up the *wa*ter."

Theo sat on the bathtub edge. One hand swirled water in the tub. Sam should be doing this. Sam was a nurse; they knew about these things.

He could hear Sam in the guest room. He heard impatience and irritation in his footsteps toward their bedroom. Well? Tough shit. Theo was not a happy camper either. He wished Mrs. Cristobel were there. Or Thalia. Or Rosy. Anyone who had ever given a child a bath.

He had bathed an infant once, of course, as part of his obstetrics rotation. He had bathed adult burn victims—a terrible, painstaking process. He had never bathed a five-year-old girl. Theo sighed.

The next time Natalia needed her bath, he would fill the tub with water and *then* tell her it was time for her bath. And now what to do—now that the tub was filled? Just call her to it?

Drops from the faucet blipped on the water's surface.

What could be so complicated here? He was the father; she was the child. She needed a bath.

Surely she could undress herself, and he could then disappear.

Not far. Not so far as downstairs where he could not hear her if she stood suddenly then slipped and cracked her little head.

After calling her to her bath he would go to his den and futz around in there until she had finished. But could he assume that she had not squandered her bath time making boats from floating soap? Could he assume that while he had left Natalia in the privacy of her bath she had been attending to critical areas: her armpits, the folds of her labia? And her anus? Could this be assumed? And was it appropriate to question her as to her attention to these parts, or should he leave her to soak a long time just in case? And did the child know how to shampoo her hair? Should he just walk right in for the shampoo part? Knock first, then walk in to do the shampoo?

He was making a big deal out of nothing. A bath was a bath. He was a doctor.

"Natalia?" he called from the top of the stairs. "Natalia!"

Did she say, "What?"

"Your bath is ready."

He heard an exasperated sigh. In a moment she trudged up the stairs dragging Roger by a leg.

"It's all ready," Theo told her at the bathroom door.

Natalia surveyed his work. She twiddled her fingers in the water. "It's cold," she said.

"Then we'll just add some hot," Theo suggested, turning the spigot. "You tell me when it's the way you like it," he said, bending, swirling the water.

"Why do I have to take a bath?"

"Because you are a human. How do you shampoo your hair?"

"With shampoo." What did he think?

"I mean, can you do that? Or does your mommy do that, or Mrs. Cristobel?"

"They do."

"Before your bath or after your bath?" Now things were moving along. A bath required only a take-charge attitude.

"After."

"OK, you get undressed and get your bath and you call me when you're ready for your hair. I'll just be in the next room."

Relieved, Theo departed the bathroom, leaving the door slightly ajar—the better to hear her, the better to know if she were to slip.

He sat in the leather reading chair in his den. He paged a medical journal until he was aware of silence in the bathroom. No water stirred; there was no distracted singing in the tub. He walked about the den. After a time he heard the sound of water sloshing. He returned to his chair.

He was annoyed with Susan. If she wanted a vacation, why not just say so in advance. She was checking out another practice was what she was doing, he thought indignantly, sneaking off to become a partner at some hotsy-totsy practice in the sun and dumping the kid in *his* lap. What was this, revenge for years of his inattention? He hadn't wanted a child. *She* had. He had just been doing a friend a favor. Did that mean he had to baby-sit while she plotted to leave the practice they had opened together?

He flipped through the journal. He tossed the magazine to the floor.

And how long did she think she could leave the kid here? Clothes for a week. He couldn't do this for a week. And why did she need a week? How long could it take to fly to San Diego and check out a practice? Have an over-priced dinner with a bunch of over-priced doctors? Oh, she'd milk this trip—drag it out for a few extra days on the beach while he did her work, *her* rounds. Of all the goddamned gall, dumping the kid on him and flying off to meet with total strangers. They'd probably offer her a live-in nanny. They'd probably offer her a young, live-in stud.

"I'm done!"

Theo sighed. How could the child be clean already? Should he make her soak longer? After the hair part?

She sat in the tub up to her belly button in soapy water. A soggy wash cloth was draped over the tub edge. A good sign.

"O-*kay,*"Theo said, taking up a bottle of shampoo. He turned on both faucets and adjusted the temperature and when it felt comfortable to him he said, "Put your head under."

"I can't. There's no *room.*"

"We have to get your hair wet first."

She looked up at the wall above her. "Now you put the *show*er on." Fool. Dummy. "But you let the *tub* out first," she instructed, pushing the plug release.

"Right," Theo said, turning spigots, pulling out the shower knob. The plumbing choked. Water gushed, then fanned, drenching his own head and shirt in a shock of frigid water. He clawed for the shower release.

Natalia shrieked. She scrambled to the far end of the tub. "You have to pull the curtain first!" she yelled, wrapping herself in the plastic liner. Didn't they know *any*thing here?

Theo punched the shower knob. His shirt clung, cold on his skin. He knelt in a collecting pool of water on the floor tiles. A lock of wet hair fell over one eye; he raked it back.

"There must have been water in the pipes," he explained lamely.

"Here," he said, tugging at the outside shower curtain. "Let go, Natalia. We'll just pull the curtain closed, then we'll get your hair shampooed."

With one arm inside the curtain, Theo reactivated the shower, warm now. He extended the shampoo bottle.

"It's not No More Tears," she whined. "That will hurt my *eyes!*"

"Natalia, this is what Sam and I use. Every day. It's not going to hurt your eyes. Just keep them closed."

"*No!*"

"Natalia, please. Do as I say—just get your hair wet, and I'll shampoo it!"

"*It burns my eyes!*"

"You haven't even put any *on* yet! Get under the shower. Do as I say."

When she refused to move, Theo, half inside the shower now, turned the shower head on her.

She emitted one piercing screech then stood—head bent, as if resigned to dismemberment—as Theo, his entire torso leaning into the shower, went about the work of lathering her thick, black hair. Never mind the watch, the cold shirt, the wet trousers. This child would have clean hair if he had to climb into the shower with her. *Damn* Susan!

Theo stood in the doorway of the guest room. Natalia was curled in sleep, her knees drawn up toward her chest. A thumb was in her mouth; fingers wrapped her nose. She embraced her animal, a raccoon. Its masked face lay on her neck. One black eye held a point of light.

He would not make it through a week of this.

Sam's toiletries had been returned to their bathroom. Sam's photographs had been returned to the dresser top. Theo opened Sam's closet. His shirts and slacks hung there again, each article separated by an inch or two of space. His shoes were lined on the carpeted floor, and the vacuum cleaner tracks could be seen no longer.

He had brought it all back. Everything. Everything was the same as it was—except that Theo's daughter slept now in the room down the hall.

When Sam padded up the stairs, Theo considered in bed that he had to say something, that he had to explain that the child in the next room was his. But how?

Sam stopped briefly at the guest room. Theo heard the soft sounds of Sam's feet on their bedroom carpet, the familiar rattle of the ball bearings in Sam's closet doors, the soft clink of a belt buckle and of a clothes hanger hung. Then he heard the sound of water running behind the closed bathroom door and the toilet flushing and the pause, the waiting until the toilet sounds had stopped before the door was opened, then the feet again on carpet.

Sam slipped into their bed, careful not to touch, not to make the mattress move. Not to disturb.

Theo's arm hissed through the crisp sheets. He touched Sam's back. He patted his back twice and rested the flat of his palm there, on Sam's warm skin.

"Thanks," Theo said. "I really didn't know she was coming."

"You do what you have to do," Sam said in the dark. "You're on your own tomorrow, though. I have to leave for work at 6."

"I'll be all right. I'll think of something."

Sam grunted.

"You know, she's a cute kid," Theo offered.

"But very screwed up," Sam said.

"She's in a new house. She hardly knows us."

"Theo, she doesn't even know who her *father* is. She told me *you're* her father. Can you beat that?"

"Really…" Theo said, but allowed this golden opportunity to pass. "What'll I feed her for breakfast?" he asked.

"Send out for pizza." The blanket was jerked to the right.

"Theo…? *The*-o!" Theo's shoulder was being shaken.

"What?"

"*Are* you?"

"What?" Theo asked.

142

"Her father. *Is* she your kid?"

"Why would you say that?" Theo asked, begging for time. Tomorrow. After dinner. Later in the week.

Sam sat up in their bed. "Theo, I don't want bullshit. I want an answer."

"Yes."

"Well, why the fuck didn't you tell me that?"

I forgot? I've been busy?

"I don't know," Theo said.

"You don't know? You don't *know?*"

"I was going to. It just—"

"It just what? *Slipped* your *mind?* You're making me goddamned nuts! The fucking *pizza* man tells me he's having a baby. The fucking pizza man tells me what kind of birth control he and his girlfriend use, and I don't even *know* them! What the hell is going on here?"

"Sam, you'll wake her up."

"Well maybe I should!" Sam exclaimed in a strangled whisper. He jumped up from the bed. "She apparently knows more about this than *I* do!"

"I was going to tell you."

"Well what were you *wait*ing for?"

"Will you calm down? Sit down a minute. Sit down."

"You have a five-year-old daughter, and you don't tell me?" Sam paced about the bed in the dark. "We've been together for six years and you don't tell me you have a *daughter? What* were you waiting for, your first *grand*child?"

"I'm sorry. It was just…very complicated."

"Complicated," Sam repeated. "I am a trained health professional. I have a master's degree in nursing. I *know* where babies come from!"

"It wasn't what you're thinking, Sam."

"What're you telling me, we got a virgin birth here?"

"Susan and I—"

"Were visited by an angel?"

"Come on, Sam."

"Then you fucked."

"No. We didn't."

Sam paused. One arm pointed at Theo in the streetlight. "You're a sperm donor."

"Yes."

"Theo, what is so goddamned *com*plicated about that? That's even less complicated than fucking. And even if you two did it normally, that's not something that would freak me out. What freaks me out is you didn't *tell* me!"

Sam stood in the light of the street lamp at the end of the bed. Theo lay motionless under the covers. He could think of nothing ameliorative to say. He could not explain it to himself. This was the lecture he expected and deserved and now found acutely embarrassing. He hadn't explained to Sam about Natalia years before because the explanation could come in the far future. He had participated in a simple act of science. All he did was do a friend a favor.

There was a long silence in the bedroom. Finally, Sam sighed. His hands moved to his naked hips. He shook his head in the streetlight. "Theo," he said, "I have to think about this."

Theo expected Sam to stalk down to the living room sofa. Instead, Sam got into bed, settled himself, and was silent.

Theo did not know what to say and so said nothing.

Chapter 17

When Theo woke, he was alone in the bed. It was 8:12 a.m. He thought with a start that he had overslept, that he should already have been to the gym, that he should already be doing rounds at the hospital. He realized that it was Sunday, that Natalia slept down the hall, that he had to feed her a breakfast—of something.

He rubbed his palms over his face. He dragged fingers through his bed-mussed hair.

This would be no lazy Sunday morning. There would be no listless hours of coffee and the Sunday papers in the late winter sun on the living room sofa. He had a child to feed. And to entertain.

On the way downstairs Theo checked the guest room. Natalia was not there.

The dining table had been set: linen napkin, place mat, and silver; cereal, sugar, jelly, and sliced oranges. There was a note on the table beside Natalia's place mat:

Natalia—
Milk is in the refrigerator.
Press the toaster bar down and wait.
—Sam

She sat on the living room floor before the television in her over-sized T-shirt. The raccoon sprawled across her lap.

"Hi, Natalia," Theo said.

She ignored him.

"Aren't you hungry?"

She watched cartoons. She shrugged her shoulders.

"There's breakfast there for you."

She shrugged. "*I* didn't know whose it was."

She did not know how to read. "How about if you come to the dining room and have something to eat?" Theo offered.

She shrugged. In a moment, she stood as if in great annoyance. She carried her raccoon by the neck. Theo indicated the place setting. She sat. She positioned the raccoon at the side of her place mat. She waited.

"How about if I eat with you?"

She shrugged.

In the kitchen the coffee machine had been set up for him. He needed only to press the start button. There was a note from Sam on top of the Sunday papers:

Will be home by 4:30.

S.

Theo started the coffee. He pressed the toaster bar. He removed a carton of milk from the refrigerator and took it to the table.

"Would you like me to pour it?"

She shrugged. He poured.

She added sugar to her cereal. She stirred. She ate a spoonful. She looked straight ahead, chewing.

"How is it? The cereal?"

"It's not the kind *we* have."

Theo laid a place for himself opposite Natalia. She spooned cereal.

"Want some toast?"

She shrugged. She made a face. Because her eyebrows went up, he took this as assent.

As he waited in the kitchen watching coffee trickle, he wondered if he should butter her toast. Did Susan run a no-fat house? He decided to butter. Having assembled his coffee, the newspapers, and toast at the dining table, he sat across from her and considered that this might be the only normal moments of this Sunday: coffee and the papers.

Natalia plopped a great glob of jelly at the center of a piece of toast and spread this with the jelly spoon. Jelly oozed and fell on her thigh. She looked up to see if Theo had noticed. She scrubbed her leg with the napkin.

Theo scanned headlines. Natalia chewed cereal very slowly, looking past him.

Her hair was awry—black as his own, with none of her mother's honey highlights. She was a thin child and—he was surprised to notice—her aunts all over. She was her grandmother also, in the sepia photographs in worn-cornered albums his father kept at the lake.

"Could we turn off the television?" Theo asked.

"I'm listening to it."

"Would you pass the sugar, please?"

Natalia lifted the sugar bowl. She clanked it to the tabletop at the length of her reach and nudged it inches farther in his direction with her knuckles. She submerged cereal pieces. She spooned, she chewed. She stared at a place past his shoulder.

As a doctor, Theo would have been equipped to talk with this child. As a parent, a stranger, he felt inept and helpless. Even embarrassed. What should he say?

"When is my mommy coming to get me?" Natalia demanded, picking up her toast.

"I don't know."

She watched the spot over his shoulder.

"Maybe in a week," Theo added.

A week. An eternity. Natalia bit toast. She chewed. For the first time since he entered the room, perhaps for the first time in their lives, Natalia looked directly at him.

"Where *is* my mommy?" she said. The bowl of her spoon tapped the surface of her cereal milk and made tiny waves there.

"She's on vacation."

The spoon slapped the milk. Her neck was long like Thalia's and Cassie's. The dark, Tithonus eyes narrowed.

"Are *you* going to take care of me?"

"Yes?" Theo asked.

She dropped the spoon in the bowl of bloated cereal. Her eyes fell. Her thin shoulders slumped. She had abandoned all hope.

They sat at the table across from each other in silence, the abandoned child and the reluctant father. Certainly Theo had not asked for this six years before when he appeared at the appointed time at the offices of Susan's gynecologist. What had he been thinking when they sent him down the hall with that absurd little plastic cup to the tiny washroom with a toilet and beige wall covering beginning to curl at its border with the sink? What had he thought about as he jerked off with one hand and held the stupid plastic cup before the moving head of his dick with the other? With a plastic cup in your hand, you do not think about the best sex you ever had. You do not play in your mind for long the face or body of a fantasy lover. You think about how you must hold the too-small plastic cup in your left hand so as to catch all of what you are urging with your right; you think about how you cannot let any of this elixir fall into the barren bowl of the sink because your dear friend with whom you have cut this deal is down the hall, spread-eagled and draped on an examination table, waiting for every fecund drop you can express in order to bathe one expectant egg—which had become this little girl of no faith who frowned now into her sodden corn flakes across the table.

They sat in silence—he rereading the same paragraph, she slapping at the middle of the small, white pond of her cereal bowl.

"Clare, I'm sorry to bother you on a Sunday," Theo told their office manager. "Susan had to leave town last night...I don't know...I don't know that either. Maybe a week. I'll have to fill in for her. Do you know what she has on for tomorrow?...Johnston's tomorrow?...At 7 a.m.? And then what...Clare, I've got that keloid lady at 10...No, no. The one you can't see her nose anymore...? Clare, that's not funny."

"Thalia, I need a favor. Can you come over for an hour or two about noon...? My partner had to leave town suddenly and she left her daughter here." *She's also my daughter, your niece.* "I have to do Susan's rounds at the hospital. And go by her house to get something...She's five...No, he's working today...Well, you could bring the kids over here if you want...Thalia, I'll give you a thousand dollars...A little joke, Thalia."

"Susan, what the hell is going on?"
"I'm having a vacation."
"You could have given me a little warning."
"This is an unscheduled vacation."
"Susan, are you there checking out another practice?"
"Is that what you think? If I were going to check out another practice, Theo, I'd just tell you to your face."
"Well then, I don't get it," Theo said crankily.

"So? You don't get it," Susan snapped back.

"Why didn't you tell me if you had to get away?"

"I *told* you, Theo. I told you a couple of times, but *you* didn't want to listen."

"I listen to you. You think I don't listen to you?"

"Bullshit. I've been running and running and I never get a break. I told you that. I told you I couldn't manage anymore. Friday I had a laryngectomy and I had to walk *out* on it, Theo. I was scrubbed and gowned and ready to go and I just stood there. My hands would not stop shaking and I knew that if I made the first cut, I'd cut the patient's fucking head off. Don't you just hate it when you do that? A guy comes in with cancer of the larynx, and you cut his fucking head off? There. No more cancer worries, Mr. Lukas. We got it all! You just can't do that, Theo, cut patients' heads off."

"Susan? Are you all right?"

"Actually? Yes. I'm sitting here on this beautiful deck of this beautiful house watching this most beautiful ocean. And it's 9 a.m., and I'm having a goddamned Bloody Mary. And I have had several realizations already today, mainly that I have not been paying attention. I just kept getting further and further off track, and I didn't even know it. And when I allowed myself to get taken in by the *four*-flusher last night, that's when I began to come to my senses and got the hell out."

"What four-flusher?"

"That... *Gar*lington person."

"You did go out with him?"

"As it turned out, we didn't."

"At least you've still got some sense."

"We stayed in."

"I take it back."

"Theo, I've beaten myself up enough about him. You don't need to kick the pulp."

"What happened?"

"I don't want to talk about it."

"Susan—"

"It's history. Besides, I've thought it all out. If it weren't for Garlington, I wouldn't have had the sense to get on that plane. He probably did me a favor."

"Susan, did he do something to you? Did he hurt you?"

"Why would you say that?"

"Did he?"

"No. Look, the whole thing was my fault. If I hadn't been so horny, I would never have agreed to see the man. But I was very horny and Garlington is very sexy, at least from all appearances. Enough said. I learned my lesson."

"What happened?"

"Oh, what the *hell*...We were supposed to meet for dinner downtown. After I walked out on poor Mr. Lukas, I called Garlington to cancel. He suggested I just drop by later for a drink at his place. So I did. And he showed me around..."

"Including the bedroom with the incredible view?"

"Yes, if you must know, and it does have an incredible view. The whole place is to die for. The man's got elegant furniture, except he hasn't got a couch yet. No big deal. We sat on the floor in front of the fireplace. He poured me a drink—which I did not touch, by the way..."

"God knows you didn't go there for a drink."

"Don't be bitchy."

"Then what?"

"Are you getting off on this?"

"Not so far. Then what?"

"He admired the fire and I admired him."

Theo made a disparaging sound.

"The man *is* absolutely gorgeous." Theo heard ice cubes clink.

"Then what happened?"

"We made small talk until I got bored. Then I undid his belt."

"You didn't."

"I did. And then I said, 'Fuck me.' "

"Jesus."

"I did. Theo, I was completely shameless. I wanted that man *in* me. I wanted to get laid. I didn't want soft music and conversation. I didn't want foreplay. I was the whore of Babylon."

"So you did it."

"No. I unzipped his slacks, and I hauled out this…*slab* that actually bounced, God help me, on my leg. I've never seen anything like it. But then, you know whereof I speak. I actually had sweat running down my forehead; I swear I've never been so horny in my life. In about three seconds, I had hung my $1,100 Donna Karan suit all over his mantel, which probably came from the Vatican, and I was ready for Nirvana…

"And you know what he said?"

"No?"

"He flipped the condom I handed him over his shoulder and he said, 'Roll over.' Can you believe that? I am the horniest woman in the world, and he told me to roll *over!*"

"You didn't, Susan."

"What do you think I am, *crazy?* I said, 'No way you're putting that there, with or without a condom.' And you won't believe what came next; you won't believe the pig. He turned on his back and he told me to do *him!* I said, 'No, no. Regular. And use the condom,' and then he lifted that thing up and he said, 'Take it.' I got back into the pieces of my Donna Karen and I walked out.

"And the really weird thing was, I looked back—and he was masturbating on the floor with one hand, and he had the other one in his mouth. I drove home. I called the airline. I came here."

"How long are you going to stay?"

"As long as it takes to catch up with myself. As long as I'm having revelations. I had another one this morning that you're not going to like. I've decided if you don't agree to hire an associate, I *will* look for another practice. I cannot go on this way. Did you hear me?"

"I hear you. Fine. We can do that. You got any ideas?"

"Anyone with a surgical license. I want you to get started on that now, Theo. Before I get back. Will you?"

"Yes." Where would he find an associate?

"Thank you. Now, would you put my little sweetie on?"

"In a minute. When do you *think* you'll be coming back?"

"I can't answer that. Put her on, would you?"

"Listen, Susan. This isn't working out real well. I don't know what to feed her. I don't know what to say to her. I don't have any No More Tears. She doesn't even like me. She totally ignores me, Susan."

"How does that feel?"

"I don't *like* it."

"You've joined the club."

"Susan, I don't think it's at all unfair to place a limit on this. I don't know anything about taking care of little kids. And I'm sorry you're feeling stressed, but I'm saying that a week is asking too much."

"What was the last thing I asked you to do for me?"

"Take care of Natalia," Theo replied defensively.

"No. Hire an associate. Before that I asked you to take care of Natalia. I haven't asked another fucking thing of you in years, Theo Tithonus, and I don't want to hear any more about it. Did you pick up Rula?"

"Who's Rula?"

"Theo, I *told* you. The goddamned cat. She hates being alone, even overnight, and if you don't pick her up soon, the neurotic little shit'll take my house apart...Did you tell Natalia that you're her father yet?"

"She told Sam I was."

"Maybe I said something last night; I can't remember. But even if I did, she doesn't get it. You owe it to the child to have a real talk with her."

"Now just a minute. I'm taking care of the kid, aren't I? I'm hiring a new associate. You want me to bring a neurotic cat into my house. I'm filling in for you at work, doing *your* operations and *your* rounds—which means twice a day trips to the hospital, just for starters—not to mention I have to see *your* patients at the office. I think that little talk can wait."

"No. It can't. Put our little precious on the phone now, please."

He called Mrs. Cristobel to find out about the burglar alarm at Susan's house.

Would he be picking up more clothes for Natalia at Dr. Zack's?

No. She had enough clothes. He would be picking up the cat.

Then he would also need cat food from the cellar stairway. And litter. And the litter box. And the toys. They could be any-where.

Natalia's?

The cat's. And he might as well bring some of Natalia's toys. He was to ask Natalia what she wanted. And the refrigerator—he'd have to clean out anything perishable, vegetables and such, and especially the pork roast Mrs. Cristobel left there to defrost. He was to take that to his own home. And he was to turn lights on in Dr. Zack's bathroom and over the kitchen sink before he left. And turn down the thermostat—no sense in wasting fuel oil. And he'd better arrange for *The Inquirer* to be stopped. No sense advertising that Dr. Zack was away. And the mail too, come to think, so burglars wouldn't see it piling on the hall floor. And, Lord, the medicine in the refrigerator door! He'd need that for sure.

Natalia's?

154

The cat's.

Why did the cat need medicine?

It kept it from getting "funny."

"Thanks for coming," Theo said in the first floor hallway.

"You're lucky I'm here," Thalia grumbled. "I take that back—
I'm lucky I'm here. I was going to bring the kids, but I couldn't
take them another minute. Be glad you don't have any. I hate
mine. It's not like when we were growing up," she said on the
stairs. "It's fluoride or chlorine or something in the toothpaste.
Then their hormones start pumping, and they forget every bit of
sense you ever taught them. I was about to kill Bradley Junior."
She stopped and glared down at him from several steps above.
"Five minutes it took me to walk down to the 7-Eleven for the
paper, and what do I hear when I'm walking back to my house?
I can't describe it! No, I *will* describe it: rap music blaring out of
my house at 3,000 decibels. The stupid jerk had thrown his bedroom windows wide open. And what do I hear all over my neighborhood? 'Fuck the bitch; uh, wanna fuck the bitch; 'cause I need
some cunt; uh, gotta get some cunt.' I nearly *died*!" Thalia continued up the stairs. "You believe that? 'Uh, gotta get some cunt'?
I raise my son to be respectful of women, and what does he become? His *father!*"

"You left the kids home?"

"Are you kidding? They'll never be home alone again in their
lifetimes. I dumped them at Cassie's."

Thalia tossed her coat on the work island, pushed up the
sleeves of her smart blouse, and turned to him. Long, green-
beaded earrings swung at the sides of her face. Her black eyes
were no longer slitty—gone, the angry, indignant Thalia. Thalia
the angel of mercy stood now at the work island awaiting her in-
structions.

"What's her name?" she asked.

"Natalia."

"Like 'Thalia,' " she observed, smiling. "So? Where is she?"

"In the living room. Playing Nintendo."

"Another invention of the devil. Well, you better get along. I told Cassie I'd be back by 2:30. Go on. I'll introduce myself."

She walked into the dining room, dragging a fingertip across the surface of the dining table as she passed. "I want this if you ever die," she said. She turned and smiled mischievously. "I've taped my name to the underside." She moved on to the living room.

He watched her a moment as she crossed the living room carpet toward the child, whose back was to her, and heard her say, "Natalia? I'm Thalia. Hey, that's a rhyme." And watched as the child turned—in some surprise—to face her and Thalia paused in her tracks and tilted her head as if she were having déjà-vu.

What had he been thinking all these years? That he could wait until the day when he gave Natalia away at her wedding? Invite the family? There goes the bride. By the way, she's your niece, your granddaughter. Quick, give her a kiss; she's leaving for her honeymoon.

It had always been easier to say nothing, even knowing that eventually he would have to say something. Easier to write periodic checks to Susan and to tell himself that he had done his part. Easier to make casual and meaningless inquiries about the child to her mother over lunch than to explain to his family how he had fathered a child through doing his friend a favor, then acted for years as if he had washed his hands of it. Of her.

Becoming a father was not so hard to explain. Men—even boys—fathered children on beach blankets. But, having virtually ignored this child's existence for years, he did not think he could now explain his behavior to his sister. Better to wait until she saw her perfect brother as a headliner on *Geraldo* among a pantheon of reviled "Fathers Who Don't Acknowledge Their Kids."

Theo put on his coat and checked for his keys. He glanced into the living room at the red T-shirted ragamuffin manipulating a control pad. Thalia sat on the floor. She seemed to be examining the child's black hair. For split ends? For genetic links to her own?

There was his daughter. Ready or not.

Yes, sir, that's my baby. No, sir, I don't mean maybe.

And he was not ready.

Chapter 18

Theo collected objects at Susan's house. There was no cat. In fact, he could not remember ever seeing a cat in her home.

On the second floor he turned on the light in Susan's bathroom. Evidence of her encounter with Garlington lay in the sink—a diaphragm case, a tube of spermicidal jelly.

He searched the second floor, a chaos of rejected clothing and hurried travel decisions, checking under beds, chairs, and in closets. There was no cat.

He wrapped the pork roast in a grocery bag. There was so much in the refrigerator that would spoil. Should he pack the milk? Natalia used milk in her cereal. And the eggs? He and Sam did not eat eggs. Did Natalia? He packed the eggs. And plastic bags of lettuce. And pears. So many pears. Yellow ones. Green. Brownish burgundy. Natalia must like pears.

And from the cupboards, cereal. An array of cereals. He packed several kinds in brown paper bags.

In the cellar stairwell, with some distaste, Theo tied the kitty litter box into a trash can liner. And in another trash bag, extra litter. And dried food boxes with happy cat photographs on their sides. And cans from the cellar shelves. From dozens stacked there, he chose gourmet beef and liver, savory chicken in gravy, and no-ash mackerel.

He walked down the cellar stairs into the basement calling, "Here, kitty, kitty, kitty…kitty, kitty, kitty?" There was no cat, only gray, damp concrete and spaces of dark from which small streams of water ran toward a drain hole in the center. And mildewed storage boxes sealed with masking tape. And deck furniture draped with plastic painter's drop sheets.

There was a sudden sharp crack followed by a terrible shaking. His heart raced. The furnace kicked itself into life.

"I hate this," he said.

His loot covered an entire kitchen counter.

In the living room he crawled from sofa to side chairs, peering under them and saying "kitty, kitty" and "here, kitty." And finally, "goddamn it!" and "come out, you little fuck!"

He was about to leave the litter box, leave food and water on the floor, and come back tomorrow or better—send Mrs. Cristobel—when a living room drapery moved. He saw the outline of a large mound bulging at the level of the sill. He parted the drapes. Balanced impossibly on the narrow ledge of wood was the fattest cat he had ever seen. One yellow eye and one brown eye regarded him from a head the size of a golf ball stuck, it seemed, on a furry watermelon.

"Oh, good lord!" he said.

After loading his car at the back of Susan's house in four trips with trash bags and brown bags, after leaving the back door braced open and turning down the thermostat, Theo returned to the living room for the cat.

When he pulled back the curtains the second time, the animal was clearly annoyed.

"Come on, pussy," he said soothingly. He slid his hands down both sides of its obese middle. "You're going to Uncle Theo's."

In spite of a long, bell-shaped growl, he lifted. The cat's great weight tensed. Tiny, clawless feet raced and pattered for purchase on the narrow ledge. Little ears flattened. A little mouth opened revealing spiky, little teeth.

"Don't you even think of biting me, you little bastard," he snarled, carrying the wiggling thing, which did not seem capable of bending at its middle, to the kitchen. He pocketed the medicine bottle at the refrigerator door.

As they passed through the back door, the fat body jerked and short legs raced in place. Somehow the animal wiggled and kicked its great girth up toward his shoulder until it was facing back toward the kitchen. Theo was squeezing the animal hard now, afraid it would leap over his back. He hurried across the deck and down the steps toward his car, one hand covering the little, twitching face, the other snatching at the door handle. He pulled the door open and threw the writhing weight through the opening. He slammed the car door closed. In the blur of a millisecond, the animal was up and over the seat and had vanished into the back among the bags and sacks.

"Jesus!" Theo gasped, his buttocks resting against the fender.

The house checked, the alarm reset, and doors locked, Theo returned to his car. The cat was not visible. He opened the driver's side door just enough to pass himself through and pulled the door to. He sighed. He hooked his seat belt. He turned the key in the ignition.

With the car's first vibration, the cat flew out from under his legs and rebounded off the seat next to him. "Get away!" Then the large, terrified shape bounded to the surface of the dash where it banged its head again and again against the windshield before skittering down and across his lap to the driver's window, where it heaved helplessly against the glass. He hauled the animal onto his lap and pressed his forearm against it. He threw the car into reverse, and they lurched backward. Instantly there was warmth in his lap. Warmth ran down his thighs and into his

160

crotch as he backed out into the alley. A terrible odor rose as the cat crawled up his chest. Incredibly, as he clamped the beast with his arm, hair detached from its sweaty body.

His lap was wet. His chest was wet. A puddle of liquid poop oozed between his legs and onto his butter-soft, hideously expensive, buff leather seat.

The air was fetid. His forehead dripped and his stomach lurched with nausea as he careened—his new, panting, and balding boarder cemented to his chest—down Spruce toward the Schuylkill River, his daughter, his lover, and his life of hourly change beyond any expectation.

Chapter 19

Theo dropped the clammy animal to the laundry room floor. Its feet spun briefly on the tile, and it was gone up the stairs.

He reeked. He would empty the car later.

He slunk through the dining room to the third floor stairway. As he ascended he called back, "Thalia, I'm here! I know I'm late, but could you stay another 15 minutes?" He did not wait for an answer.

"Honey?" Thalia said to Natalia. "I have got to go. I have to pick up my kids."

Natalia turned to her, surprised. "Are you coming back?"

"Well, no. Not today."

"Tomorrow?"

"No, honey. I'm a teacher, remember? I have to be a teacher tomorrow."

"But who will *be* here?"

"Theo will." Thalia dropped a remote pad to the carpet. "And soon you'll be back in your own house. When your mommy comes back."

"Can't *you* stay?"

"No. I've got to get home. Theo will take real good care of you."

Natalia turned back to the television. "I want my mommy!" she blubbered.

Thalia shrugged her shoulders at Theo. "Don't worry," she said to Natalia's back. "I'm off," she told Theo and, in the kitchen as she picked up her coat, said "Amazing."

"What?"

"She reminds me so of Mother."

"Amazing," Theo said.

They sat—Theo, Sam, and Natalia—at one end of the dining table. The surface was covered with cartons and bowls of Chinese food: lo mein, pork fried rice, shrimp fried rice, Ta-Chien chicken, wanton soup, egg drop soup, pork, a beef dish, another noodle thing, a large platter of appetizers. Theo had "arranged" dinner.

Natalia sat at the head of the table. Her raccoon's snout rested on the rim of her plate. Sam and Theo sat to her left and right.

Sam ate with chopsticks; Theo and Natalia used a fork and a spoon. Theo had abandoned thinking up subjects of interest to children. He ate with gusto. Natalia seemed to find the food unpleasant and played with hers. Sam had had Chinese for lunch.

"Mrs. Cristobel never gives me this," Natalia muttered.

"This is Chinese," Sam said.

"I know."

"Do you want to try your chopsticks?" Sam offered.

"I can't."

"Would you like to try? It's more fun."

"I can't." She separated straw mushrooms from beef with her spoon.

"Did you ever try?"

"Yes." She looked out toward the living room ahead of her. She returned to the separation of her food.

"When?"

Natalia shrugged.

"Probably the chopsticks were too long for your hands," Sam said. He removed Natalia's chopsticks from her place mat and took them to the kitchen. The sound of sawing was heard.

"Sam, what are you *do*ing?" Theo called. "Those're lacquered!"

"Lacquer this!" called Sam from the kitchen.

When he returned, Sam moved his chair closer to Natalia's.

"Do you remember my name?" he asked. "My name is Sam. Of course, I already know your name. You are Natasha."

"Na-*ta*-lia," she corrected.

"Natalia," Sam repeated. "I am sorry. I will not make that mistake again. It must be that you have the air of the steppes about you. Well, never mind. Are your right- or left-handed?"

Natalia shrugged. She held up her right hand.

Sam positioned a shortened chopstick in the Y of her thumb. He showed her that she must counter press with her ring finger.

"There. Push that broccoli piece to the other side of your plate…Now that brown thing. Push it over next to the broccoli. Excellent. Now, pick up the broccoli." Sam waited with an expectant smile. "Well?"

"Stab it?" she asked.

"Lesson number 2." He took up her other chopstick. "This one you hold sort of like a pencil. No—keep the other one where it is. And holding this one like a pencil, you tap the bottom ends on your plate to get them even. Go. Tap. Good. Now, squeeze the bottom ends together. Again. Again. Now, spread them apart a little…and pick up that brown thing. Squeeze…lift…and put it in your mouth."

"N-o-o-o!"

"Why?"

"Because I hate them. They're slimy."

"No problem. I hate them too. Look at my plate; I have all my mushrooms piled up in one place. They're terrible and disgusting. I never eat them. But these vegetables here are very delicious. Pick that one up," he pointed. "It's crunchy. Pick it up. Yes. Eat it. Eat it, Ninoshka."

"Na-*ta*-lia!"

"Natalia. That one is very delicious. Eat it."

The vegetable piece fell to her plate.

"Are they even? The ends? No, they are not. You see? Tap. Tap. The ends. Now, pick it up again. Yes. Eat. Yes. Excellent. Perfect."

A small smile appeared as she chewed.

"Now, Nadia—"

"Na-*ta*-lia…! Really," she said. Flat. A statement. *Like her mother in exasperated moments,* Theo thought.

"Do you rike po?" Sam asked, reaching for a carton. "You must try po." He spooned. "Rittle cubes. Velly easy. You try now. And tiny egg wo from pupu plattah? Velly easy."

"What's po?" she asked suspiciously.

"Meat of pig," Sam said, taking his own place again.

"*Eeee-oooh.*"

"Pig good for you. Make hair curly."

Theo watched this interchange with pleasure and envy. Natalia, his daughter, had spoken more to Sam in these moments than she had to him all day. He watched Natalia tweeze her cubes of pork as she watched Sam pluck duck breast and lychee nuts from his plate with chopsticks. He noticed that when Sam was sure Natalia was watching, he lifted individual grains of rice to his lips. Sam did not watch Natalia. Rather, he turned to her occasionally and smiled, apparently at pleasure in his food, with no interest in Natalia other than her company at the table.

"Sam?" Natalia asked.

"Natyavanska?"

The corners of Natalia's mouth curled up. "Nah-*tah*-lee-ah!"

"Sorry. An effect of the vine. You vish?"

"Can we find Rula now?"

"Rula."

"We *have* to find her," Natalia said. "She's hiding someplace. She didn't have her dinner."

"Who," Sam inquired, "is Rula?"

"Rula Lenska," said Theo.

"Rula Lens-ka? Who is Rula Lenska?" he asked Theo.

"Um, it's a cat," Theo replied. "I had to bring it from Susan's."

"A cat named Rula Lenska?"

"She'll die if she doesn't have food," Natalia declared.

"That's not likely," Theo remarked. "She weighs 25 pounds."

Natalia darted Theo a glare. "Can we find her now, Sam? Please?"

"Yes. But first you must eat four po or four beef or four pupu and seven vegetable of your choice. Eleven pieces. With chopstick. Then we find Miss Rula Lenska."

"Maybe she got outside," Natalia said with concern. "She's never been outside."

"She's probably upstairs," Theo suggested. "Growing new hair."

"New hair?" Sam asked.

"Another movie," Theo said.

Theo cleaned up the kitchen. He transferred food from cardboard cartons to Tupperware.

Sam was being pleasant. More than pleasant. Sam seemed to be adjusting. And when Susan came back in a week, their lives could return to normal.

And he'd make this up to Sam. He'd be attentive from now on. And when Susan got back and was settled in, maybe he'd take Sam on a vacation. Let him choose the place.

Theo loaded the dishwasher with care—plates in the plate

places, no glasses on the bottom rack—the way Sam did it.

They would start fresh. Go back to the old days when going to work was something you endured until you could get back together. Back to the days when you got a blue veiner just talking together on the phone.

What had he been thinking? That Sam would be furious to learn Theo had a child? A lot of men had children. Billions of men. Had he thought that Sam would actually disapprove of his being a sperm donor? Of course, far better to have told Sam years ago—before the donation came to visit.

He sponged the countertops. He moved objects: the toaster, the food processor, the ice crusher used only twice in his memory. He moved the flour and sugar cans. And the tall, glass pasta jars. He sprinkled Comet where these objects had stood, then added a bit of water to the Comet and worked a paste into tiny, stained scratches in the Formica.

And he would sit Natalia down sometime this week. Yes, and Sam too, when he explained to Natalia that he was her father. He would not need to go deeply into this, just enough that she would know the basics—that she had a father, and not an irresponsible one.

Theo wiped away the Comet paste with a refreshed, damp sponge. He dried the countertops with paper towels. He lined up the counter objects. Just wait until Sam saw this. The new Theo. He might even learn to cook. Easy things at first: fried chicken and spaghetti. Then move on. To *beouf bourguignon.* To *choux à limousine.* No more pizza. No more Chinese.

When he had wiped the sinks dry, he poured vodka into a short, crystal glass. He added ice. He ground pepper over the ice and leaned against the work island to admire the orderly room.

Tomorrow the new Theo would begin to emerge—the mindful, attentive, and considerate Theo. *Just look at this kitchen,* he thought. The new Theo had already begun to emerge.

Sam held the fat, striped Rula Lenska to his chest. "You'll never guess where we found her," he told Theo.

"Guess!" Natalia begged, bouncing on her toes, one palm on the belly of the beast.

"In the washing machine," Theo said.

"N-o-o-o!" Natalia said, joy in her eyes.

"In the attic. The attic crawl space."

"N-o-o-o!" cried Natalia.

"You tell," Sam told Natalia.

"In the *books*!" she said, delighted.

"What books?"

"No, wait! *Way* up." One small hand rose as high as Natalia could reach. "In the room with all the books!"

"In your den," Sam said.

"Isn't that just…great?" Theo said.

"No, wait!" Natalia cried. "We walked back and forth, back and forth everywhere looking for her." She walked back and forth, her fingers bent claws now before her face. "We walked right under her and we didn't even *see* her! *I* saw her first. I saw her tail moving under the shelf."

"She did."

"And now we have to give her her dinner," Natalia said.

"Does she like Chinese?" Theo asked.

"She *only* eats cat food."

Theo removed several cans from the cupboard. "Take your pick."

"She likes kitty meat loaf the best."

"We don't have kitty meat loaf."

"Then she likes the fish one the best."

Theo opened a can of mackerel and began to fork the contents onto a bread plate.

"No! Just half. She gets half in the morning and half in the night. And water. We have to always have water in a bowl for her."

When Sam placed the cat before her food, she smelled the dish and darted—her belly flesh flapping from side to side—around the corner toward the stairs and the third floor.

"She's in a strange house, Natalia," Theo explained. "She'll eat when she's ready. Time for bed."

"*Not!*" Natalia scowled. Skinny arms crossed a skinny chest.

"Yep."

"My mommy lets me stay up until the news."

"Your mommy's in California," Theo said firmly.

"Come on," Sam said. "I'll take you up."

To Theo's surprise, Natalia complied without objection.

"Thanks," Theo said in the dark.

"For what?"

"For being so good to her."

"She's all right."

"I did sort of spring her on you."

"There was no 'sort of' about it."

"I don't know what I was thinking."

"Nothing, probably," Sam replied. "I've let this one go. We'll make this amnesty night. If you have any more surprises, this is the time. Think hard, Theo. You got a wife and three kids in the Poconos? Maybe you've sold our house, and we're moving to Detroit? Now's the time, Theo. I'm willing to start with a clean slate."

"No more surprises, Sam. I promise." Theo snuggled closer in the bed.

"I'm holding you to that."

Theo nodded against Sam's shoulder. "It's going to be different, Sam. I promise."

"I've got to leave here by 10:30 tomorrow. I've got a meeting...Theo?" Sam nudged. Theo grunted.

169

"Did you hear me? I've got a meeting at 10:30."

"Ten-thirty."

"You going to the gym?"

"Hospital."

"What about Natalia?"

"PlaySchool."

Chapter 20

Sam sipped coffee in his ratty, terry robe. Natalia sat across from him. Her face was very near her cereal bowl, near the snout of her raccoon. She spooned. She stared at a space beyond Sam. It was 7 a.m.

"Natalia? Is Theo taking you to PlaySchool?"

She shrugged. She spooned.

"Did Theo talk to you about going to PlaySchool today?"

"No."

"How will you get there?"

"I don't know."

"Do you know where PlaySchool is? The address?"

"It's in Philadelphia."

"Terrific," Sam muttered. Primly squeezing his beltless robe at the neck and waist, he stalked to the kitchen. He dialed Theo's pager. He punched in the number of their home phone and slammed the receiver to. "Right. No more surprises," he huffed. He folded one side of the robe over the other, hugged himself, and returned to the table.

"You want a pear, Natalia? We have lots of pears."

"They're for snack time. We're 'sposed to eat fruit at snack time."

"At PlaySchool," Sam said.

"Yes," she told the wall behind him.

The doorbell rang. *Theo,* Sam thought. *Here to pick her up already, and she—still in the T-shirt she slept in and hair looking like a brush pile. Well, let him handle it,* Sam decided.

The bell rang again, two short and impatient bursts. Sam stirred but did not stand. Theo had forgotten his door keys again and was too impatient to drive around the block to the laundry room door.

"Somebody's there," Natalia observed.

"It's Theo," Sam sighed. He stood holding the robe to him and trudged to the stairs. The doorbell rang again, three sharp blasts. "You know?" he shouted on the stairs, "Somebody ought to give you a memory for Christmas!"

The bell sounded yet again as he crossed the first floor hall. *"How* do you remember your *name,* for God's sake?" He snapped the dead bolt. He jerked the door open. On the doormat stood a 50-ish woman in a cloche of blue feathers, a long fabric coat, and holding a Macy's shopping bag. Her eyes dropped, then her jaw. She breathed in and looked quickly into the shrubberies.

"Oh! Excuse me!" Sam cried, grabbing for terry cloth. "I thought you were somebody else!"

The woman sniffed toward the clipped hollies. A car idled at the curb, a man in the driver's seat. "Are you Dr. Tithonus?" she asked doubtfully.

"No," Sam said, giving this stranger no purchase.

She glanced at the house number. "Is Dr. Tithonus in?"

"No."

"And when do you expect him?"

"Who are you?"

The woman frowned. Clearly her name was none of this derelict's business. "I told the doctor I'd be here at 7."

"What for?" Sam wrapped one naked leg around the other against the cold.

The woman was losing her patience with this person in the

dreadful bathrobe. The man in the car leaned across the car seat and peered uneasily from the passenger window.

"When is Dr. Tithonus expected?"

"I don't know."

The car horn tooted. The woman turned toward the car then back to Sam. She began another tack. "Is Natalia Zack here?"

"Yes. Why?"

"Obviously you don't know anything," the woman remarked. Sam bristled. The woman stood taller. "I am Anna Cristobel. I will be working here until Dr. Zack returns."

"Working where?"

"Working *here,*" she said, pointing at the doormat.

"And just what is it you *do?*" Sam said with some irritation.

" 'Do?' " she said. "I do everything. What do *you* do?" She eyed the clenched and unspeakable robe.

The man in the car rolled down the passenger window. "Anna?" he called.

"What do you want, identification? Is that what you want?" The woman dropped her Macy's bag to the mat and snapped open her purse. She was experienced at disabuse. She jerked out her wallet and flipped it open. "There!" she said. She shook the wallet at Sam. "Anna Janine Cristobel. That's me."

"Anna?" the man called again from the car.

"Hush!" she called over her shoulder.

"Who's that?"

"My *hus*band," she said, as if to dispel whatever vulgar implication.

"Are you Susan's maid?"

"I am Dr. Zack's housekeeper," she corrected.

"And you're supposed to work *here?*"

"I *am,*" she scowled.

"I didn't know." Sam opened the door to her. "No one told me."

Mrs. Cristobel did not seem surprised to hear this. She waved the car off. "It's all right!" she called irritably.

"I still don't understand why you're here," Sam said, holding the door wide as Mrs. Cristobel edged her Macy's bag past him. "If I'd known—"

"You'd have put some *clothes* on?" the woman asked behind her back.

"Oh, there's my little love!" said Mrs. Cristobel in the kitchen, opening her arms to the child who came running. She hugged and kissed Natalia and said, "But, baby, your shirt's on backward. And God love ya, just look at that hair! Lordy, it'll take me an hour to get you ready, and we'll miss our bus!"

"Where do you keep the cleaning supplies?"

"For what?" Sam asked, showered, shaved, combed, and dressed now in hospital scrubs.

"Everything. Are *you* a doctor?" she added.

"I'm a nurse."

She nodded but did not seem to approve.

Sam leaned against the dining room door frame. "Mrs. Cristobel, could we just talk about a couple of things?"

"Well?"

"Who hired you to come here?"

"If you mean who's paying me, Dr. Zack's paying me. Two weeks ahead, so you needn't worry."

"Two weeks?"

"Except for my petty cash, which she forgot, but I have enough of my own for today."

"And what are you supposed to do here? Take care of Natalia?"

"That and everything I do at Dr. Zack's house." Mrs. Cristobel folded her arms over her breasts. "And you? Do you live here...? Or are you just visiting?"

"This is also my house."

She assessed this information. "So you'll be having your dinners in?"

"Certainly."

"I see Dr. Tithonus brought the pork roast from Dr. Zack's. I'll make that for tonight. I do it with bourbon sauce and apples, which I see you've got. Dr. Zack likes Natalia to have lots of fresh vegetables, which I see you haven't got. Or salad makings, either. I do salad every dinner, so I'll need to do some shopping. I'll be needing a key to let myself in and out. I'll discuss the petty cash with Dr. Tithonus when he returns."

"You can discuss the petty cash with me."

Mrs. Cristobel seemed doubtful.

"What do you mean by 'petty cash?' " Sam inquired.

"Dr. Zack always keeps $200 in one of her vases. I take out what I need for the shopping and my cab fares and such, and I put in my receipts. She replaces the petty cash as needed."

Sam took out his wallet and extracted some bills. "Here is a hundred," he said, extending the money. "Dr. Tithonus will give you another hundred."

She paused. She took the money, one eyebrow raised.

"There'll be no need for you to do housework," Sam said.

"I'll not be sitting on my fanny watching *Oprah* all day," she announced.

"The house is clean."

"There's plenty to keep me busy."

"Like what, for example?"

"The room Natalia's in, for example. And the office next to it. And all the curtains are long overdue for a washing—"

"We have them dry cleaned."

"They're perfectly washable in Woolite," Mrs. Cristobel retorted. "You'll be leaving for your work soon?"

"Yes."

"Then if you'll tell me where the cleaning things are, I'll get started on *my* work."

"I told you, the house is clean."

"I don't call dust balls under beds 'clean.' The windows need doing, inside and out. I use ammonia and water. And I'll need a good lot of paper towels." She ran a finger across the dining table then pointed at its surface. "Wax buildup. From Pledge, I'll wager, or some other lazy person's spray-on. I use tung oil—pure tung oil with clean flannel," she added. "That's the best. And if I were you, I'd tell my regular cleaning people about tung oil and flannel. If you'll show me where the laundry is, I'll get started on the curtains and the windows. I suppose they don't pop out?"

"No."

"I'll manage."

" 'How's it going?' 'How's it *going?*'" Sam shouted into the phone. "Number one, she's pulled down every curtain in the house. Number two, she stripped the bed *I* just *changed.* Number three, she threw my goddamned Pledge in the trash; and Number four, why the fuck didn't you *tell* me that woman was coming here this morning?"

"Mrs. Cristobel."

"*Yes,* Mrs. Cristobel, who the *hell* do you think?"

"Sam, I—"

"Theo, you cannot keep doing these things to me. You know *why?* Because I am not going to let you. Do I withhold things from you? No I do not. I have never withheld one goddamned thing from you. I even warn you before I let out a *fart!* You don't tell me anything, and, Theo, I have *had* it!"

The phone went dead in Theo's ear.

"Oh, my God!" Mrs. Cristobel shrieked, backing against the washing machine.

"Sorry. I didn't mean to startle you. I'm Dr. Tithonus."

"You scared the bejesus out of me!"

"I'm sorry. Is Sam upstairs?"

"If you mean the man who was here this morning, he left, then he came back again, and then he left again an hour ago."

"To work?"

"Looks to me like he left bag and baggage."

"He packed a bag?"

"Two," she said.

What remained in Sam's closet were things he seldom wore. All his work clothes were gone. His jeans and pointy-toed cowboy boots were gone. The framed photograph of his parents which he kept at his bedside was gone. There was a bare spot where the digital clock radio always sat. His two shelves in the bathroom medicine cabinet had been stripped.

"Did Mr. Meacham leave a note?" Theo asked Mrs. Cristobel in the kitchen. "Or a number?"

"He didn't tell me, if he did."

"I have to get back to the hospital. If he calls, tell him to call me there or at my office."

"I'll be picking Natalia up at 3," she said. "I'll be needing a key."

"I'll give you the one for the front door."

"He gave me a hundred dollars toward the petty cash," she said. "Dr. Zack always gives me $200. And we'll have to decide on a place."

"A place for what?"

"The petty cash."

"Can't you just hold on to it?"

"And if I'm mugged on the street? Indeed not."

"Can't we decide on that tonight?"

"I'll have to be leaving at 6. I have my samba tonight."

"You dance?"

"Cards," she said. "You *will* be back by 6, doctor?"

"No, I can't," Theo said. "Seven. 7:30. I have to cover for Dr. Zack."

"I can't stay after 6 Mondays, so you'll have to make your arrangements," she said. "I'll have your dinner prepared." She began to descend the stairs to the first floor. "Pork roast—I make it with bourbon sauce," she called back.

Theo stood at the kitchen work island. He drummed his fingers on the butcher block.

Sam would be back, he thought. Oh, he'd stay away the night to make his point. And not call. For sure not call, to cause Theo worry.

Theo snorted. He should have told Sam about the housekeeper. But he couldn't remember everything, could he?

He removed all the bills from his wallet. He had $63. He put $50 on the cutting board and a salt shaker on the money.

"I could only leave you $50," he told Mrs. Cristobel as he passed the washing machine. "I'll stop at the bank and get you more."

Mrs. Cristobel measured out Woolite. "You'll be back by 6," she said.

"Yes. Samba."

"And shall I have Natalia fed early, or will you be wanting to eat with her?"

"I don't know. Feed her."

Chapter 21

Clare, you're going to have to reschedule these patients."

"Most of them can't be."

"They'll have to be. I can't be running back and forth from the hospital like this. This is my third trip back here, and now I have to go back there again and do…somebody, I don't know, and then you tell me I have to come back here again and see more?"

"Four."

"Well, I can't. I have to be home by 6."

"Then you tell 'em," Clare said, tossing manila folders across the counter. "They're all up for surgeries. And we haven't even talked about Susan's Thursday and Friday schedules, and when you see that list, you're gonna cut your damned throat's what you're gonna do. And I'm not staying past 5 today. I've been here since 6:30 this morning trying to figure all this out. I got my own things to do."

Theo glanced at his wristwatch. Fourteen minutes before 6. The drive home took 20 minutes, and this woman, Susan's patient, would not listen to reason.

He squirmed. "Mrs. Rosenwig," he began anew, "let me review your situation—one more time.

"You have a tumor in your parotid gland. It was very slow

growing; it's not anymore. You can see that for yourself.

"I can't give you the sorts of guarantees you seem to be asking for in this operation. Facial nerves are very tightly imbedded at the site of the tumor. When we remove the growth, there's always a chance there could be some paralysis to that side of your face. I said 'could,' not 'would.' "

Mrs. Rosenwig's feet jiggled.

"We have a very good track record with this kind of tumor," Theo continued. "Especially at the stage yours is in just now. But as it grows, the chances of damage increase.

"Now, I understand the part about you and Mr. Rosenwig having nonrefundable airline tickets to Maui," Theo said impatiently. "I understand about your condominium time-share."

Theo stood in frustration. "But Mrs. Rosenwig, your tumor is doubling in size every six to eight weeks, and if you wait until after you get back from Hawaii to have it out, not only will you increase the risk of nerve damage but you also take the chance that the tumor itself will paralyze the whole left side of your face. That could happen spontaneously. While you're *golfing* or something."

Mrs. Rosenwig crossed one athletic leg over the other. "I don't golf, doctor. I play tennis. I'm third seed at my club."

"Well, what if a *tennis* ball hits your tumor, Mrs. Rosenwig?" Theo pulled the fingers of one hand suddenly down one side of his face, distorting his eye and cheek and lips. "We might not be able to repair that kind of damage."

Mrs. Rosenwig shifted her weight on the examination table. "Look, doctor. I *get* it. Dr. Zack already went through this. I know what the risks are." Mrs. Rosenwig sighed. "Here's *my* objection: The part I'm having just a little trouble adjusting to is what happens after the operation. Saliva running out of my ear when I eat?"

Theo grinned. "Not out of your ear, Mrs. Rosenwig. There

180

could be some moisture. Beside your ear."

This was little solace to Barbara Rosenwig. "Doctor, we entertain. When I say 'entertain,' I'm talking four, five times a week. Fancy New York restaurants—Lutèce, places like that. While my husband's patrician clients are touching napkins to their lips, I'm supposed to sit there mopping *spit* off my ear?"

"Moisture."

"Doctor, you can say that till the cows come home. It's spit."

Theo looked directly now at his wristwatch. "Mrs. Rosenwig. What more can I say? If you have this operation now, there is a slight chance you could lose a little facial control." He threw up his palms. "If you don't have this operation now, you could look like Quasimodo. Consider the alternatives. Look, you're a very worldly lady. If you can't come up with a subtle way to get a little spit off your cheek, I think you better turn in your hostess cards."

"I like you…You got balls. OK, screw Maui. When do you want to operate?"

"Thursday. First thing. I'll have Clare set it up. And don't worry, Mrs. Rosenwig. I'm good. Now if you'll excuse me, my daughter's waiting."

Theo tossed his lab coat through the door of his office. *My daughter,* he thought. The first time he'd ever said those words.

Mrs. Cristobel stood in the kitchen in her coat and blue feathered cloche. "When Dr. Zack's going to be late, she calls."

"I'm very sorry to hold you up."

"Your dinner's in the microwave; Natalia's had hers. And her bath."

"Did Mr. Meacham call?"

"No." Mrs. Cristobel picked up her Macy's bag and gloves. "Natalia's watching the television. No television after 7. That's Dr.

Zack's rule. She's to be in bed by 8...You have children, doctor?"

Just that one, he thought.

"Well, I'll give you a word of advice. I raised four of them myself, and bedtime's the worst. But if you're firm and you don't take nonsense, they go to bed when they're told. I'll just let myself in in the morning. Good night."

Theo removed his coat. The evening stretched before him. What would he do with it?

What would he do if Sam were here and Natalia were not?

And what would he do if his pager went off and he were called to the hospital? Take Natalia to the hospital with him? Drop her off at Thalia's or Cassie's?

Maybe Sam would come home after work. Just walk in as if nothing had happened. What if Sam did not come home? Ever.

In the living room, Natalia sat cross-legged before the television. She had positioned her raccoon next to her so that it also watched television.

"Hi, Natalia."

She turned briefly then ignored him for the African animals that cavorted on the screen.

"What're you watching?"

She did not answer.

Should he sit with her and watch African animals? Should he eat now instead, in the quiet of his den? Or eat after bedtime? Eat alone in the quiet house after she slept?

No, he thought, suddenly inspired. They should have their little talk. Their very important talk.

"Natalia, would you turn that off, please?"

She seemed not to hear.

"Natalia, turn that off for a few minutes. I want to talk to you."

"This is my program."

"I'd like to talk with you about something."

"When it's over."

What could be more important than what he had to tell her? There were always African animals on some channel. He walked to the set. He turned the television off.

"I was watching!"

"I need to talk with you for a little bit."

"I watch this every day. My mommy lets me, and Mrs. Cristobel said I could!" She pointed the remote at the screen. A lioness tore flesh.

Theo leaned and stabbed the power button. "It's important that we have a talk."

Natalia pointed and clicked. The lioness revealed her bloody maw.

"Na-*talia*," Theo whined, offended. He pressed the power button.

Natalia's eyes narrowed. She pointed and clicked. Lion cubs leaped into the ripped belly of a gazelle and pulled at entrails.

"Na*talia*!" Theo said sharply. He jabbed power.

The child's face screwed up. Her head tilted back. Her eyes closed and her mouth formed a silent scream. Dramatically, she threw herself across her lap to the carpet and wailed: "I'm allowed to watch this *every night*. I'm al-*low*ed!"

"All right, all right!" Theo returned power to the set. "We'll talk when it's over." He left the room.

He sat on a kitchen stool drinking peppered vodka.

Ten more minutes. He could have waited ten more minutes. This was no way to win over a child. He hadn't needed to barge into her television time, to usurp her private time for something about which he had kept his silence for years.

At 7 he'd go back in and they would talk. They would have a quiet time together, father and daughter, and he would tell her about being her father. About what that could mean to their futures.

Natalia, I am your father.

No. Too…abrupt.

Natalia, I'm very sorry I intruded a while ago. That was inconsiderate. Thoughtless.

But I was so anxious to tell you this important thing. To share with you…that I am your father.

No.

To tell you that I'm your daddy, sweetie.

To tell you, sweetie, that I'm really your daddy.

Natalia, I'm your sweetie daddy, honey.

Theo guffawed into his glass.

Impalas leaped behind closing credits.

"Natalia, honey. It's 7."

"No. Frogs is next."

"Natalia? No TV after 7."

"I *have* to. My teacher *said.* We're *learn*ing frogs!"

"Mrs. Cristobel told me no TV after 7."

"I *have* to watch. Mrs. Hellmann *said.* It's *home*work."

I'm your father, and I say no.

"Are you making this up, Natalia?"

She rolled her eyes. She sighed. "Mrs. Hellmann SAID we have to watch the program about the frogs. Do you want me to get in *trouble?*"

"Natalia. It's 7:30. Turn that off now."

Obediently, she pointed the remote and turned the television off. "But I don't have to go to bed yet."

"No. Not till 8. We have a half hour." Theo lowered himself to the carpet next to Natalia. He crossed his legs. Natalia squiggled to make several more inches between them then regarded a wall.

Theo pushed a forefinger into the carpeting. "Natalia? There's something I've been wanting to tell you…"

She turned her raccoon to face her. She arranged its tail. She waited.

"Do you know…who your daddy is?" Foolish though this sounded to him, it was at least a beginning.

By manipulating its front legs, Natalia caused the raccoon to walk toward her. "My mommy and my daddy are divorced," she said nonchalantly.

"Who told you that?"

"Billy Bastian."

"Who's Billy Bastian?"

"He's my friend." The raccoon pranced back and forth at her knees.

Theo pressed five fingers into the carpet. "Well, no. Not divorced exactly." What did he tell her now? That she was illegitimate?

Natalia, you're a bastard.

"Natalia? Years ago—before you were born—your mommy wanted to have a baby. To have you." Theo made random finger holes in the carpet pile. "And I was your mommy's best friend, you see, and so she asked me." Theo smiled in what seemed to him a very parental way.

"Asked you what?"

Theo made rows of parallel finger holes in the carpet. "Your mommy asked me to be your daddy."

The raccoon leaped over her legs. "Then you got divorced."

"No. Not exactly."

"Then, what?"

He had not expected the marriage part to be so critical. Did he need tell her now that he and her mommy were never married?

"Natalia. Your mommy and her husband were divorced. Your mommy and I weren't divorced."

"Then why don't you live with us?"

That wasn't part of the deal.

"Because," he indicated the walls, "I have my own house."

"You don't like us." The raccoon paused to listen.

"Of course I do. Your mommy and I are very best friends."

Natalia waited for more.

"Do you understand what I'm saying to you, Natalia?"

"No."

"What I'm telling you is, *I'm* your daddy, Natalia."

"If you're my daddy..." her chin rose, "why don't you ever come see us?"

This was a good question.

He could think of no answer that did not make him out to be a lout. "Well, I will," he vowed. "When your mommy gets back from her vacation, I'll come and visit you every weekend," he heard himself say. "And you can come over here and stay too. Would you like that?"

"No," she said. She stood. "Now I have to find Rula." And she was gone.

"Natalia," Theo said at the doorway of his den. "Turn that off. It's time for bed."

She flipped channels with the den remote and ignored him.

"Natalia, you turn off that TV. Now. It's time for bed."

The screen's images shifted yet again.

Theo walked to the set. The screen became a tiny point of light.

"No!" She pounded the remote on the arm of his leather reading chair. She glared at Theo.

"Yes," he said calmly. "Bed."

"No!"

"Come," he said, standing beside her, reaching toward her.

She folded abruptly into her lap.

"Natalia."

Little hands wrapped under her knees then clasped.

"Natalia."

What did one do now? He was the adult. She was the child. He was the father.

"Natalia," he repeated sternly.

Silence.

He bent and lifted her like a medicine ball into his arms. Immediately her back arched. Her arms rose straight above her head. Her legs descended together like a diver's. She dropped through his arms, a dead weight, to the floor and lay back, eyes squeezed closed, teeth clenched.

"Natalia, I am not going to argue with you," Theo announced.

She did not move.

He bent, lifted her stiff like a plank into his arms and carried her toward the hallway and her room.

She thrust her body in all directions suddenly—squirming, throwing herself out, a sack of snakes. When he held tight, she twisted her head toward him. She sank her teeth into his biceps.

"Je-sus *Christ!*"

She dropped to the floor like a stone.

Blood seeped through Theo's shirt. His arm swung up above her and she flinched, grimaced for a blow. Theo caught himself mid-arch. The muscles in front of his ears bulged, and suddenly he dropped to the floor also, and like a jungle beast, rolled her, and closed his teeth on the fabric of her little trousers high upon her buttock.

She shrieked.

He held on, not cutting but pinching severely, as she, shocked, screamed and squirmed to pull herself away. He opened his jaws and released her. "If you *ever* bite me or anyone else again…" He allowed the threat to hang.

He hauled Natalia to her feet by her armpits, grabbed an arm, and pulled the wide-eyed child toward the hallway and the guest room.

Pork and fat congealed on Theo's plate. His bourbon-soaked apple slices darkened in their sauce.

You just couldn't go around biting people. She couldn't, nor could he. He had never bitten a human in his life, and who did he choose for his first victim? His daughter.

Some father. Her second night under his roof, and there he was, down on the floor biting her bum.

Theo could not sleep. Having gone to bed mind-weary, he was restless now. He rolled, alone in the bed, onto his bitten biceps and flinched. Was he due for a tetanus shot? Never mind lock-jaw; the kid was probably rabid.

Where is Sam sleeping? he wondered. If he was sleeping. Surely he had gone to stay with a friend. Tommy Warhola, maybe. Certainly he wouldn't go to the Cinco de Mayos, whose lives were a Mexican travelogue and whose home smelled more than remotely of kennel. He must be with a friend. Not like Sam to throw money away on a hotel.

Unless, in anger, he had driven to the Ritz after work, handed over his car, and checked in and showered to go out for a night on the town.

It was the packing of the pointy-toed cowboy boots which gave Theo pause. Why, leaving in a lurch, would he have bothered to take them at all when he could have come back for them?

Unless, having showered in some vast marble bath at the Ritz

188

and shaved and applied a drop or two of Obsession, he put on fresh Levis and that favorite deep-green shirt and pulled on the boots to saunter, rusty-haired and hairy-armed and hot, to cruise the bars?

The image of Sam—his Sam—shoulders bracing a wall, beer bottle dangling, and that small, mysterious smile, set Theo again to tossing. Theo had seen the appreciative glances, the warm and welcoming smiles that Sam could illicit from men on the make.

He wouldn't do that. Not Sam. Not *his* Sam.

Unless he had decided that he and Theo were finished. For good. Unless Sam believed that there was no hope for the new Theo ever emerging and had decided today he wanted no more.

Theo had not been the most attentive of lovers for some time. Theo had let sex take a backseat to work. Theo had let sex, once their primary epoxy, become a very thin paste of flour and water.

Nor had he been attentive in other ways. And not just toward Sam. He had virtually ignored Susan when she most needed his support and understanding. God knew he had ignored their child, the sharp-fanged little hydrophobe, who slept, finally, in the room down the hall.

Well, he still had his work. At least his work made him feel good and was the one aspect of his life which satisfied. And in a year, he would become chief of surgery. To have that kind of position and influence? To be able to change the directions and politics of health care in one of the finest hospitals in the country? Such an unexpected boost to his career.

But would he be an effective administrator?

Not if you looked at the many questionable examples of his personal life. Not if you looked at the botch he was making of his life on 26th Street. Not if you weighed in how well he supported his friends or considered the complete failure of his second full day of parenthood.

Or if you threw in his driving away the one person who had

always been there for him.

No, from those points of view he was a very lousy administrator.

So his private life was a little thin. And getting thinner.

At least when Micari handed him the job of surgical chief, he would take that position and run with it.

Unless Garlington snatched up that ball himself.

Such a user. Such a creep. Such a piece of shit in the workplace and on the streets. At least Susan had not become one of his statistics—or worse—in the bedroom with the incredible view.

Thoughts of Timothy Garlington began a new round of tossing.

Chapter 22

T heo has hired a housekeeper."

"A housekeeper? *I'm* the one who needs a housekeeper," Thalia groused on the phone. "Were you over there?"

"Of course not," Cassie replied, drawing doodles on her phone pad. "I called him. I was afraid his friend would answer but when a woman did, I thought I had the wrong number. She told me she was Dr. Tithonus's housekeeper."

"She didn't say she was Dr. Tithonus's and Mr. Meacham's housekeeper?"

"Well, that doesn't sound very chic, does it? Anyway, Theo's the one paying her. *He* can't afford a housekeeper on what he makes. I doubt he even pays Theo rent."

"Probably not."

"You'd think he'd be embarrassed to be kept, wouldn't you?"

"Well, he is cute, Cassie, I'll give him that."

"He's not cute at all. He looks common to me. And Irish."

"I don't think 'Meacham' is Irish. I think it's Scotch."

"Well, what's the difference, Thalia? Really. And those freckles. And no nose to speak of. The man is not cute."

"*I* think he's very cute," Thalia said.

"Oh, Thalia. Honestly," Cassie said, dismissing her. "In any case, he'll be out of there before long."

"Why do you say that?"

"Thalia, Theo is 46 years old."

"What's that got to do with it?"

"He'll be marrying Susan Zack one of these days. Mark my words."

"Cassie, are you on drugs, or something?"

"Thalia!"

"Well, what are you babbling about? The man is as gay as a goose."

"I always *thought* he was. And I never understood why Theo let him live in his house so long. Generosity is one thing, but five years is a bit excessive."

"I can't believe I'm hearing this."

"What are *you* babbling about, Thalia? Would you let a friend live in your house for five years? A lesbian? I doubt that very much."

"Cassie! *Theo* is as gay as a goose. They are *both* gay as gooses."

"Theo is *not* homosexual, Thalia. That's just absurd. How do you explain Susan Zack? You said yesterday he had her child staying there. How do you explain that? Anyway, he's dated her for years. They go everywhere together."

"It's very simple," Thalia replied. "He and Susan are friends, and that's that. She's a convenience. For social reasons. Could Theo take his 'friend' to hospital functions? Of course not. And what's her daughter got to do with the price of beans? I can't believe you're so naive, Cassie."

"We'll talk no more about it," Cassie said with finality. "And I hope you are not spreading such nasty innuendo around in public."

"You just go ahead and dream on, Cassie."

"Anyway, that isn't what I wanted to talk to you about. I've had a new will drawn up for Daddy, and I want you to look it over before I send it to him."

"You don't just write a will for somebody, Cassie."

"Why not? I wrote the last one. Why wouldn't I write this one?"

"Did he ask you to?"

"Of course not. Daddy's in no condition to be doing anything as complicated as this."

"Isn't that why God invented lawyers?"

"Thalia, I didn't write the will myself. My lawyers did. All Daddy has to do is sign it."

"What's it say?"

"It says precisely what we discussed here last week. I've had Rosy put in for a flat $30,000. Cash on the barrel head."

"I've been thinking a little more about that…"

Cassie considered that she might have made an error.

"Cassie…maybe we did jump the gun a little. Probably we should wait awhile. See what's really happening? Theo *is* a doctor, Cassie. If he says it's the diabetes, then it's probably the diabetes. Don't you think?"

Cassie regretted giving Thalia $10,000. That was dumb, dumb, dumb. Better to have kept her lean and hungry. And compliant. But then, how long could it take $10,000 to burn holes through Thalia's pockets? She owed everybody and his brother.

"Thalia, dear, there is a world of difference between diabetes and abuse. Are you really willing to look the other way while that woman does God knows what to Daddy?"

"I was just thinking that it *could* be his insulin, Cassie. You have to admit it could be."

Cassie sighed for effect. "I'm not completely opposed to that, Thalia. Maybe you're right. Maybe we should wait a few months. Of course, watch the situation very closely in the meantime…. I would just need for you to make arrangements to repay the loan I made to you. I'm going to need my $10,000 back fairly soon."

"But you said I could repay that with the $10,000 Daddy's going to give us."

"Well, that *was* our plan, Thalia, but if you want to wait now and see how things work out, *I* won't have *my* $10,000 from Daddy."

"I can't believe $10,000 could mean a thing to *you,* Cassie," Thalia said abruptly.

Cassie scrolled delete symbols in a column down her pad. "Contrary to appearances," she said indignantly, "I am not *made* of money." She drew little French curves in another column. "Warren did leave me some lovely things, and just because I have a home on Delancey Place, everybody seems to think I'm a wealthy woman. What they don't know, and what you don't know apparently, is that this house was mortgaged to the hilt when Warren died. The bank could have foreclosed. They could have taken my home."

"Cassie—"

"That all fell on *me,* Thalia, and you more than anybody should know what it feels like to suddenly lose a husband you depended on. And Warren's business? I don't even want to get into the problems that caused me. He told me *nothing* about the business before he died," Cassie said as bitterly as she could manage. "I work 12- and 14-hour days just to keep that concern afloat." She began a border of dollar signs across the top of her pad. "No, indeed. Ten thousand dollars means as much to me as it does to you."

"Cassie, maybe—"

"Ten thousand dollars doesn't even meet my weekly *pay*roll, Thalia."

"Cassie—"

"As I think about it, though," Cassie said with resignation, "Maybe it is time I did some economizing. I could get by without Mrs. Wimmer, I guess. If I left work a little earlier each day, I might be able to keep things up."

"I'll come to your office tomorrow and look at the will."

"Thalia, I don't mean to badger you with my own problems, believe me. I want you to feel good about this entire situation."

"No. Every time I think about that woman getting even a penny, my blood just boils. But what about Theo? Will he cooperate?"

"Daddy's signing his will does not require Theo's cooperation. Besides, it's up to us girls to resolve this, and he'll be relieved that we did. You'll see. You come by my office and look this over, and that, as they say, will be that. Lord, Thalia, it's 10 o'clock and I've *got* to get to bed."

"Yes, you get some rest. You do work long days, Cassie."

Cassie hung up her phone. She smiled slightly. She pushed her notepad aside and reached for an investment portfolio.

The phone rang.

"Cassie, I was just thinking," Thalia said. "I don't have to sign this will, do I?"

"Thalia," Cassie sighed. "Where is your head these days? This is not *your* will, this is *Daddy's* will. All you have to do is look it over and be in agreement with what I'm doing."

"Cassandra, don't patronize me. I was just thinking…Oh, I don't know what I was thinking."

Having finished again with her sister, Cassie opened the portfolio folder. She looked at the computer printout of the buying activities of her vice president, Stuart Flowers. Her jaw dropped.

"Oh, my God…Greedy, deceitful ingrate!" She rubbed her temple. She sat back in her chair. "How am I going to cover *this* up?"

Chapter 23

She told me you bit her," Mrs. Cristobel said, buckling a galosh.

"She bit me."

Mrs. Cristobel tugged at the second rubber boot. "She never bit me," she grunted, bending over. "Seems to me adults have no place biting...I'd never assume to be telling a parent how to raise their own," she said with a sideways glance to let him know she knew now. "I never bit any of mine." She straightened herself, her backside well against the kitchen cabinets. "I suppose you'll be biting me next..." she said without a trace of a smile. "You didn't like the pork roast?"

"No, it was fine."

Mrs. Cristobel glanced at the unfinished plate in the sink.

"I wasn't hungry," Theo explained. "Mrs. Cristobel, there's no way I can get home before 7:30 tonight. In fact, you better count on 7:30 at the earliest every night until Dr. Zack gets back."

Mrs. Cristobel frowned. "I'll stay. But that doesn't mean quarter to 8. And there'll be cab fare to be paid. I live almost to Glenside, and that's 20-some dollars—even with no traffic."

"Use the petty cash. I'll say good-bye to Natalia. Is she upstairs?"

"Dressing for school," Mrs. Cristobel said at the sink, scraping his pork roast from the plate. "She said she's not speaking to you.

196

She said you weren't her father because fathers don't bite little children."

Mrs. Cristobel flipped the disposal switch.

"That's a very pretty outfit, Natalia," Theo offered from the doorway of the guest room.

She tugged at a sneaker.

"I was thinking maybe I'd rent a movie for us tonight. Would you like that? You could stay up late."

"No."

He had expected a shrug.

"I have to go to the hospital now," he said.

Natalia worked her shoe.

"Natalia. Listen. About when I bit you? We shouldn't bite people. But when you bit me, I was very angry. Do you understand that?"

Natalia struggled with the sneaker.

"Would you like me to help you with that? How about if I tie them for you?"

She stood. She walked past him, her laces dragging the hallway floor.

Chapter 24

T heo sat on the bench before his locker in the surgical dressing room. He had finished the tedious repair of a depressed cheek fracture. His scrub suit was blood-spattered and blotchy with perspiration. He was exhausted and irritable and now needed to get cleaned up to perform one of Susan's surgeries. His day was already too long, and he had many hours to go.

From behind the row of metal lockers, he heard someone humming "Begin the Beguine." Millard Roberts, Theo thought. Now he would have that melody running through his tired brain for the rest of the day.

Theo removed his damp scrub shirt in one pull and pitched it with a high, overhand shot into the laundry cart. His scrub pants followed. He hoped a shower would recharge him.

"Ah, Dr. Tithonus," said Timothy Garlington at the intersection of lockers.

Theo looked up. "I thought that was The Hummer."

"Who?"

"Never mind," Theo told him.

Garlington primped before the mirror. He adjusted white French cuffs at the wrists of his jacket. "Dr. Micari has invited me to lunch," Garlington said casually.

It was the slight, scoffing set of Garlington's lips in the mirror which most disgusted Theo.

"I suspect he wants to tell me I'm being considered for chief of surgery," Garlington mused. "I think I'd make a pretty good one," he told the mirror.

"Not with your sense of protocol," Theo muttered.

Garlington began to comb his sandy hair. "Oh, I don't know. Dr. Micari and Dr. Steinhower seem to think I have a fine grasp of protocol...I haven't seen Susan in a few days," he added. "She was incredible Saturday night."

Theo removed shampoo from his locker.

"I'll tell you," Garlington continued. "She is one hot little fuck."

Theo saw himself leaping naked over the locker room benches to destroy this man's face. He closed his locker door quietly. He stood. He smiled. "Funny," he said. "That's not the way I heard it."

Garlington's head lifted slightly at the mirror. "Huh?"

Theo turned his back and walked toward the showers. "I heard you had to choke the rooster."

Under the shower, Theo wondered at the anticipation he once felt at seeing this predator, at the thrill he had felt at finding notes from Tim Garlington in his dorm room—in a book he had been reading or folded into a pants pocket—each of them saved carefully and stored in its envelope in a Contadina tomato paste box which had traveled with the other boxes of his life, move after move. How could he have been so smitten?

Not at all fresh from his third surgery and fourth shower of the day, Theo raced the green Jaguar across the South Street Bridge toward the backlog of patients who waited at the Medical Tower on 17th, his own patients and Susan's. He could not keep up this pace. He could not handle both their practices, even temporarily. He could not juggle his time between her surgeries and his own, his patients and hers, and Susan was absolutely correct: What would they do when he became chief of surgery if they did not take on an associate?

If he became chief of surgery.

While he had stood bent over a splayed leg teasing nerves, Garlington had politicked over Crab Louis for the job Theo had been told would be his own.

There was nothing for it, Theo thought as traffic halted abruptly at 26th Street. He had no time for schmoozing with Micari. He could not dash about the hospital afternoons putting out grass fires torched by Garlington and his toady, Millard Roberts, or steal time from wholesome evening bite fests with his daughter.

Natalia retaliated for Theo's distracted, poor attentions by ignoring him for her cat Rula Lenska, whose listless, endless patience with the child had begun to rankle Theo. Could he be less interesting than that hairy slug?

Bad enough to fail as a parent, he thought, laying on the car horn. His life partner had also become a casualty of his indifference. *Erstwhile life partner,* Theo corrected himself. Where was Sam as he sat in dead traffic at the corner of 26th and South? Was this a work day for him? Theo could not remember. Was he at his hospital at that moment—or shopping happily for tables, chairs, and breakfronts?

He had deserved to be walked out on, Theo reflected. He should have warned Sam years ago, sat him down and said: You must know this before we move in together—before we buy this house, these things, before our lives become entangled in lawyers and mortgages and social arrangements—be aware that I am your worst nightmare. If it's thoughtfulness you want, take a walk. If it's consideration you yearn for, run for your life. I've never even acknowledged my own daughter.

And he would now pay the price of his silence—and pay

alone. And live this life which was beginning to resemble a medical internship: no time to think, except inside a car; no time to deal with others' needs, let alone his own. His was a life of time accounts always overdrawn.

Susan would decide to live in California and abandon their cannibal child to him. He would have to give up his gym, then he would develop stress diseases and grow fat like Rula Lenska. His patients, short changed, would gradually abandon him. His practice would dwindle; his income would dry up. Sam would take a lover who could show him he loved him.

"Move it, asshole!" Theo shouted in the closed sedan.

And stop your goddamned whining, Theo chastised himself, insinuating the car into another lane. He was not a whiner. He was not a carper. He was a responsible, take-charge guy and his life had not gone begging yet. He ought to be sorting out solutions.

They needed a medical partner. So find a medical partner. Advertise? Invite some vapid, yuppy resident up from Houston for a free Philadelphia weekend; offer half their practice, a red BMW, and paid lifetime fees at a golf club? Jesus.

"Boldini!" Theo shouted. "Oh, Boldini! Why not Boldini?"

"I know," Theo whispered to Clare, his harried office manager. "I know, I know! I'm here already. But first get me Barry Boldini."

"Mrs. Conway had an appointment at 2," Clare hissed. She's becoming very bitchy."

"Becoming?"

"Mrs. Moranski's been here an hour and 20 minutes."

"What's she doing here? I thought we were done with her." Theo looked out into the waiting room. "Which one is she?"

"The one who looks like Jack Palance. The one passed out on the floor? From boredom?"

"*That's* Mrs. Moranski? God, Clare. We can't do anything for her," he quipped. "Wake her up. Tell her to go home."

"Theo. Please? Would you cut the shit? I'm not having a good time here. Just get in there and get started."

"Get me Boldini first. I'm going to save our lives, Clare," he said, moving toward his office.

"Wait! Here," she said, holding up a fistful of telephone messages.

"Clare, call those people back. Really. What do I pay you for?"

"This is my last day, doctor."

Theo closed his office door. He surveyed his desk. Paper was piled in seven, eight stacks across the surface. It would take him a whole day just to do paper. He rifled his phone messages. He tossed them on the desk. He changed from jacket to white lab coat.

Susan looked good in a white lab coat. Susan looked sensational in a white lab coat. Rockette legs in stiletto heels and always, always just a little cleavage. He would tell her when she got back. He would tell her every day how wonderful she was.

Theo shuffled paper piles. Insurance junk. Insurance junk. He'd try to come in early one day.

He lifted the phone. "Clare, any luck with Boldini?"

"Are you nuts? I've had three death threats out here. I quit!"

"Barry! Barry! I have the greatest idea. You're going to love this, Barry!"

"It better be a short idea. I'm scrubbed. RoseAnne's holding the phone to my ear. What?"

"Meet me at the White Dog. Six-thirty."

"I can't."

"Seven, then."

"I can't tonight."

"Breakfast. The Ritz-Carlton."

"I can't afford it."

"You can, Barry."

"I just bought a house I can't afford. I got three kids I can't afford. And I have to have a root canal tomorrow morning, and I can't afford that either."

"Friday then. I'll buy. Seven? The dining room?"

"What's up?"

"See you Friday at 7."

"Mrs. Moranski, I am late. I apologize," Theo said, breezing into an examination room.

Mrs. Moranski, on her back, seemed to awake from a sleep. She waved a hand in the air. She did look like Jack Palance, Theo thought as he prepared to remove her stitches.

"You look absolutely beautiful. We'll get these out, and I think after one more visit you and I are breaking up."

The wall phone buzzed. Mrs. Moranski stirred.

"Excuse me," Theo said.

"Theo, it's your sister," Clare announced with great annoyance. "She insists she talk with you. I told her you're busy."

"Which sister?"

"How the hell would I know? You just got started with Moranski. Mrs. Conway has pulled a gun. She says she's taking one of us out every five minutes, Theo."

"Volunteer to be first, Clare. What have you got to lose? It's your last day. I'll take the call in my office. Mrs. Moranski?" he said to the pink and blue face. "I'm sorry. I have a family matter to attend to. It won't take long, I promise."

"You said that last time."

"I did?"

"What the hey," she said, waving him off. "Go on. I'm only the patient."

"Theo!"

"Cassie?"

"I have to talk with you. Immediately."

"No! I mean, I can't."

"I can be there in 20 minutes. I can't discuss this on the phone."

"Cassie, I just can't. I've been operating all day; I'm hours behind; there's a goddamned riot going on out there in the waiting room."

"Then I'll come over at 5."

"Cassie, I just can't."

"Then I'll meet you at your house after work."

"Seven-thirty."

"Seven-thirty? Oh, all right!"

Mrs. Cristobel waited in the kitchen in her coat. "Mr. Meacham called. He said he'd call you back."

"Did he leave a number?"

"No. Your sister Cassandra called. She won't be here until 8:30." Mrs. Cristobel gathered her purse and Macy's shopping bag. "You forgot to put money in the petty cash. I spent $51 of my own on groceries today and I don't have enough left for the cab. I'll be satisfied with $20 until tomorrow."

"I'm sorry. I forgot." He gave her three 20s.

"Don't you have anything smaller? The cabbies say they can't make change. Tips, you know. I like to be ready when they say that."

Theo gave her a five and some ones. "That's all the cash I have."

She counted the bills. She handed him a twenty. "You can pay me back tomorrow. Your dinner's in the refrigerator. Natalia's watching the TV. A homework assignment about frogs. I told her she could, if it was for school." She was gone.

The dining table was set for one. There were vacuum cleaner tracks in the carpet. The table glowed. The tassels of the oriental rug in the living room all lay in the same direction. Natalia and her raccoon watched television.

"Natalia?"

She turned in annoyance then looked back at the screen.

"Natalia. Off."

She did not respond.

"Turn the television off, Natalia."

"We *have* to watch. My teacher said."

"Once, yes. Twice, no."

"Mrs. Cristobel *said* I could."

"And I say you can't. You conned her into letting you watch that again. Turn it off."

She ignored him.

Theo walked to the television. He punched the power control. Natalia picked up the remote control.

"Don't...touch...that...button."

She clicked. A male voice droned, "...but the young tadpoles have many enemies in the pond..."

Theo bent and punched the power control.

Natalia clicked. "...relatively few survivors. About half are eaten by fish: the stickleback, young trout now several inches long..."

The TV went off.

The TV went on. "...dragonfly nymphs, resembling prehistoric monsters..."

"All right," Theo said with authority, "you're going to bed. Now...either you go to bed, or I carry you to bed."

He took her hand. He pulled.

"NO!" She fell to the rug, limp. Theo lifted her. Natalia assumed divers' point. He held on.

Tiny teeth bared.

Porcelain bridgework glistened back.

"I'll *go* my*self!*"

"I'm very embarrassed," Cassie announced in the kitchen. "Your friend is here?" she asked quietly, looking about. "Could we talk privately?"

"He's not. You want a drink or something?"

"I don't want a drink. I *need* a drink. Ouzo on the rocks?"

"No ouzo. Vodka?"

Theo prepared drinks while his usually self-possessed sister paced.

"You haven't had your dinner yet," she observed as they passed through the dining room. Clearly whatever she had come to talk about was more important than his dinner.

Cassie took a seat on the sofa and folded one long leg over the other. Theo sat in a wing-back chair and waited.

"Is your little guest still here? Natalie, is it?"

"Natalia." He nodded toward the second floor. "She's sleeping. I think."

"It's none of my business, but doesn't Susan have family she could leave the child with? This has got to be a major inconvenience for you. What do *you* know about children?"

In spite of himself and what he perceived to be the coolness of the water, Theo plunged. "I don't know anything about children, but I'm learning very fast. Cassie, Natalia is my daughter."

Cassie's drink stalled halfway to her lips. "What?"

Theo felt his face redden. This was the part he found most difficult—not acknowledging that he was a parent but feeling he needed to explain how he came to be one.

"But how?" she asked. "Well, I don't mean *how*. I get that part. But why have you kept her a secret all these years? Why didn't you tell us?"

"There was no reason to tell you," he prevaricated.

"No *reason*? I can think of three very good ones right off the bat. She has two aunts and a grandfather. A whole family, Theo. *Cou*sins. Bradley Junior and Martha. Theo, I don't understand this at all." Cassie downed a finger of vodka. "You've been keeping this a secret to protect Susan, haven't you? Well, that's all very noble, Theo, but I can't imagine anyone getting seriously bent out of shape over a little...indiscretion. Good lord, you're both doctors!"

"It wasn't about Susan. It was about me. In the beginning, I didn't say anything because of a sort of...deal Susan and I had. Then I guess it just got to be a habit. Or something," he explained lamely.

Cassie leaned forward. "Look. I don't want to give you advice when God knows I have enough problems of my own, but I think you'd better just sit Susan down and agree with her to have a life. To*ge*ther. For the child's sake, if no one else's. What if something were to happen to one of you? Or both of you, God forbid? Where would the child be then? Thalia and I couldn't do a thing for her. She'd go to Susan's family."

"Susan hasn't got family."

"Good lord, Theo. Then we'd *have* to take care of the child. What in heaven's name were you waiting for?"

Theo squirmed in his chair.

"You know," Cassie continued, "it's not as if you and Susan were rock stars. You can't just go and do anything you want, have a child and not get married."

"Cassie, we don't want to get married."

"Theo, you are 46 years old. *And* a father."

"And I'm gay." There.

Cassie frowned and did not speak for several seconds. She placed her drink on the coffee table. She leaned back. "Well," she said softly, "who is the dummy now?"

"What do you mean?"

"All the ignorant things I must have said to you over all these years…And Warren. How you must have despised Warren."

"Why?"

"If he thought there was one in the room, he'd tell all the worst homosexual jokes he knew."

"I don't remember any of that."

"Sam is your…what do we say, partner?"

"Yes."

"He must think I'm Lucrezia Borgia…I've virtually ignored him for years."

"He left me the other day. I don't know if he'll be back."

"Because of Natalie?"

"Natalia. Because of me. I took him for granted. He got fed up."

"I'm sorry. Truly I am."

"Thanks."

"Thank you," Cassie replied.

"Jesus. For what?"

"For telling me all this." She stood. She crossed to his chair, her eyes full. She kissed him on the cheek.

"Well," Theo blushed, "you didn't come over here tonight to get an earful."

"No," she said wistfully.

"How come you called?"

"Oh, that…" she said offhandedly, "I had this chance to make you a good investment, is all. There'll be others."

"Something's wrong. Isn't it, Cassie?"

His big sister's hands trembled. She clasped them together. She returned to her place on the sofa and swirled ice cubes idly with a finger. "My problems pale in the face of yours." She seemed to make a decision. "Theo, I am very good at what I do. Very good. I have taken a company that was falling apart and turned it completely around…Before he died, Warren let the business go. Oh he was clever in his day. He started with nothing, and he created a financial need the likes of which Philadelphia had never seen. And he had connections." She looked at her hands. She shook her head. "He knew *everyone*, Warren did. When we gave a party, everyone came. They came from Chestnut Hill, Radnor, Paoli, from New Hope. Paul and Julia Child stayed over in our house when we gave a party. Warren helped her invest when she got syndicated, did you know that?"

"I knew you knew her," Theo said. "In fact, I met her once at your house. We talked about to-*mah*-toes."

"But Warren stopped paying attention to business. And the business went away. One by one, his clients went over to the young turks. Warren taught every one of those kids how to do it, and that's how they repaid him. But *I* got it back," she said. "Not all the old accounts, but I rebuilt a strong client base. Bitler and Morant is now the fastest growing investment firm in the Delaware Valley. Did you know that, Theo?"

"No."

Cassie seemed sad. "Theo…something very bad is likely to happen soon."

"What?"

"I've called in every chit I have in this town. Every media favor I'm owed. But I'm afraid the you-know-what is going to hit the fan, as Thalia says."

"What are you talking about?"

"My vice president is Stuart Flowers. Do you know him?"

"I don't think."

"I'm afraid he and I are about to get our 15 minutes of fame. He's going to be indicted before the weekend for insider trading. Do you know what that is?"

"Using what you know to make money for yourself?"

"A bit broad but essentially correct. Do you know Grandmère's Meat Pies?"

"Who doesn't?"

"His father owns it. Stuart Flowers set up an account in my firm for himself using a false name. He managed to accumulate a great deal of money, which is bad enough, but he also placed four of our largest clients into an investment that is now completely worthless. Teshigahara is a Japanese firm whose stock has been going through the ceiling of the Nikkei. I forbade my employees to trade in that stock because I knew the managers of the company were simply running up its value. Stuart Flowers got greedy. He invested himself and these four clients behind my back, then he pulled his own money out. This morning, Teshigahara announced bankruptcy.

"I can't let my clients take a bath; they're far too important to my firm. I have to replace their losses."

"With your money?"

She nodded. "Theo, if I don't bale them out before this nitwit is indicted, I'll lose every client I've worked to get since Warren died. I may lose everything if Bitler and Morant gets caught up in the Flowers' publicity."

"How much do you have to pay out?"

"Two and a quarter million dollars."

"Jesus. How can you do that? I mean, come up with that?"

"This afternoon I arranged to sell all my own investments."

"What about Flowers? He's the one who made the money. Why can't he put out his own money? Or get his old man to help him?"

"The phony portfolio is being liquidated. The money will be placed in escrow and be tied up in the courts for years. The father called me, I guess just to find out how bad things were and to see what my position was going to be. He told me that as far as he was concerned, his son could 'stew in his own frigging juices.' An apt metaphor from a man who makes meat pies," Cassie said with faint amusement.

"This afternoon I mortgaged my home. To the max. I can

scrape enough together to pay off the investors, but I don't have enough to float my business…I came here tonight to beg for a half a million dollars."

"Cassie, I don't even *have* a half a million dollars…Do I?"

Cassie regarded him as if he had lost his mind. "What do you do with the quarterly reports I send you? Don't you *read* them?"

"I save them. They're all up there."

"Theo—*I* save them. *You're* supposed to *read* them. God, you're as thick as Thalia…! I apologize," she said, holding up a hand. "I have no call to be annoyed with you. It's just that I seem to be the only one in this family who understands money, and you all make me very crazy sometimes.

"You have a half a million dollars, Theo. You have quite a bit more than that—not even counting the value of your medical practice."

"Then, if I have enough to lend you, you better borrow it."

She shook her head. She smiled ironically—then lovingly, to his surprise. "Thank you. I appreciate the sentiment, more than you'll ever know. Especially for it's naïveté. But before I would borrow that kind of money from you, I'd need to be assured I could pay you back. With a nice profit. *If* Bitler and Morant does not get sucked into the Flowers publicity and *if* I'm able to get the word out that none of my investors was harmed financially and *if* the rest of my clients don't make a mad dash for my competition, then I would borrow some of your money. In my own defense, I want to point out that I've made over $600,000 for you in the past four years."

"*That* much?" Theo said with some wonder.

"It is shocking to me that you didn't know that. But the point is, if you were to lend money to me, you'd be risking only the profits I've made for you and none of your initial investment."

"It doesn't matter, Cassie. You decide what you need, and if I have it, you can use it."

"I need $32,000 by Friday to cover payroll and my operating account."

"You'll need more than that."

"Probably."

"Then, you sell what you have to sell of mine to keep you going, and we'll talk about the rest later."

"You don't know what this means to me."

Theo thought for a moment. "What about interest?"

"Certainly I'll pay you interest. To save my business? I'll pay the highest bank rate."

"No."

"No?"

"No. Here's the deal: If you borrow my money, you back out of Dad's affairs."

"What do you mean?"

"I mean, you don't interfere anymore. If he wants Rosy to have all the insurance money, you let him give it to her. You and Thalia both. If he wants her to have all his stock and property and whatever, you let him give her that. And you keep your mouth shut."

"I can't do that!"

"Then there's no deal."

"I'd have to talk to Thalia about this," she deflected.

"You don't have to talk to Thalia about anything. You just drop it—whatever you two have been cooking up. Those are my terms."

"But it's apples and oranges, Theo. My business problems have nothing to do with what that woman has been doing to Daddy."

"She's been doing nothing but good for Dad."

Cassie adjusted herself on the couch. She scowled. She smiled appeasingly. "Theo…"

"It's not negotiable, Cassie."

A Gucci pump jerked. "*Christ,* I hate to borrow money!" She glared for a moment at her drink. "Very well," she said. "You have my word. This is only the third time today that I've been asked to bend over a barrel. It's all *very* humiliating."

"I'm sorry."

"Oh? *Screw* it." Cassie smirked. After a moment she said, "Can I ask you another favor, Theo?"

"You want my medical practice too."

"Do you think I could just *sneak* upstairs and take a peek at my new niece? I won't wake her. I promise."

"Are you OK?" Theo asked when she came down the stairs.

Cassie swiped her cheek with the back of her hand. "She looks just like Mama."

Dear Dad and Rosy,

I hope I'm not taking the cowardly way out. I should drive up there and talk with you, but there isn't time right now.

I am going to be 47 in August. That is not very old, but it is too old to have waited to share with you at least two important aspects of my life. I have been thinking a lot tonight, Dad, about what you've preached to us since we were little kids: the importance of living what you call an "authentic" life. I haven't been living very authentically and apologize for not telling you sooner that:

1) You have another grandchild. I have a daughter whose name is Natalia. She is five. My medical partner, Susan, is her mother.

213

2) Your son is gay. (That's me.) And it doesn't matter a whole lot whether you like that or not. I'm afraid this is one of those take-it-or-leave-it situations. I am what I am.

I assume you are both wise enough to waste no time worrying about how you might have messed me up when I was a child and to wonder instead if I am happy. I am, pretty much. Most important, I am taking steps to make myself happier. This letter is one of those steps.
     Love,
     Theo

At 2 a.m., Theo stood beside Natalia's bed watching her sleep. She hugged her raccoon. It rose and fell with her chest.

Her hands were so small. Her hair was as black as his own, a tangle on the pillowcase.

He did not remember when her birthday was. He had never bought her a toy. Instead, he bought certificates of deposit in her name. At least, he justified, with more regularity than he bought cars, but as he did most things—from a safe distance.

He watched the little girl breathe, watched her hand quiver and twitch in sleep, watched her eyes roll through dreams under their lids. Should he wake her? Nudge the bony shoulders through Susan's ridiculous T-shirt? Explain to the child that her absent father wished to make amends? That although two in the morning was maybe a bad time, it was the only time he had to give to her today?

Natalia slept.

Theo watched, his throat froggy.

Forget the gym. So what if her daddy wasn't honed by rowing

214

and StairMaster machines? Certainly chubby daddies were as capable of love as thin daddies. Instead of his going to the gym, they'd do breakfast with Daddy then, perhaps, a drive with Daddy to PlaySchool. They would leave Mrs. Cristobel to her housekeeping, and alone in the car, they would talk about life.

How could he help her manage her life when he had so much difficulty managing his own?

Were daddies who found frogs leaping to their throats lately up to such a daunting task?

Natalia frowned and moaned in her sleep.

Theo covered a tiny hand with one of his own.

"No bad dreams," he whispered.

There was no breakfast with Daddy.

Theo woke to Mrs. Cristobel's voice on the stairs: "Natalia, we are going to miss the bus! Is that what you want? You *want* to miss the bus?"

Chapter 25

Theo paid for his salad and coffee at the staff cafeteria. "Theo!" trilled a woman's voice across the dining room. "Theo!"

Sondra Micari waved and gestured from a table near the center of the room. Theo hesitated. He had hoped to wolf his lunch and head back to the office from hell. Could he just wave back, he wondered? But she was half standing now, and there was no avoiding Sondra Micari.

"Join us," she commanded. "This," she said, indicating a smiling, well-dressed woman of a certain age, "is Pauline Ziggenhoffer. Dr. Theo Tithonus."

"—Heuffer," corrected the woman who beamed at Theo as if he were lunch.

"—Heuffer," repeated Mrs. Micari. "Pauline is absolutely indispensable to me. Unfortunately, she has to rush back to town." She gave Pauline Ziggenheuffer a pointed look. The woman began to gather her tray and possessions. "But I have a few minutes," the woman offered.

"No. You don't. Sit, Theo. You have your hair appointment, and you know how much you hate to be late. Over here, Theo. Pauline has just come up with the fabulous concept for a fundraiser—a musi*cale* to be held in her own magnificent home, using talent from our hospital staff! Pauline, we'll talk more at the meeting tomorrow." Mrs. Micari squeezed Pauline's hand.

"Good-bye, dear."

Pauline Ziggenheuffer lingered with her tray. "So nice to meet you," she told Theo.

"Yes!" Mrs. Micari piped. "Good-*bye*, Pauline."

When the woman was out of earshot, Sondra Micari leaned to Theo: "Good, galloping *Jesus!*" She threw herself back in her chair and struck her forehead. "Did you ever hear a dumber idea in your life? I'm trying to book Toni Braxton, and she wants to have a musi*cale?* In her *liv*ing room? It's not easy, believe me." Mrs. Micari's eyes narrowed. "Well, I'm glad *you* showed up. Now tell me, what's going on with Susan?"

"Susan," he said, surprised.

"Right. Your partner. The one who's among the missing?"

"She's on vacation." Theo poked his salad greens.

"That's not the scuttlebutt."

"What do you mean?"

"I heard she snapped out. In the OR."

Theo regarded Sondra Micari across his steaming coffee.

"Theo, you're being protective; it's not necessary. I'm not a nasty little gossip. What's going on?"

Theo pulled the lid from a thimble of artificial creamer. "She's been working too hard. She needed a break, so she took a trip."

"I know that. Is she all right?"

"Sure."

"And Natalia's staying with you."

"How'd you know that?"

"I called your office this morning. They said you were at home. I called your home. Susan's housekeeper answered. People do not lend out their housekeepers. *Ipso facto,* Natalia is staying with you."

"Yes," Theo said warily. "How come you called, Mrs. Micari?"

"It's 'Sondra,' and we're coming to that." She leaned closer and said very low: "Theo—are you Natalia's father?"

"Huh?"

"Oh, would you just give up this ingenue thing? I'm *try*ing to *help* you."

"But why would you ask that?"

"You and Susan go everywhere together," she said. "Natalia looks more like you than *you* do. You're her father, the way I see it."

"OK," Theo said, dumbfounded. "Yes."

"Tuh-riffic!" Mrs. Micari cheered across the table. "I said so. That's what I told Marvin," she squealed. "I told him you are the father of that child, but he didn't believe me." Her brows knitted. She glanced left and right. "Now listen. I haven't much time, but we have to talk. There is something happening that you probably haven't got wind of yet, and you and I must nip it in the bud. We must stop it *cold,* Theo. De*rail* it." Her voice became conspiratorial. "Do you know what that snake-in-the-grass Garlington has been spreading around about you? He's told Marvin, and he's told Margaret Steinhower, and I don't know who else that you have no concept of either hospital politics *or* administration, and that you are *queer,* Theo! Timothy Garlington wants to be chief of surgery, and that scum will stop at nothing. Frankly, I think anyone who would try to ruin a man's reputation by calling him queer is beneath contempt!"

Theo was both angered by Garlington's hypocrisy and touched to have such an ally in Mrs. Micari, whom he hardly knew before her annual surgeons' dinner. To what extent has she been involved in his nomination for chief? She had been nothing but warm toward him. Theo decided to trust his intuitions.

"I *am* queer," he whispered.

"Well, of *course* you are, Theo!"

"How did you know?" Theo asked, taken aback.

Sondra Micari sighed with exasperation. "Theo, what do you think? I was born yesterday? My *brother* is gay!"

"You have a gay brother?"

Sondra sighed. "Theo, I am beginning to doubt your perceptions. You *work* with him. You've probably scrubbed with him hundreds of times. Wiley is my brother."

"Wiley Branstetter?"

"Yes. Isn't he a dear?"

"He never said anything."

"That's just like Wiley. He's incredibly shy. He says you're a superb surgeon and that no one would make a better chief than you. That's only one of several reasons I've been pushing you with Marvin. Marvin is also a great surgeon, but I'm afraid he's a very poor judge of character. He needs beating with a stick now and then.

"But that is neither here nor there. Right now, I'm concerned about this Garlington person and his influence over Marvin and Margaret. Look. By the new year, Marvin and I will be back in California—and good riddance to the East Coast, *I* say—but I have become very involved with this hospital, and I especially care what happens to Marvin's department. Garlington may be brilliant when it comes to inventing surgical tools—God knows Marvin's impressed—but the man will not be an asset to our hospital, and I am going to do my damndest to see he doesn't get that appointment. But I need your cooperation."

"Thank you, Mrs.—Sondra."

"Have you got any dirt on the son of a bitch?"

The invitation tempted Theo. He wanted to tell Mrs. Micari that Garlington must be the original pot to call the kettle black. He was even tempted to tell her about nights—about mornings he himself spent wrapped with Garlington in tangles of sheets damp with bodily fluids. About the rich, unattractive nurse Garlington had married for money.

"No," he said.

"You probably wouldn't tell me if you did."

"I don't know."

"That's honest. Here's the way I see it, Theo: The 'queer' part doesn't mean a rat's ass to anyone, except Margaret Steinhower and a few others. I wouldn't even bring it up, but we have to deal with it. Marvin idolizes Margaret Steinhower. She knows that and that she's got Marvin wrapped around her little finger. She hates gays, so anything Garlington tells her is grist for her mill because she's plugging Garlington for the appointment. Of course, it's a little known fact that Garlington's plugging *her.*"

"He is?"

"Yes. But don't dare repeat that. I haven't even told Marvin. He thinks Margaret Steinhower walks on water. As far as dealing with the gay part goes, if I were you I'd bring my daughter here to the hospital to show her where Daddy works. Parade her around. If you have a surgery scheduled, drop her off at our day care center. I guarantee you the news will be flashed through every floor of this hospital before you return to pick her up."

"I couldn't do that."

"What are you, embarrassed?"

"No, but I can't use my kid to look like something I'm not."

"Well, why the hell not? Theo, wake up. You have to fight fire with fire. This creep is painting you every color but attractive. Do you want Timothy Garlington to be chief of surgery of the *Hos*pital of the Uni*ver*sity of Pennsyl*van*ia?"

"No."

"Neither does anybody else. Except, apparently, my husband and Margaret Steinhower. Were you ever president of anything?"

"I'm sorry?"

"The Medical Association? The Board of Plastic Surgery, or whatever you people call your club?"

"No...I was captain of the soccer team my senior year at Hopkins."

"Well, I suppose that's a start. You better let me handle the political side of your reputation, and you handle the queer part. I've got to get going. Half of the hospital's board of directors are coming to dinner tonight and I haven't even got a clean girdle. You can be sure I'll get your name dropped at every opportunity." Lifting her lunch tray in one hand, she placed the other on Theo's hand and squeezed. "I sure hope you and Sam enjoy entertaining. Lord knows you'll be doing enough of it. We hope you will, anyway."

"You know Sam?"

"No—how I know about him is an amusing story which I'll tell you sometime." She leaned. Her eyes crinkled. "HA! Won't that knock their socks off? You and Sam receiving all those stuffy surgeons at the Four Seasons? You've got to invite me to your first social function as chief. I'll fly back from Palm Springs just to watch!"

Sondra Micari wended her way through cafeteria tables, bending briefly to speak, waving and smiling graciously.

Theo considered his salad. And, with some uneasiness, his potential hospital appointment.

He parked his shining, green Jaguar on a war-zone block near Thalia's school and glanced at his watch. There was time for 15 stolen minutes with Thalia before rushing back to the Medical Tower. He could steal 15 minutes if Clare did not page him from the office.

Entering The Passyunk, he wondered if the health department ever visited the place. Thalia raised her hand and waved from a booth at the far end of the diner. The counters were worn, pink Formica. The ceiling was the color of grease—or of nicotine. He and his sister were the only customers.

Her clothes, from her days of plenty, were too chic for such a dive.

"You come here often?" Theo asked, settling himself onto a cracked Naugahyde seat across from his sister.

"Isn't it charming? My students love it."

Theo looked about with distaste. An aproned woman approached their booth with a wet dishcloth. Her piled, bleached hair was ensnared in black netting.

"How'zit?" she asked, streaking the tabletop with her rag. She leered at Theo. "You been holding out on me, Thal, or what?"

"Ida, this is my brother Theo."

"You have been holding out on me, girlfriend."

"He's a *doc*tor," Thalia stage whispered.

"I'd leave my Dougie for a doctor," she told Thalia. "You married, hon?"

"Yes," said Theo quickly.

"You wanna fool around?"

Theo blushed.

"We're just having coffee, Ida. Coffee?" she asked Theo.

"Fine."

"How 'bout pie? You want some pie? I got banana cream. Bee-u-tee-ful. Made it myself."

"Nah. Just coffee," replied Thalia.

"Goddamned skinny people," Ida muttered as she left.

"Heart of gold, that woman," Thalia remarked. "So…you feeling all right?"

"Why wouldn't I?"

"You called me. You never call me."

"Of course I do."

"No, I always call you."

"Thalia, that's not true."

"Sure it is."

"Thalia, it's not."

"When was the last time you called me? Other than Sunday to baby-sit?"

"About the meeting we had about Dad," he said. "At Cassie's house."

"I called you."

"No, I called you. To tell you what time the meeting was."

"No. Cassie asked me to call you. I called you from school. On my break. What was another time?"

"Thalia, this is silly," he said, looking for a dry spot to rest his elbows on the water-tracked table.

"So to what do I owe this honor?"

"Could we change places? Would you mind? So I can see my car?"

"I can see it. What's left of it…" she said. "Relax. There's no market over here for Jaguar parts. So. What's up?"

"I wanted to talk to you about something."

"That's a shock."

"Cut me a break."

"Let me guess, given the rarity of this occasion. You want to tell me you're gay."

"What? No, Thalia."

"You're not gay." Thalia sat forward. Her pendent earrings swung at her long neck.

"That's not why I wanted to talk."

"So you're *not* gay."

Theo rearranged the salt and pepper shakers. "I'm having some trouble with this conversation."

"Hey. It's only me, old Thalia?"

"Listen," he said. "Would you just listen?"

"I'm listening." Thalia examined her polished nails.

"Thalia…you know that Susan and I are very close."

"Sure."

"It's a very long story. But Susan and I…we…" He stopped speaking as the waitress approached and placed Thalia's coffee, then Theo's. The waitress looked into Theo's lap. "Wadya weigh? You don't mind my askin'."

"Huh?"

"Wadya weigh?"

"One seventy-six."

"How tall'r ya?"

"Six two."

Ida licked a corner of her mouth and left.

"You and Susan what?"

"Susan and I...have a child," Theo said softly.

"Then you're not gay," Thalia said. Her eyebrows arched.

"Thalia, what is this? Could you just listen?"

"I'm listening."

"We have a daughter."

Thalia positioned the elbows of her impeccable suit on either side of her mug. "Natalia."

"Yes, Natalia is my daughter."

"Why have you kept her a secret?"

Theo shook sugar into his coffee. His fingers were granular and sticky from the bottle. He extracted a wad of tiny paper napkins from a stained dispenser. It would be the same until everybody in the world knew. You couldn't just say you had a daughter; you had to explain how you got one. "It was just...I don't know."

"Well," Thalia said. She fished in her purse and took out a cigarette.

"Thalia, you don't smoke."

"No," she said, lighting up with a practiced flourish. She inhaled deeply.

"When did you start smoking?"

"When Bradley left me for Dolly Parton." Thalia looked out the diner window. "Things change. It took me 15 years to decide that tits weren't essential to a happy life. Now I'd buy a pair. You know anyone who does tits...? Well, this is certainly embarrassing."

"What do you mean?"

"There I was at your house meeting my niece for the first time, and I didn't even know she was my niece. I sat there playing Nintendo until I was cross-eyed. I didn't even know who I was playing with."

"I should have told you. I wanted to tell you."

"I guess I'm supposed to feel better?"

"I'm sorry. I really feel bad about that. I do."

Thalia French inhaled.

"Thalia? Could I ask you a really big favor?"

"I refuse to baby-sit again until the child and I have been introduced."

"No. Do you think you could tell Bradley Junior and Martha they have a cousin. I mean, about Natalia?"

"What'll I tell them, Theo? That the stork flew over your house? They know more about sex than I do."

"Maybe I better tell them."

"No—you'll tell them it was the stork. If I'm confused, they're going to be…What am I supposed to tell them, anyhow? That you're ambidextrous? They're pretty comfortable thinking you're gay."

"Why would they think I'm gay?"

"Because I told them you were."

"Why would you do that?" Theo asked.

"Why the hell not? I'll tell you something, Theo. You better start tuning in to the Learning Channel. Pick up a few pointers on parenting. I told my kids because they asked me."

"Why would they ask? I'm not some kind of flaming queen."

"You and Cassie. You've both got your heads buried in the same pit. It doesn't take a rocket scientist to conclude that a 46-year-old man who has never married and lives with a guy just might prefer guys. You know, I'm *not* going to allow my kids to grow up into mean-spirited little homophobes, especially when they have an uncle who may or may not be a pansy. Now explain to me, in my native language: Were you and Susan an item, or what?"

"She wanted a child. I was the…donor."

"You make it sound so antiseptic."

"It was." Theo's face felt very warm.

"Are we talking turkey baster here?"

"Thalia…"

"You've got to understand I'd be a little curious. You did this at home or what?"

"No. It's, uh…a process."

"Seriously, just the two of you?"

"No. A clinic. We went to a clinic."

"What do you put it in? The sperm, I mean. When you give it. I always wondered."

"Thalia."

"Theo, my kids are going to ask. They're not going to be satisfied with 'a process.' I know them. Come on, what do you put it in?"

"A cup."

"What kind of cup?"

Theo squirmed.

"All right. I'll deal with the kids. And you better let me handle Cassie. I'll just tell her you shtupped your friend Susan. She's not going to be able to handle the gay part."

"I told her already."

"When did you tell her?"

"Last night."

"And *now* you're telling me."

"I didn't plan on telling her first. It just happened."

"I don't mind. I don't mind being the last to hear everything."

"Thalia, it's not as if I planned it."

Thalia crushed out her cigarette.

"Thalia, could I ask your opinion about something else that's happening?"

"Why not?"

"I'm up for a very prestigious position at the hospital. There's another doctor who wants the job too. He's been telling some important people certain things about me, that I am gay. The ironic part is, he and I had a thing together 20 years ago."

"Was there a question in this?"

"Well, what should I do? Should I expose the guy for what he is? Or, now that I'm sort of out with my kid, do I play it like I'm straight? For the record?"

"Theo, I have always looked up to you. But about certain things, you seem to be as blind as a bat. If you expose the guy, you become what he is. If you use your daughter as a foil, you don't deserve to be her father."

"I see that. I understand that. But what do I do?"

Thalia sighed. "I am definitely in the wrong business. I ought to be working with the hearing impaired. You know, I stand on my soapbox all day in front of my students, and I tell them to respect truth. Make that the center of their lives. And about half of them look at me as if I were speaking Swahili. Theo, the truth will make you free. Don't you get that?"

"I know. I know. I mentioned that to Dad the other night, even. 'Living the authentic life?' "

"You talked to Daddy?"

"No. I wrote to him. I figured it was the safest way. But I made a clean sweep—I told him about Natalia and that I'm gay."

"Safe or not, that was pretty ballsy," Thalia grinned. "Of course you know you'll be disinherited, and he'll never speak to you again. His health will get worse, and then he'll die. And it'll all be your fault. But just think, Theo: You will be free."

"I've worried about all that," Theo said ruefully.

"So," Thalia said, "when are we coming to dinner?"

"Dinner?"

"Isn't that the part in the script we're up to now? We all gather at your house—Cassie and me and the kids and my asshole husband, with whom I will have naturally and blissfully reconciled, and Daddy and Rosy and you and Natalia and Sam? Sort of a Greek Easter with the Waltons? Like all good, dysfunctional families, we pretend that none of our problems exist?"

"I don't think dinner's in the script. Sam's gone. He left me."

"How come?"

"I think the last straw was, I didn't tell him about Natalia."

"You didn't tell me either, but you don't see me running down the block."

"There was a lot of other stuff. All kinds of things I let go by the boards."

"He'll be back."

"I doubt it."

"He will."

"Polyanna speaks."

"You know why he'll be back?"

"No, Thalia. Today I can't think of a single reason."

"Because he's a Walton too."

"You're a very sick woman."

"It's genetic, dear."

Chapter 26

He thought as he tossed in his bed, sleepless again at midnight, that until so recently he had had an uncomplicated life. An enviable life. Not very long ago he fell asleep when his head hit the pillow. He awoke with enthusiasm for his work, for its challenges which he looked forward to meeting and in which he took pride. He had a peaceful life, a pleasant one. How had it all turned about so quickly?

The conundrum on which he could not sleep this night was not only his resentment of his recent losses, but also his frustration—no, he admitted, his anger—that he was not being allowed to be the way he was, gay the way he was. Where was it written, in *The Manual of Gay Lifestyle* that he was required to even react at all to the likes of Timothy Garlington and Margaret Steinhower? Or to gays who might not approve of his firm choice to toe a thick line in the sand between his social and professional lives? Where was it written that he was required to handle Garlington's outing of him with aplomb? What would Garlington say next? That Theo was HIV-positive? There would be a kiss good-bye to his successful surgical career.

Know thine enemy? He had known his enemy before Garlington became one. And loved his enemy with great enthusiasm.

Fight fire with fire? That was hardly Theo's style, but perhaps Sondra Micari was correct in her assessment that being passive would get him nowhere. Should he out Garlington in return? Theo took great pleasure in the fantasy but could see nothing to be gained.

The ringing telephone first startled then thrilled him. *Sam,* he thought. *Finally.*

"Good morning."

"Do you know what time it is?"

"I hope I woke you," Susan said.

"I haven't had a night's sleep since you left. When are you coming home?"

"Who said I was?"

"Susan. Don't play with me."

"My, aren't we testy?"

"I'm not having a good time."

"How is she?"

"I'm looking into reform schools."

"That bad?"

"She's not my child, Susan. She can't be. They mixed up the cups or something. She doesn't like me. She won't talk to me. She won't do anything I ask her to do. We fight every night about television, going to bed, clothes, food. Everything is a battle with that kid. And she bit me the other night," Theo added, touching the scab on his shoulder.

"You're looking at it the wrong way. Isn't this better than indifference?

"To be honest, I'm calling this late because I didn't want to talk to her. Isn't that terrible? Don't take this personally, but I really didn't want to talk to you either. I'm making this call out of an annoying sense of obligation I've decided to get rid of so I won't have anything important to think about. I'm sitting on a deck a hundred yards from the water line. There's a white moon trail on the ocean. The temperature is 76, slight breeze...I slept 11 hours last night. Ten the night before. I don't know what the date is.

Do you know what that feels like?"

"No."

"I love this."

"Good."

"There's a little restaurant I go to every night down the beach. I eat the same dish every dinner. It's made of crab."

"When are you coming home, Susan?"

"I don't know…How're you? How's Sam?"

"I don't know. He moved out."

"Wow."

"Is that all you can say?"

"Yes."

"Seriously—when are you coming home?"

"Seriously, I don't know. When I get slept out. When I can't remember what my schedule used to be."

"I need to know."

"They were telling me at my little restaurant that the grunions come tonight."

"Who are the Grunions?"

"Little fish. The females lay their eggs in the sand. The males come and spread their milt…Isn't that a turn-on?"

"I found us a new associate, I think."

"Good. That's wonderful."

"Don't you want to know who it is?"

"No."

Chapter 27

The Ritz-Carlton waiter floated an open napkin onto Barry Boldini's lap then seemed to fade into the woodwork.

"And will they feed me with a spoon?" Barry asked Theo.

"Of course. We'll each have our own personal feeder. You're not supposed to do anything at the Ritz except enjoy."

"I could get used to this."

"Maybe you will," replied Theo.

"You look like something the cat dragged in."

"I feel like that. No sleep. How about you?"

"It goes," said Barry. One thick eyebrow arched. "You should take a vacation."

"I can't. I'm driven."

"So I hear."

"What do you hear?"

"What should I hear?"

"I don't know." Theo looked about the bright dining room. "Maybe nothing."

"There is talk," Boldini said. "Not around me. They know better. But I hear the edges of it."

"It's Garlington," Theo said coolly.

"He's a jerk. Everyone thinks so. But why's he grinding an axe for you?"

"I haven't told you because it might not happen. I'm up for chief of surgery."

"Theo, that's wonderful!" Barry Boldini extended his hand across the table. "Think of it. I'm the friend of the chief of surgery."

"Don't count your chickens."

"But what about Steinhower?"

"She's leaving. Don't tell anybody."

"Why did she accept the appointment?"

"Another line on her resume? What's this talk you hear?"

"The tattle used to be that you and Susan were lovers, of course."

" 'Were?' "

"But now folks are saying you got gay. There's a major new player in Gossipland."

"Garlington."

"No. The Hummer. He never used to, but now he sings like a bird. He and Garlington are inseparable buddies these days. Tables for two in the medical lounge? Thing is, Garlington never mentions your name. He gets The Hummer to do all his dirty work. The Hummer's telling everybody who'll listen that you sleep with guys."

"What do you think about that?"

Barry rested his elbows on the table. "I don't think anything about that."

"Did you know I was gay?"

"Sure. How's Sam?"

"You know Sam?"

"Through softball. The hospital league. We're both umpires. He didn't tell you?"

"No. Does that bother you, Barry? That I didn't tell you?"

"I figured you'd get around to it. Before you retired. How is Sam?"

"He left me."

"Ouch."

"It just happened."

"And Natalia?"

"You know about Natalia too?"

"Yeah. Susan told me. Years ago." Barry's green eyes crinkled.

"You never said anything."

"Neither did you. Anyway, it's your business."

"I'm beginning to think nothing is my business...Barry, I asked you to breakfast because I wanted to try something out on you. I want you to consider joining our practice, Susan's and mine."

Barry Boldini sat back in his chair. His coffee ice cream skin seemed to darken. He did not smile. He drew a couple of lines on the tablecloth with his fingertip.

"I am very, very flattered," he said after a moment. "And I am deeply touched. You are the best surgeon I've ever worked with or even seen working. I've never scrubbed with Susan, but I know she can cut circles around any man on staff. And I am proud to call you both my friends. But I can't do what you're asking.... Beverly and I are so far in debt. Including medical school and the house and the car and her grad school tuition, we owe about a quarter of a million dollars. I can't even pay for the root canal I had yesterday."

"Forget the debts for a minute. Would you like to join the practice?"

"I would love to. But I'm in a hole I can't dig out of. I'm too deep in debt to buy into a practice."

Theo's jacket brushed his china. "Barry, during the past four years Susan and I have each taken $275,000 out of our corporation. We will guarantee you that annually for the next five years. You pay the corporation $100,000 a year for five years, after which you own a third. Could you swing that?"

Barry's hand raked his curly hair. "Do you know how much I make now working for the hospital?"

"I could maybe guess."

"I make $37,700 a year. Out of that I pay taxes of $8,000, give or take, and $3,000 toward my student loans and nine thou to the mortgage company; and then there's the orthodontist and the car payments and Beverly's school and transportation and the kids' clothes and our clothes and a tiny bit to my parents." Barry sighed, then he grinned. "I'm being ridiculous, aren't I? Why can't I get by on 275 grand a year?"

"You'll do it?"

"I'd be crazy not to."

Theo stood from his chair, banging the table edge. China rattled. Coffee sloshed. "Barry," he said. "Could I kiss you?"

"Not here," said Barry, looking about the dining room of the Ritz-Carlton Hotel.

Theo sat, barely able to contain himself. "You couldn't start this afternoon, could you?"

"I've got a contract with the hospital through July."

"Four months—I can handle four months. I wonder if Susan can handle four months."

Theo sat at eye level next to Susan's patient. Her chart lay in his lap.

"Mrs. Bellagraff," he said, regarding her with his most radiant bedside smile. "Your nurses tell me you want a local anesthetic instead of general anesthesia. How come?"

Mrs. Bellagraff arranged the fold of her sheet. Her makeup was severe, an older woman trying to appear young.

"My friend had like what I have," she said. "She had the local." Mrs. Bellagraff's smile was forced and frightened. "They let her stay awake during the whole operation."

"Your friend could not have had what you have. Your tumor has grown almost all the way around your jawbone," he said, pinching his own jaw halfway toward his mouth. "This is going to be a very noisy operation," he said with a look of distaste. "You don't want to listen to all that sucking and stuff. Really."

"I won't mind," she said.

"I'm going to have to take out a good deal of tissue. You don't want to hear while I'm doing that."

"I've heard worse."

Theo glanced at the chart. "Mrs. Bellagraff?" He lowered his voice to a whisper. "How old are you? Really?"

Mrs. Bellagraff eyed her unconscious roommate. "It's there. On those papers."

Theo slid his chair closer to the bed. "It says here you're 53," he whispered. Theo raised one eyebrow. "And there are a lot of question marks after that."

"Well?" she asked, daring him to question hospital records.

"Sixty-eight?" he said softly.

Mrs. Bellagraff's mascaraed eyes widened then closed. "Nine. How did you know?"

Theo ignored the question. "Listen…you wouldn't be afraid you won't wake up from this operation, would you?"

Mrs. Bellagraff's chin quivered. "Maybe."

"You don't need to worry about that. You'll wake up just fine."

"How do you know?"

"Because you've got a heart—excuse me—like a horse."

"Are you sure?"

"Yes. Will you let Dr. Branstetter give you some sleep medicine?"

"Maybe."

"Good."

"Doctor?"

"What?"

Mrs. Bellagraff leaned toward the bed rail. "How did you know?" she whispered. "How old I am?"

"Your hands."

Mrs. Bellagraff examined the backs of her hands. "Shit," she said.

Theo's name droned through the hall intercom.

"May I use your phone, Mrs. Bellagraff?"

She was intent upon her hands. Theo dialed. "Dr. Tithonus," he said.

"Hold for Dr. Micari," said a bored voice. Theo felt a surge of adrenaline. This could only be trouble.

"Theo," said Marvin Micari, "are you involved?" Micari did not wait for an answer. "I would like you to come by the board room."

"Yes, Sir," Theo replied and hung up. It was 10 o'clock. He was due at the office at 10:30. He would not make it. He calculated his odds. If he called Clare at the office to tell her he would be late, he would have to endure her abuse twice—on the telephone and again when he arrived at the office. He opted for once.

"Mrs. Bellagraff," he said, standing. "You're not to worry, do you hear?"

"Doctor," she said. She motioned him closer with a glance toward her still unconscious roommate.

"Mrs. Bellagraff?" Theo said, stepping closer to the bed.

She examined her hands, palms down. Her skin was wrinkled and nearly transparent. "Can you do something about…these?" she asked.

Theo took her hands in his own. He felt the knobby, arthritic knuckles. He pretended to examine her hands with great interest.

"What would I do about them?" he asked after a moment. "These are wonderful hands."

"They are?"

"You don't get hands like this overnight, Mrs. Bellagraff. Look at them. They're marvelous."

"They are?"

"Yes. They're your hands."

When he left her, she was holding the backs of her hands before her as if they were mirrors.

Theo stood before the receptionist of the executive offices on the top floor of the Hospital of the University of Pennsylvania. He had left his white coat in his locker and was dressed in subdued trousers and a jacket. His tie was colorful, though not loud.

"Dr. Tithonus to see Dr. Micari," he told the too-happy woman behind the desk. She wore a red, Orphan Annie dress and a string of pearls of a color unknown to the Pacific.

"Yes, doctor," she burbled, smiling many large put perfect teeth. "Please have a seat." Her lips did not seem capable of closing completely.

Theo wandered in the direction of claw-footed chairs placed in a row but did not sit. He stood before a wall of windows overlooking Philadelphia. He could see the front of his own house facing the Schuylkill River. He could not locate Cassie's house, a five block walk toward the city's center. There were patches of grass beginning to green the parks. There were splashes here and there of yellow forsythia. No leaves on the trees. No fountains threw water yet. The city waited for the true arrival of spring.

He wanted to go for awhile where spring had arrived. Take a long weekend. With Sam. Walk the warmed streets of Charleston; drink designer cocktails facing azaleas from sidewalk cafés. He missed Sam and that empty space grew more painful each day.

"Doctors will see you now," said the receptionist at his side. Her smile was gaping and very pulled back.

She led him down a hall past her station, past the elevators.

Her Orphan Annie dress flapped at her knees. "Doctors" would see him now? Would there be standing room only? An amphitheater filled with white coats and unsmiling faces and him presenting his bizarre symptoms on a raised center dais?

The receptionist walked ahead, turning now and again to be sure Theo was still with her. Her jaws were clenched, her lips parted in a rictus smile. Did she expect he might cut and run?

She paused dramatically before tall, paneled double doors. She grasped their curved handles simultaneously and, with some ceremony, pulled the doors wide to reveal a vast room with a high ceiling in the middle of which was the longest table Theo had ever seen. The table, a gleaming, dark expanse of wax and varnish, was surrounded by arm chairs with high backs, each placed precisely the same distance from its neighbors and from the table itself.

"Ah, Theo," came the voice of Marvin Micari from somewhere at one side of the room. The center of the table was illuminated from the ceiling; its ends disappeared into obscurity. The great doors closed with synchronous finality behind him, the sound suffocated in thick pile carpet and regency silk draperies over windows sealed from the city outside. The huge, silent room smelled of polish and money and power. Was this the place where budget cuts were made?

"Please," said Dr. Micari off to Theo's left.

Dr. Micari was seated near the head of the table. A woman sat beside him, her back to Theo. She did not turn.

Theo waded through a harbor of deep blue fiber. There were antique buffets and commode tables overlit at the sides of the room. The walls were hung with oil portraits of stern and gloomy men in white mutton chops, full beards, and goatees. There were some contemporary faces as well, but few spaces remained on the walls. None of these people looked friendly. Or happy.

Dr. Micari motioned toward the opposite side of the table's

end. As Theo came round, he saw that the woman was Margaret Steinhower.

"Dr. Steinhower," he said.

"Dr. Tithonus." Short. Not very sweet. She seemed to have spoken to his crotch.

There were name cards at each chair place. Theo looked to Dr. Micari for direction.

"Anywhere, Theo. Dr. Steinhower and I are addressing the board in a short while. I asked you to meet us here because we have very little time before that meeting."

Theo took a chair facing Micari and Steinhower. He found himself sitting at the seat assigned to the dean of the school of medicine.

"Lovely room, isn't it?" Micari said, looking about.

This was not the adjective Theo would have chosen. "Impressive," he said, trying to make himself comfortable in an unforgiving chair.

Margaret Steinhower regarded Theo without expression. He had never scrubbed with her. He could not recall ever conversing with her. A thoracic surgeon, she was the terror of her residents. They called her The Ginzu Knife.

"There is much history here," Micari said redundantly, looking at the boardroom walls.

Margaret Steinhower glanced at her watch. She turned toward Micari. "Marvin," she said, "suppose we cut to the chase?"

"Yes," Micari said. "A very good idea, Margaret, given the time." He looked across at Theo.

Theo shifted in his chair.

Margaret Steinhower opened her file folder. She examined the top sheet through the bottoms of her reading glasses. Strands of hay-colored hair had escaped her French twist. Theo noticed that she had had minor eye work and a rhinoplasty. He took her to be about Cassie's age.

Margaret Steinhower slid two typed sheets across the table toward him.

Theo looked at his own curriculum vitae.

"Is this essentially correct?" she asked.

"Outdated. Essentially correct," Theo said.

"Impressive background, doctor."

"Thank you."

Dr. Micari moved his own folders to one side then back to where they had been. He smiled vaguely at the shining board table.

"What we have to say here shall go no farther than this room, Theo," Micari said. "As you know, Dr. Steinhower was named to be chief of surgery upon my own retirement at the end of this year. The entire board of the hospital and I were unanimous in Dr. Steinhower's appointment, even in view of her expressed decision to leave our hospital in the near future to accept a teaching position at Harvard."

Theo permitted a frown.

Dr. Micari smiled fawningly at Dr. Steinhower. She ignored him. She looked directly at Theo.

"Dr. Steinhower deserves this honor," Micari continued. "More than any other, for her years of work at this institution."

"Thank you, Marvin. You are too kind," Margaret Steinhower said to Theo. "What Dr. Micari is attempting to say is, although I accepted the appointment, upon reflection I feel that the interests of continuity at this hospital would not be served by a half-year term. I informed Dr. Micari yesterday that I must refuse the position."

Dr. Micari shook his head at this tragedy. Theo tried to look deeply concerned himself. He recrossed his legs.

Dr. Steinhower regarded Dr. Micari. Dr. Micari regarded Dr. Steinhower. They both looked at Theo. It seemed as if he were expected to speak.

"And then?" Theo asked.

Dr. Steinhower's eyebrows flicked. "And then," she said, "We began to discuss—"

"Other candidates," Micari jumped in. His face was grave. He bore his great responsibilities with considerable effort. "My first choice for the position of chief of surgery was you, Theo."

Theo considered "was" to be the operative word in this sentence. He had never asked for the position. He had never sought it out. He wanted the job, he admitted. He would enjoy the opportunity to wipe out bureaucratic foolishness which interfered with good medicine, to re-institute standards lost in cults of personality. He wanted this position in spite of his very complicated life. But after Micari's dubious prelude, his chances seemed grim. Why, then, the charade of this interview? Theo began to feel annoyed.

"We have been informed—" Micari began. There came a sharp glance from Margaret Steinhower. "It has come to our attention," Micari amended, "That you might, um, be…"

"Are you a homosexual, Dr. Tithonus?" Margaret Steinhower asked.

What is this? he wondered. He had expected something abstruse. Something more subtly crafted. Devious, even. Couldn't they have somehow laced the question of his being gay into the fabric of a university hospital's role in shaping the future course of medicine? "Dr. Tithonus, how do you as a (possibly, presumptively?) gay physician stand on the following issues of Patient Rights?", or "Theo, do you, uh, *per*sonally feel that this year's budgetary constraints upon the department of surgery in any way reflect either an ethnic or a—forgive us for saying—*sex*-ual bias?"

Dr. Steinhower regarded Theo from across the table through the bottoms of her reading glasses. Her lips were pursed forward. Dr. Micari began to draw small boxes on the tabletop with the tip of his little finger.

Theo directed himself to Dr. Steinhower. "Is the position we are discussing somehow limited as to sexual orientation?"

Dr. Micari cleared his throat and looked up. "The Hospital of the University of Pennsylvania is an equal opportunity employer," he said. What could Theo be suggesting?

"Then the question is moot," Theo replied.

"Not exactly," Dr. Steinhower replied. "In determining who will hold this important appointment, Dr. Micari and I must assure ourselves—*and* the board—that there will be no taint of, shall we say, reverse bias?"

"I don't get it," Theo said.

"Dr. Tithonus," said Dr. Steinhower, "I have been a surgeon all of my adult life. I have personally witnessed many incidences of homosexual people using their 'sexual orientation,' as you call it, to see that others of their per*sua*sion received promotions far more deserved by normal people."

"Margaret," said Micari softly.

"Marvin," said Steinhower, cutting him off. She addressed Theo. "I'm sure you know what I mean, doctor? I will not permit that to happen where I work."

"I don't know where you've worked, Dr. Steinhower—"

"It doesn't matter," she interjected. "This sort of thing has not only happened to associates of mine; I now find myself a victim of this practice. At this very hospital. It is all part and parcel of the homosexual agenda."

"Excuse me? 'Homosexual agenda'?"

"You deny there is one?"

"Dr. Steinhower," he said. "If there's a 'homosexual agenda,' I can assure you that there's only one item on its list and that's to have a happy life."

"*At* the expense of normal people?" snapped Dr. Steinhower.

"I've been a surgeon here for 15 years," Theo replied. "I've never even heard of this happening."

"Margaret," Micari said appeasably, "Perhaps we should focus here on whether Dr. Tithonus might use his own, um…gayness inappropriately. In the position of chief of surgery," he added.

Steinhower ignored Micari. "Dr. Tithonus, don't pretend to be naive. I know what I'm talking about. And I can tell you that attempts by homosexuals on the staff of this hospital to malign the reputations of straight people are going to backfire. Big time."

"Margaret—" said Micari.

"I really don't know what you're talking about," said Theo evenly.

"Oh, don't you?" huffed Steinhower. "Then how do you and your homosexual friends explain the grotesque rumor that has recently emerged concerning me?"

Dr. Micari's eyebrows arched. "What rumor, Margaret?"

Steinhower smiled thinly at Theo. "Although you people apparently think so, I don't live in an ivory tower, doctor. I do keep my ear to the ground. I have my friends here, and I hear what's being said. Don't think for a minute I don't."

Theo was nonplussed. "I'm afraid you've lost me."

Steinhower closed her folder. "Marvin, I told you we'd be wasting our time on these people."

Micari fidgeted in his chair. "I think you've lost me too, Margaret. Now, if you're talking about 'The Ginzu Knife,' well, I think really that's probably an affectionate term the residents use. Don't you think so, Theo?"

Her head jerked toward Micari. "What Ginzu Knife?"

"It's just a *term,* Margaret. All residents do that. Why, mine used to call me 'Dr. Magoo!'" Marvin Micari giggled.

"I don't find this at all amusing, Marvin. Doctor," she said to Theo, "take my advice: As soon as our meeting has terminated, I think you had better gather all your little homosexual friends together downstairs, and you put a lid on this. Do we understand each other?" she said venomously.

"A lid on what?" Theo asked. "The Ginzu Knife?"

Dr. Micari shook his head. "I don't think Theo started that, Margaret."

"Marvin, this is *all* a part of their agenda, don't you see? They think that by making up lies, pretty soon everybody's going to be*lieve* them. It's just a simple-minded political tactic, is all it is. Now you *hear* me, doctor," she told Theo. Her eyes were slits. "Don't think you can paint *me* with the same tar brush as you because you're not going to get away with it—any of you homosexuals. I am *not* a lesbian! I have *never* been a lesbian, and I have two children to prove it! Now you and your cronies march right back to your war room, mister, and you put a stop to this because I'll tell you something, you don't screw with Margaret Steinhower. *Get* it?" Veins pulsed at Margaret Steinhower's neck.

"Dr. Steinhower," Theo said after a moment. "I hadn't even heard you were a lesbian."

"I'm *not* a lesbian, goddamn it!"

"*Mar*garet," said Dr. Micari.

"I mean, the rumor," said Theo. "Who told you this?"

"I don't have to reveal my source, doctor. But *I* know how it got started." She shoved her folder to one side. "Marvin, I think you can ring for the next candidate."

"I don't believe this," Theo said.

"Marvin," she said scoldingly. "We're short of time."

Theo stood. "Doctor?" he said to Margaret Steinhower, who had already dismissed him and now looked off into the vague, dark end of the room.

Dr. Micari rustled papers nervously. "A decision will be made quite soon, Theo. You'll be informed, of course."

"Doctor?" Theo repeated. When Margaret Steinhower did not reply or even look in his direction, Theo placed his knuckles on the table across from her place and leaned on them. "I'm not a litigious person, Dr. Steinhower, but if even a breath of talk reaches me that you've suggested I've spread rumors about you, you can trust that I will sue your butt off." Theo straightened. "Good-bye, doctors." He rounded the vast table's end and crossed the blue gulf of carpeting toward the double doors.

Behind him he heard Micari mumble and Steinhower reply, "Well what did you expect from that sort, Marvin?"

Theo pushed through the huge doors and left them gaping behind him.

"Good-bye, Dr. Tithonus," trilled the receptionist as he passed her. "You have a nice day now."

Theo jabbed the elevator button. He looked at his watch. And on top of that charade, he'd have hell to pay at the office. He pushed the button several more times and waited for the elevator to arrive.

Someone sat in a claw-footed chair in Theo's peripheral vision. Someone moved his blond head behind a palm frond. Theo smiled at the closed elevator doors.

Without consideration as to what he would do or say, Theo turned and walked toward the row of claw-footed chairs. Garlington, his head at an awkward angle, regarded the ceiling. Theo took a chair next to Garlington's. Garlington neither moved nor spoke. Theo straightened his tie. He laid one arm over the other.

"What a complete surprise to find you here," he said, not unpleasantly.

Garlington moved his head to a more comfortable position but did not speak.

"I just had the weirdest experience. Margaret Steinhower just accused me of spreading a rumor that she's a lesbian. You know anything about that?"

"Tithonus," Garlington said, looking straight ahead, "kill yourself—do the world a favor."

"Cute," Theo said. "Not very witty but cute," he added. "I've been thinking a lot about you lately. Thinking a lot about 'an eye for an eye.' I've been wondering if I would suffer, say, a loss of self-esteem if I began to play your game."

"You haven't got the balls for it, Tithonus," Garlington snarled next to him.

"Oh, I've got the balls," Theo said, his tone relaxed and conversational. "You remember kissing them? The thing is, I've spent some time lately getting closer to my cultural roots...I'm Greek, I guess you know that. My people have made a fine art of vengeance. We're not like Catholics. When it comes to issues of justice, we believe that the ends do justify the means. We feel absolutely no guilt whatsoever. Greeks..." Theo shrugged his shoulders, "just don't *give* a shit."

Dr. Timothy Garlington and Dr. Theo Tithonus sat in delicate antique chairs in tailored tweed jackets and sharply pressed trousers facing a wall of glass high above the city. The receptionist fingered her strand of simulated pearls. Her smile was small and distracted. She thought that these were the very handsomest men who had ever sat in her receiving area. She would tell the girls at lunch about them—especially about the sandy haired one, Dr. Garlington, who had stood at her counter and looked down at her as if he were Nick Nolte and she, Barbra Streisand. Dr. Tithonus was very handsome too, but just a little odd, she thought, sitting there smiling and talking to himself.

"This will really tickle you, Garlington," Theo was saying. "You know, I saved every one of your old notes and letters from Hopkins? Every one. Carried 'em around with me in a box all these years." Did the body stiffen ever so slightly? "I guess I'm a pack rat at heart. In fact, just last night I was rereading the very first one you sent me. You were such a romantic back then, Garlington. Remember? You dropped that note through the slots in my locker for me to find after soccer practice. *Very* fancy stationery. Very tasteful; I was impressed. Ecru? With raised black letters at the top?" Oh, the body was definitely stiffening. " 'Timothy Randell Garlington III,' it said."

Garlington's head snapped toward Theo. His voice was chilling. "You wouldn't."

"Oh, yes. I would," Theo said to the window wall. "You were so rash. You didn't even say 'Dear Theo.' You went right for it. Remember what you said? Probably not." Although Theo continued to look out the window, he tilted toward Garlington. "You said you wanted to slide your tongue down my frenulum." Theo chuckled. "Imagine. There I was a premed student at the Johns Hopkins University, and I didn't even know what a frenulum was. I had to look it up!" Theo shook his head at this reverie, then he turned to Garlington and grinned malevolently. He put his hand on Garlington's knee and wiggled the leg. "But I sure knew what 'suck your thick, hard dick' meant! Ha, *ha!*"

Garlington looked ill.

Theo's face transformed. His black eyes glowered. His face was cold with anger as he turned again to Garlington. "Here is what you are going to do, Timmy boy. You are going to find a way to erase this Steinhower rumor completely and any connection of my name to it. Today. And if there is one more word of gossip from you or your little stooge Roberts, one more mention of my name that is not complimentary by you or by him in the cafeteria or in the surgical locker room or in the goddamned parking garage, a copy of that note goes to every…fucking…employee in this hospital. Top to bottom. And I guarantee you, there's gonna be a stampede to *Gray's Anatomy.*"

Garlington stared out the windows.

"And if you ever say a vulgar word about Susan Zack again, or even so much as approach her for a lasagna recipe, I will rip your fucking colon out and strangle you with it." Theo smiled. "You have a nice day now," he said, and strode toward the elevators.

As he stood inside waiting for the elevator doors to close, Orphan Annie led an ashen Garlington past, on their way to the boardroom.

"Timmy," Theo called out in a stage whisper, "don't forget the word for the day: fren-u-lum!"

The elevator doors closed and the car began its descent. "Yep!" Theo hooted. "He would've said that."

Stalled in traffic outside the hospital, Theo performed boxing feints at his steering wheel.

On the South Street Bridge he admired the skyline of his city, bold against threatening, late winter clouds.

He was pleased with himself. He had discomfitted his enemies. He had emerged, if not victorious, at least proud and intact. Perhaps the truth did make you free. Even embroidered with fibs.

And who needed their position? He did not work for position. He worked because he loved what he did.

What he needed to do now was to learn to work for love as well. And he would do that. He would find ways to put his personal life back together. Not all together, he amended, remembering that Sam appeared to want no part of him. But at least the rest.

Chapter 28

Each time he began to place a call, each time he lifted the bizarre telephone to dial, he returned the receiver to its cradle.

Sam Meacham had fallen victim to a sort of paralysis of the will. He wanted to call. He wanted to hear Theo's voice and say, "How're you?"

He wanted to fill his half-unpacked bags and load them into the trunk of his car and drive back to 26th Street. Place his things back on their proper shelves. Prepare a special dinner. Sit down to it and to Theo and to the life he had for years considered happy. In spite of everything.

And not sleep alone any longer in the bed in there, which—though undeniably chic, in this undeniably upscale sub-let, in this undeniably chi-chi Washington Square building—was beautiful but cold, a bed he and Theo would never have chosen.

He was, at the moment, reclining in a piece of black leather and teak furniture which he knew to have cost five of his and Theo's mortgage payments. He was, for the cost of this apartment's utilities, the caretaker of a collection of cleverly-lit contemporary art which he knew to be of museum quality. He could, from his position in this amazing chair, look into part of a kitchen which had taken most of a year to construct, could see from his friend's sleek chair dark reflections of marble countertops there—shipped, he knew, from Thailand. These rooms belonged in a magazine. Sam belonged somewhere else.

He had many times concluded in this sleek, impersonal place that his leaving home had been largely a matter of pride. Of being correct. Not of being right; there was a difference. He could be right and pack up and go home to 26th Street and his and Theo's own worn surfaces. But if he packed up and returned, he could not be correct. And he might forever lose something he could not quite put his finger on.

Nor had he had taken his stand with Theo entirely out of vanity. Partly, yes. Natalia, the heretofore unknown child. An unknown housekeeper coming in and claiming dust bunnies under his beds. Wax build-up—how dare she?

No, this was not all about vanity. There was the larger issue. Of equality.

Sam did not feel unequal exactly. He felt unequal inexactly.

Theo had never played games of profession: he the doctor, Sam the nurse. Or games of intellect; certainly that common field was level. Nor was there any form of sexual competition in their relationship. Each usually ended up getting what he wanted from the other. There was between them no top or bottom, no wished-for length or girth. They liked each other's crotches.

But in the day-to-day something did not come out even for Sam. When he added up the days, there were too many when he was left wanting. No matter how many times or in how many ways he gave to Theo, he did not feel he got back anything approaching equal.

Sam often rationalized that this was because of the way in which Theo had been socialized. There was no changing that. The older Theo got, the more he became what he was: not a man who could tell you he loved you in spite of how many times Sam might show how easy a thing that was to do; not one to dare to wear his heart upon his sleeve. Theo simply took the ways in which you tried to show him that you loved him as his just desserts, ate them, and moved on to the next event. And seldom offered to wash the dishes.

He had never set out to change Theo; had never seen Theo as a mirror in which he might one day see his own reflection. But Sam admitted that he had always hoped that by his own quiet example Theo might gradually become more the thoughtful and demonstrative man Sam thought he had fallen in love with.

Was he beating a dead horse? Sam wondered as he lay in the incredible, modernist chair. You could lead a horse to water, but...

Pick up his friend's strange phone which seemed to wish it were something else and dial this time?

And say what?

I'm coming home?

And to what?

Resolved as I am to accepting your laws of emotional latitude, I am also resolved that...

I will take no more stands?

You win. I will continue to give and to find satisfaction in being left wanting?

And at the sacrifice of what?

No. He could not.

However, if Theo were the dead horse, Sam thought, he must certainly be the mule. What was he holding out for, and why the importance of these dug-in hooves?

It was not pride which kept him from dialing, he thought with despair. It was a fear of the loss of some inchoate integrity which prevented him from picking up the absurd phone and returning to 26th Street. And he was correct in this. Wasn't he?

His father had always called him bullheaded, had said many times that compromise was not Sam's long suit. Nor had Sam called his parents since leaving 26th Street, knowing what their own stand would be. His mother would caution that he discuss things with Theo, "work things out." His father would press for details.

What could he tell his father? That Theo was useless in the laundry room? That he ordered in pizza too often? Even the large issues—of Natalia, of Theo's seeming to love his work above loving Sam, and of his forgetting birthdays and not calling when he was late—would fall upon deaf ears. His father was much like Theo in all these respects. His father would even chortle at the part about Natalia's parentage. "Well, isn't *that* something?" His parents adored Theo as he was and would take no sides against him.

And Sam loved Theo, even as he was. And admittedly would be hard pressed to make a list of negative ways in which Theo had changed since the day they met over a bin of cabbages and collard greens. He remained the same old Theo, in some ways absent minded and in others so acute. And beautiful to look at. And endearing, if truth be told, for his naive humor and even— yes, even—his unaccountable reserve. And there was no one on Sam's many horizons more easy to be with—or anyone with whom he preferred to be with—over Theo.

So why was he living in this drop-dead sublet among no objects he himself would have chosen save the clothes he brought with him, his clock radio, his parents' photograph, and the wonderful, pointy-toed cowboy boots that now twitched side to side at the ends of his Levis?

Because there was some fucking *prin*ciple involved here.

Chapter 29

Theo and Natalia trudged across the field of Schuylkill Park, which his house faced. It had been snowing for many hours. Natalia allowed him to hold her mittened hand in his glove. He allowed her to set the pace. She waddled in her boots and puffy jacket, one small child's step ahead of his. Her brown hood pointed the way toward the dark woods and the river beyond. Theo scanned the vast, white meadow for muggers and turned often to look behind them. Although they seemed to be the only people out in this freak March storm, Theo did not want to get close to the woods.

Natalia's boots creaked as she pushed forward in the eerie evening light. She said something.

"What, baby?"

"I'm *not* a baby."

"What did you say, Natalia?"

She stopped abruptly. She squinted up at him, her face to the falling snow flakes. Her nose was already running. What would he do about that? "I said, 'You said we were going to play in the snow.' "

He had asked her after her dinner in the warm house behind them if she would like to go out in the snow. Had he said "play?" He might have said play; he could not remember, but he had envisioned a brief foray out and back.

"Fine," he told her. "No, that's fine. What would you like to play?"

"We'll play Make Angels."

"In the snow?" Theo said doubtfully to the sleeve of his expensive, leather bomber jacket. "Well, how about right here? You can make a neat angel here," he said, pointing vaguely at the virgin snow just ahead of them.

"No," she replied. "Then people will walk on them." She indicated the far end of the field and the Cyclone fenced tennis courts. "There."

"I think they locked the gates for the winter, Natalia."

She ignored him and plodded forward. He followed.

There was the sound of slow, wet, and muffled traffic on the expressway across the river. There were the sounds of their feet hissing in the deep snow. Natalia snuffed mucus. Snow water trickled on Theo's forehead.

She labored toward the courts. He followed in the thin socks he had worn to work inside inadequate loafers inside squatty, shoe-high rubber Totes. The low sky glowed yellow in the lights of the city.

At the courts, Natalia lifted a hinged metal cuff. Theo pulled the gate against the snow and stepped onto the court.

"No!"

"What?"

"You'll ruin the snow! This way," she said, leading close along the inside perimeter of the fencing. "Walk in my feet."

Theo followed. He clutched the fencing from time to time—her stride so short, his feet so large. Natalia reached the midline of the court and turned 90 degrees at the netless metal post then pivoted to check that Theo was walking properly. In her footsteps.

She faced the back half of the court and pointed down. "Here," she said.

"OK. Go ahead," Theo said. "Make an angel."

"You make one here," she indicated. "And *I* make one here. Next to yours."

Theo hesitated. He was wearing the fine wool trousers that belonged to a suit. He had had to make bargains with himself before purchasing the leather jacket.

"I'll watch you, Natalia."

"You *said!*"

"What?"

"That *we* would play."

"Natalia," said Theo petulantly.

Natalia lowered herself into position, flat in the snow on the court, her arms at her sides.

Theo stood a foot or two away.

"Farther," she instructed. "You go where your wings will touch mine—just touching." She stretched a jacketed arm in his direction as his guide but did not mar the snow beside her.

Theo moved a few feet on. He crouched. Never mind the lovely trousers. Never mind the buttery jacket. A deal was a deal. He lay back in the cold snow but did not allow his head to touch.

Natalia made an exasperated noise. "You have to put your head in the snow or your angel won't have any *head!*"

Theo's head dropped back.

"Now, we both *do.* Touch my fingers. Yes. Just touch." Natalia spread her legs and her arms out simultaneously. She repeated the motions several times. Her head turned toward him. "Don't you now *how?*"

"I *know,*" Theo groused and spread his own arms and legs. Snow banked against fine fabric.

"Now, you stay there," Natalia instructed. Cautious of her snow impression, Natalia got back to her feet. She gauged distances and dropped to a perfect, new canvas on the other side of Theo. "Now you go over here," she said, pointing to her other side.

"All right. But only one more," Theo offered parentally.

"No," she said. "We have to fill this. This whole side."

"Natalia, it's very wet and cold. I don't want you to catch pneumonia." Theo brushed snow and water from his pinstriped pant legs.

"We just got here."

"All right, that's a heck of a lot of angels."

"We have to keep the lines straight," Natalia told him as she passed him on the way to yet another position. "So they're all in rows."

"Natalia?"

"You have to move your legs more or the dresses won't be good."

"I'm making men angels," Theo sulked.

"NO! My pants are soaked. Now that's enough, Natalia."

"Ten more. Each."

They stood at the gate of the tennis court in slackening snow-fall. Theo's wet trousers were sticking to his numb legs. His bomber jacket hung wet and limp from his shoulders.

"See?" she said, pleased at their work. "ALL angels on this side. No angels on that side…It's *very* beautiful," she pronounced.

"Sort of like heaven and hell," Theo muttered at the orderly host of shadows before them.

"Do you like them?"

"Yes. I do," Theo said. "They *are* very beautiful," he added with some wonder. And they were beautiful, he thought. How many? A hundred large and small angels alternating? How long since he had played in the snow? How long since he had played?

"Now we have to close the gate," Natalia said quietly. "Or people will come in and step on them."

"OK," Theo whispered in the silent park.

"We can come and visit them tomorrow night," she said. "That'll be fun too."

"OK."

She set off across the field toward the house. Theo lingered at the Cyclone fence. There had to be at least a hundred. So uniform. So strangely lit in the clouded glow of city lights. He noticed that his own angels became far more professional toward the back of the court, their gowns wider, their wings far more extended.

"Theo!" she called back. "We have to go now!"

She asked him after they got back to the house and he had changed if she could go into his room to see if she could see the angels from the house.

She got herself ready for bed without their normal hassle. She called down the stairwell, "Good night," in a small voice.

"Good night, baby," he replied without thinking, and she did not take issue.

Chapter 30

Theo and Eubeeda Jones sat at the counter of the fifth floor nursing station. They reviewed their surgical schedules for the coming week. She was, in his view, the best instrument nurse on staff, and he tried to get her on all his teams. They made adjustments on their sheets to assure that they would work together.

"I can scratch Monroe, " Eubeeda said, "But you gotta move Hammond up from 3 o'clock to 2."

"Where will I put Conway?"

"You can put her out on the street, far as I'm concerned. Calls me 'girl.' My mother can call me 'girl.' No snotty white woman's gonna call me 'girl.' Huh-uh. You better not schedule me for her at *all*, Theo. You ask me for a hemostat, and I'll be handing you a wooden stake for that white bitch's heart."

"Then get me Bernadette Poscaparo for the white bitch."

"Can't. She's off Wednesdays. I'll get you Maria deJesus. You like Maria deJesus."

"The-o! The-o!" called a woman's voice above them. Sondra Micari stood tiptoe at the high counter. She was wiggling her hand across at him.

"Could I see you for just a minute? I am very sorry to interrupt," she told Eubeeda Jones.

"I won't be long," Theo said.

"White ass kissah," Eubeeda muttered.

"Hush, Nigrah girl," Theo muttered back.

Sondra Micari could barely contain herself. She directed Theo down the hall toward a windowed day room. "I've been looking all over for you," she told him, hauling her mink coat and strap purse under one arm. Her free hand gesticulated. "Well, not obstetrics; I didn't think you'd be there."

Theo held the day room door. Sondra Micari peered in to be sure the room was empty. "Great," she said. She tossed her fur and bag across a vinyl couch. "Sit," she commanded toward a round table.

"Did Marvin call you this morning?" she asked across the table.

"No."

"Well, he will. Have you heard?"

"Heard what?"

"Oh, *won*derful!" Mrs. Micari trilled. "Because it's spreading like wildfire. It'll be all over the hospital by lunch!"

"What will?" Theo said.

"Well," Mrs. Micari began. "I heard it twice already this morning, once from Marvin at breakfast and again a half hour ago from Gigi Roberts. The women's auxiliary? I'm president of the women's auxiliary, did you know that?"

"Yes."

"This is my third term," she said proudly. She leaned forward. "The women's auxiliary raised over a million dollars for the hospital last year. Did you know that, Theo? That's not small change."

"I didn't realize," said Theo, wondering where she was going with this.

"Gigi Roberts is my vice president. Gigi is a tireless worker. She's got a mouth like a sailor, but she's just as cute as a button. I don't *know* what I'd do without her," Sondra Micari mused. "But the poor thing has absolutely the dullest husband in the world. Do you know him? Millard Roberts?"

The Hummer? The Hummer had a wife named Gigi? With a mouth like a sailor?

"I know him," Theo said shortly.

"Gigi's version is much juicier than Marvin's, I can tell you."

"Her version of what?" he asked, to move her on.

"I did everything I could, Theo, but Marvin simply would not budge. After that little altercation you had with Margaret Steinhower yesterday." Her palms went up. "No. Don't get me wrong. I'm proud of you for standing up to her, Theo. You took the *only* honorable course. However, be that as it may, Marvin and Margaret chose not to see reason and decided to make Garlington the new chief of surgery. Look," she said, turning to the windows then back to Theo. Her palms dropped to the tabletop. "I tried. I tried my damndest. But Margaret insisted on the snake in the grass, and Marvin went along because he was convinced she walked on water. At least until last night."

Theo felt resentment. And disappointment. But the decision did not come as a surprise to him. He had read this writing on the boardroom walls.

"Well," Sondra Micari said, beaming now. "That was then, and this is now! *Wait* till I tell you the rest!

"Marvin and Margaret had agreed to have dinner together last night to talk about whatever happened at their board meeting, but what she didn't know and should have is that Marvin likes his dinner at 7 and I don't mean 7:15. In any case, she hadn't arrived in the lobby yet, and he apparently got impatient and came upstairs looking for her. And who does he run into in the hall but Millard Roberts. Marvin asked Millard if he had seen Margaret Steinhower. Millard said she was probably in her office, but that she shouldn't be disturbed. Marvin replied that he'd disturb her if he pleased, and he marched right down there with Millard going 'Umm, uhh, doctor' behind him, and he rapped on her door and opened it right up, and what did he walk in on? This is the part I got from Gigi Roberts: Timothy Garlington standing there buck naked in the middle of Margaret Steinhower's oriental rug, and her on her knees mooning Marvin, and Millard behind him, while she gnawed on Garlington's you-know-what! Marvin called it 'flagrante delicto' at breakfast, but that is *not* what Gigi Roberts called it."

Theo hoped he did not look delighted. "What did they do?"

"What *could* they do?" Sondra Micari squealed. "Margaret crawled behind her desk. Garlington tried to cover himself with his hands—which, according to Gigi Roberts, cannot be done—and Marvin backed out the door. Marvin was livid, and he started to leave, but then Gigi said he opened the door again, and he yelled inside, 'Well I guess this means you're not a lesbian, *huh,* Margaret?'

"This morning Marvin had completely changed *his* tune, I can tell you. He wants to have them both dismissed for 'unprofessional conduct,' and he wants you to be chief of surgery! Now what do you think of them apples?" Sondra Micari said, sitting back in her chair with great satisfaction.

Theo took a breath. He exhaled. "No," he said.

"What do you mean, 'no?' "

"I'm not interested in being chief by default. I already decided I don't want the job at all."

"But you have to take it. This is a coup. A feather in your cap. This position will help establish you as one of the preeminent surgeons in this country!"

"Yesterday I wasn't good enough? Today I'm the best man for the job because I didn't have sex with Margaret Steinhower? No, thank you."

"You're being very childish, Theo."

"Childish," Theo repeated, offended.

Sondra Micari sat upright in her chair, her face quite stern. She folded her hands in her lap. "My life has revolved around this hospital for the nearly 20 years we've lived here. Let me tell you something, Theo. You either seize power and become an agent of change, or you end up a cipher like Millard Roberts. You have the choice. You can go home and lick your hurt feelings, or you can grab some power and change things. For patients. And for people like yourself. And my brother Wiley," she said, standing.

Sondra Micari walked to the couch. She took up her mink and her purse. She crossed the day room. "I am very fond of you, Theo," she said at the door. "But I must tell you that this is no time to be behaving like a dolt. Now you think on this before Marvin calls you." She was gone.

Theo followed the steaming path of the University of Pennsylvania's Locust Walk, his sport jacket tossed over his shoulder. The snow of the night before had been shoveled onto budding jonquils and banked against winter-weary yews, out of the way of fast moving students whose faces seemed desperately young to Theo. Given the opportunity, he would not want to be as young as they again.

He was the only person on the path who meandered. He who had not the time to meander; he whose office filled with hopeful patients as he wandered in blinding sunlight reflected on disappearing snow; he who was 46 with more life behind him than ahead considered the muddle of his life and the decision that would further complicate it.

He would accept the appointment. He might reply to Micari with ambivalence, say that he required a day or two for further consideration. But he would take the job because Sondra Micari was correct: He was thinking like a victim and licking his anger. Why not take the opportunity and run with it? Further humanize the hospital. Instead of sulking over attitudes like Steinhower's, why not grab the power and attempt to change doctors like her?

Physician, heal thyself, he thought as he strolled. Who was he to be thinking of changing other people's attitudes? He wasn't even in control of his own life. He was the most thoughtless of lovers and of friends, barely coped as a parent, and it was his intention to set out to humanize medicine in one of the great hospitals of America?

Well, he would. He had until December to humanize himself, didn't he? To make time for sleep-overs with Daddy. Breakfasts with Daddy. Driving home with Daddy after PlaySchool.

Or Nintendo with Daddy? On each occasion something, another small step toward making up for years of ignoring a child.

And he would somehow make up to Sam his having taken him for granted. Leave a score or two of phone messages at the Jefferson Hospital ER for him? Lay in its halls on a gurney until Sam finally walked by? "Hi. Remember me? I'm the jerk you tried so hard to make a life with?"

Step by painful step.

He would ease Boldini into their practice, see that Susan's workload became manageable. He would listen harder when she spoke.

Theo pulled down a branch of witch hazel. He smelled its insignificant flowers, the scent of an aftershave no longer in fashion, the first thing to bloom in the spring, according to his father. Look for it in the woods, his father said, when Draco's head stood just above the northeast horizon, his tail separating the Bears: Ursa Major and Ursa Minor.

Rock salt crackled on the wet walk under Theo's shoes. A half mile away, snow angels were dissolving on a tennis court and would not be there to visit tonight. What fun that had been, he thought with a smile. But such a transitory pleasure.

Theo imagined himself old. He imagined himself old and

comfortable. Then imagined himself telling someone that he had lived a comfortable life, one without great waves. A life, even, without profound interaction. He had had a dear friend once with whom he shared a medical practice. She retired to California.

They had a daughter once. Yes, he and the woman.

And where was the daughter now?

Who knew? Natalia never called. She didn't write.

You didn't get along?

Theo didn't know.

But he had had a lover once. For five smooth, comfortable, and uneventful years. Or was it six? Something like that. No, Theo no longer knew where he lived.

What, you fell out of love?

Things happened. Nothing happened. Theo took the responsibility for that.

But he had been a fine surgeon. That part had been good.

And suddenly Theo needed to get to his car. He no longer meandered. He needed to pull together a life.

He had parked on the fourth floor. He entered an elevator at the atrium level of the hospital and stepped back to make room for a group of second-year residents who also entered the car. "Dr. Tithonus," one said deferentially as they pressed in. "Pardon me, sir," said another.

"Hi," Theo said.

"Hey, Theo," Wiley Branstetter called back from the front of the elevator.

"Hey, Wiley."

"Hold that car!" commanded a voice out in the atrium.

Wiley grasped the door's leading edge. Passengers pushed toward the rear until Theo's back was to the wall.

"Ah!" said Wiley at the front of the car. "Another country is heard from. Good *mo*rning!"

"Doctor," Garlington replied curtly as he backed into the group.

"Your floor?" Wiley asked.

"Three," said Garlington.

The doors closed.

"Five?" called a resident a foot or two from Theo, then said to his companions, "Pray for me, guys. The Ginzu Knife wants to see me."

The car began to rise.

"Better keep your clothes on," said one of his friends.

"You kidding?" said the first. "She's older than my mother."

"You didn't hear?" asked his friend. "The chief caught her giving some surgeon a blow job last night. In her *office!*"

Theo's heart leaped.

Wiley Branstetter's head turned. He was smiling beatifically.

"You're shitting me. Who?"

The skin at the back of Garlington's neck darkened.

"The new one, they're sayin'. The inventor guy. What's-his-name."

Garlington? the name formed on Theo's lips. Timothy Randell Garlington the Third? But Theo held his peace. And his tongue. He existed today in a new state of grace.

Wiley Branstetter coughed. The car slowed. "Three?" Wiley said innocently. But Wiley Branstetter did not exist in a new state of grace today. "Dr. *Gar*-ling-ton?" he called. "Didn't you want three?"

Garlington tried to push at the opening doors.

"Oh, Christ!" said the second resident as Garlington bolted out. "That's the blow job guy!"

Garlington hurried around the corner and down a hall.

The doors slid closed.

"They say Micari's out for blood," said the second resident. "I wouldn't want to be in his shoes."

The car rose. Wiley Branstetter's smile was elfin. He looked back. "Fourth floor: stroller rentals, Dr. Tithonus."

"Guess that's me," Theo said. He grinned at Wiley as he passed.

Theo stepped out of the elevator. He stopped to search his pockets for keys.

"He's gay, you know. Tithonus," whispered one of the residents behind him.

"So am I," Theo heard Wiley Branstetter say.

"No shit?"

"Yeah. And rumor has it *he's* going to be our new chief," said Wiley Branstetter. "One hell of a fine surgeon," he added.

The elevator doors closed.

Chapter 31

When Theo returned home Saturday morning after hospital rounds, Mrs. Cristobel told him he had had two calls: one from Susan, one from his sister Cassandra. He was not to call his sister back. She would not be home. Dr. Zack told Mrs. Cristobel she would be returning from California Sunday afternoon ("Isn't *that* just the best news?"); Mrs. Cristobel would be working henceforth at Dr. Zack's house. She hoped that her work in his home had been satisfactory?

"Oh, beautiful," Theo told her. "Just fine."

The hose on the washing machine had sprung a leak, she told him. Not terrible yet, but he was to have it fixed Monday. The remains of the petty cash lay on a kitchen counter next to her receipts. He was invited to check the accuracy of her accounting. All of Natalia's clothes had been washed and put away. He was to do her packing for her the following day, she instructed. And the cat, of course; he'd have to deal with that. She could be reached at her home during the rest of the weekend but she hoped he wouldn't need to call her because her sister was visiting. Mrs. Cristobel prepared a long list of orders for his "regular house cleaner" and left promptly at noon.

"Hey, how about that?" Theo said to Natalia. "Your mommy's coming home."

Natalia did not appear to be thrilled.

That afternoon, Theo and Natalia climbed through the plastic auricles of the great heart at the Franklin Institute. They placed their hands on an electrified globe and laughed at each other's hair. They went shopping.

Theo and his daughter Natalia sat across from each other at a table for two on the first floor of Le Bec Fin. Theo wore an Italian suit and his new tie. Natalia was demurely uncomfortable in a dusty rose number with a large, lace collar, chosen with the help of a clerk at *I Primi*.

"My mommy never brought me here before," Natalia remarked, looking about the glistening dining room.

"Your mommy and I have been here lots of times," Theo said. Natalia pulled at her collar.

"Natalia, why don't you just try the pâté? It's sort of like hamburger."

"I want a hamburger, please."

"It's all ground up."

"No, thank you."

"Natalia, this is one of the best French restaurants in the country. How about if you just *try* something French?"

Natalia's lips tightened.

"Fine," Theo said. "A hamburger. How would you like them to cook it?"

"On a bun."

Natalia drew fork lines across the top of her *crème caramel.* "Theo?" she said. "When is Sam coming back?"

"I don't know."

"Why don't you?"

"Why don't I what?"

"Know when Sam's coming back?"

"He hasn't said."

Natalia dragged more fork lines, perpendicular to her first set.

"You and Sam are fairies, aren't you?"

Theo choked on his espresso. He glanced right and left. "Natalia, what are you talking about?"

"Billy Bastian said you were."

"Who's Billy Bastian?" said Theo.

"My friend at PlaySchool."

"Ah."

"He said you and Sam probably diddle." She split her *crème caramel* into halves.

Did a time ever come, Theo wondered, when there was peace? When you could just live your life?

Theo eyed neighboring tables, then he said very quietly, "Natalia, what is 'diddle?' "

Natalia squinted. "Touching pee-pees." Her head tipped back. She scanned the room and waited for confirmation or denial.

And they sat, father and daughter, at their first public meal, in this very decorous restaurant, more finely dressed than they had ever been together, stalled on the subject of the touching of pee-pees. Natalia, fork in hand, looked at herself in one of the room's many mirrors. She seemed pleased at her reflection. She even seemed to like the dress Theo had bought for her. Theo looked into his coffee for answers.

But what was the question? What was 'diddling?' No. Diddling had been defined. Were he and Sam fairies? Well, in a manner of speaking. Fairies, yes. As it were.

Theo frowned. This was many times more awkward than the dark, spongy silence of the hospital boardroom.

But why make a big deal over a simple fact of life? he thought.

270

He was the parent. She was the child. He would handle this blazing issue in an open, frank, and positive manner. He ironed his forehead.

"Natalia," Theo said, leaning far forward, the better to keep his voice low. "Fairies is a word we use for imaginary people, not real people."

"I know that. Billy means the *other* kind of fairies," she said in what sounded to Theo like a scream.

"I'm sure he does. But what Billy meant was that Sam and I are 'gay.' It's a better word. Sometimes men love each other and live together like Sam and I do. Like we did. Sometimes women love each other in the same way. But most of the time, women and men fall in love with each other. That's the way it'll be with you, I think. When you grow up."

Natalia regarded first her *crème caramel,* then Theo. "Did you and my mommy?"

"Did we what?" Theo asked.

"Touch pee-pees?"

Was there no end to this?

"No," Theo said. "Yes," Theo said, unwilling to discuss masturbating into a plastic cup.

"Which?" she asked.

"We did. Yes." She knew about pee-pee touching. She brought it up. "Your mommy wanted to have a baby. Very much. To have you. I did too. And I'm very glad we did have you, Natalia."

Natalia seemed disturbed. She patted a half of her dessert with the bottom of her fork. "It's very nasty, you know," she said.

"...Touching pee-pees?"

"This," she muttered, pointing at her plate.

They stood on the sidewalk outside the restaurant waiting for Theo's car to be brought around. Natalia embraced her coat against the March wind. Her black hair blew across her face. Theo moved closer to shield her. To his surprise, she stepped inside his open overcoat.

A dark Lincoln town car glided to the curb and stopped. The passenger door yawned open. "Oh, just *stop* that, Marvin! It's only quarter to 8." Mink-wrapped, Sondra Micari launched herself from the vehicle.

"What a lovely surprise," she burbled at the curb. "Hel-*lo,* dear," she said to Natalia. "My name is Sondra Micari."

A small hand reached out, thumb up, fingers stretched as he had seen Susan's extended hand hundreds of times over the years. Had Susan taught her this? Were handshakes embedded in DNA? "How do you do?" Natalia asked.

How do you do?

"Well, I am just fine, thank you very much. And you?"

"I am very well," replied the little Antichrist with a dignified, if distant smile. "This is my daddy," Natalia said, pulling the flap of his overcoat toward Sondra Micari.

A frog came to Theo's throat.

"Well, the goddamned thing can just sit there in the street," Marvin Micari groused behind them.

"The valet's off getting my car," Theo explained.

"Theo," said Micari, clearly surprised and suddenly ill at ease.

"How are you, Marvin," Theo allowed himself.

"Fine. Fine. You?"

"I don't think you've met my daughter, Natalia. Natalia, this is my boss, Dr. Micari."

The small hand came out again and was engulfed in Marvin Micari's. Micari grunted. "You look just like your father, little girl."

Natalia did not appear pleased to hear this. Theo wondered if it were his predominant nose or the "little girl" part.

"Theo," Micari said, "May I speak with you?" He guided Theo aside with the palm of one hand on Theo's back. Dr. Micari leaned his head toward Theo's. The eyes were watery behind little, round spectacles. "Nice coat," he said. He ran a hand down a sleeve. "Very nice. Yes...Um, Theo. I've been wanting to call you. But frankly, Theo," he said, gathering fortitude, "I've been very embarrassed. After...you know," Micari said into the restaurant's awning.

Theo offered Micari a faint but encouraging smile.

"I, uh...I want you to know that the job of chief of surgery is yours, Theo. If you will take it. I know. I *know*. And I want to apologize for all that...you know, the other day. I allowed , uh, a friendship to interfere with judgment, and I wouldn't blame you if you thought the less of me now. No, sir. But I *want* you to take that position, Theo. And you take as long as you want to think about it. A week. A couple of weeks."

"No," said Theo, shaking his head.

Micari's brow furrowed. His mouth opened.

"That won't be necessary. I accept the appointment. I would be honored."

Micari smiled weakly. "Thank you. Thank you, Theo." He gave Theo several firm, man-to-man pats on the back and turned awkwardly toward his wife. "Sondra. Come now. It's well past dinner."

His wife ignored him. "Theo, I've invited Natalia to have lunch with me at the hospital some Saturday, if that's all right with you and Susan."

"If Natalia would like to. Thanks."

Marvin Micari coughed behind them.

"I am *com*ing, Marvin!"

Theo sat in his reading chair in the den. Natalia snored down the hall. Should children snore? Should he have her adenoids checked?

A successful dinner with Daddy. A museum trip with Daddy. Shopping with Daddy. A day she seemed to have enjoyed.

And they had had conversations. And she had referred to him as her daddy. And revealed, to his continuing surprise, social skills he had not known she possessed.

She had bitten no one. Nor had he.

Chapter 32

Natalia chewed shredded wheat bits.

"Your mommy's coming back this afternoon. How about that?"

Natalia shrugged her shoulders.

"Don't you miss her?"

"Yes." She offered a soggy wheat bit to her raccoon. "Can I please stay one more day?" she asked. "I can help make dinner. I know how. Or we could go to that place again."

Theo was astonished. "But your mommy's coming home."

"I know," she sighed. "Just when we started to have fun."

"But don't you want to see her?"

"Yes. Anyway, she's never home," Natalia confided to her cereal bowl.

"She'll be home more now," Theo said. "I promise."

"She's always tired. And she doesn't take me places."

And I do? Theo thought.

"I can make hot dogs and canned corn," she offered. "Sometimes we have that on Sunday when Mrs. Cristobel isn't at our house. It's my favorite…I'm allowed to use the microwave if there's an adult."

"But I have to go to work tomorrow. How would you get to PlaySchool?"

"You could take me."

A short time ago he had been counting the days—the hours—until she would go back to her mother. He found himself deeply touched, both that she would want more of him and that the idea of more of her was not at all unattractive.

"Maybe not tonight. I think your mommy will want to be with you. But maybe a weekend? Even next weekend."

"She wouldn't let me. Unless you told her."

From noon to 3 they did the Philadelphia Zoo. They began with the petting zoo, an area which Theo thought a brilliant concept and which she quite quickly pronounced boring and "for little kids." It was amphibians that interested her. Then reptiles, chiefly snakes. Until she discovered the Hummingbird House, where for four extra dollars apiece they stood in a steaming tropical jungle inches from tiny, long tailed birds and were buzzed by them as they walked ferny, stone pathways. She talked of this place all the way back to 26th Street and asked to return there as soon as Theo could arrange that.

"*This* is my new dress," she told her mother. "*Theo* bought it for me."

"It's *very* beautiful," Susan said. She placed the dress over the back of a living room chair.

"No," Natalia corrected, taking up the dress by its hanger. "You have to hang it. The lady said. It gets wrinkled if you don't hang it. I wore it last night. *We* went to a restaurant."

"No! Which one?"

"I don't know, but Mrs. McCarty is taking *me* to lunch at the hospital."

"Who is Mrs. McCarty?"

"*She's* the *Pres*ident."

"Sondra Micari," Theo explained.

"Where'd you see her?"

"Le Bec Fin."

"Well, didn't you two get around. I'm very impressed. Sweetie, how about if you hang your new dress downstairs by the door and then go find Rula?"

Natalia ran off obediently. Susan plopped onto the sofa.

"You look great," Theo told her. "Rested. You look terrific."

"I'm a new woman. Actually, I got home yesterday," she whispered. "I was already home when I talked to Mrs. Cristobel."

"Needed a little more alone time?"

"I had almost a week of alone time. I needed together time. There was a message on the machine when I got back to call Dennis, so I called him."

"Who's Dennis?"

"The cute oncologist from Wilmington? With the buns? The one I had to cancel the date with because of you? He wanted me to come to Wilmington. I went." Susan lifted her glowing chestnut hair with both hands. "We had such a good time. God, did we have a good time. He asked me out again for next Saturday. You wouldn't mind, would you?"

"No. I owe you, I guess."

"He gave me a very thorough pelvic, Theo. Three of 'em, in fact. Two last night and one this morning." Susan's eyes sparkled. "I think he's crazy about me. He called me on my cellular as I was pulling out of his driveway this morning. I *like* this man. A lot...But I could never marry him."

"Jesus. He asked you to marry him?"

"Of course not. We've only been together once. But his name is *Pack*er!"

"So what?"

"Don't you get it? If I married him, I'd be Susan Zack-Packer!" Susan snorted. She fell into her lap and squealed.

"I'm glad you're back," Theo said.

"Is Sam?" she asked, straightening.

"No."

"What's going on?"

"Who knows?"

"Give me his number. I'll find out."

"I don't know where he is. He called once, but he didn't leave a number. He won't answer my calls at Jefferson."

"I'm sorry."

"It's not your fault," Theo said glumly. "It's mine."

"Thank you for taking care of Natalia." Susan leaned and kissed Theo. "I was a real jerk to take off like that when you had problems of your own."

Theo shrugged. "It'll work out. One way or the other. Probably the other," he added.

Susan squeezed Theo's hand. She stood. "Well, I'll get my kid out of your hair."

"Saturday," Theo said. "Why don't you drop her off before your date? She can spend the night."

"You *want* her?"

"Yeah."

"Really?"

"We get along."

Susan looked at him quizzically.

"But ask her first," Theo said.

They loaded the suitcase and the child into Susan's car. And the toys. And the bags of cat food and the litter tray. And finally, the enormous cat, who settled calmly between Natalia's legs.

"Thanks," Susan said out the window. "Very much."

"Did I tell you? I hired Boldini," Theo said beside the car.

"Boldini?" Susan said. "I love Boldini. Why didn't *I* think of Boldini?"

"Mommy?" said Natalia in the seat beside Susan.

"Thank you. For doing that."

"Mommy."

"I wasn't sure you'd handle it," Susan said.

"Oh, ye of little faith."

"*Mom*my."

"I think my faith's coming back," Susan replied and put the car in gear.

"Mommy, don't *drive* yet! We have to talk while Theo is *here!*"

"*What*, sweetie?"

"*He* said I can come here next weekend." Natalia folded her arms across her chest. "Can I or not?"

"Well, sure you can."

"What *time?*"

"We can call him about that. Later in the week."

"We'll call you later in the week," Natalia told Theo.

Susan began to back out of the driveway. "*We* made angels in the snow," Theo heard his daughter tell her mother.

Theo worked in his den. He drew the changes he would make to the face of a young woman nearly beaten to death by her ex-boyfriend. The boyfriend had concentrated on her head. He told the police that if he could not have her, he wanted to make it so that no one would want her.

That would not be so. Though she would not have the same face as before, she would—in a year or two—have a face which many would find beautiful. But because of the damage done to her, she would always look slightly puzzled. Or curious, Theo thought as he sketched in the late afternoon light. Always, even in repose, even in sleep her expression would be that of one who had just been presented with a thought-provoking idea. If she became a teacher, a university professor, she would seem slightly perplexed even by theorem which had no mystery for her. She would always look interested. But slightly at sea. Men would go bananas over this face.

The house was silent. No child watched television. No music swelled. Sam's pots did not clank in the kitchen.

Theo inventoried toiletries for his gym bag. He had not worked out for a week and would feel this the day after tomorrow.

He hung a suit in his suit bag. He draped a tie over folded trousers. The evening stretched emptily before him.

When the doorbell rang he scurried for his wallet, thinking that this was the pizza delivery man. Pepperoni with double mushrooms on thin, crisp crust—not the doughy kind.

However, it was not the front doorbell which had rung but the rear. And it was not the pizza man who stood outside the door but his sister Cassie.

"He's here!" Cassie called back toward her dark Cadillac. "We didn't know," Cassie explained. "We took a chance."

Behind her, Thalia struggled to extricate a very long box from the back seat.

"Do you need help?" called Cassie without enthusiasm.

"Well what the *hell* do you think?" snarled their sister, juggling the box and the car door.

Theo took the box from Thalia. "What is this?"

"We don't know," she said. "Daddy said it was for you. Well? Aren't you going to invite us in? We need a drink."

Theo carried the heavy box up to the kitchen and placed it on the work island.

"Vodka," Cassie said before the women had removed their coats.

"Scotch," said Thalia.

280

"We went to the lake," announced Cassie.

"We drove up this morning," said Thalia.

"It was a purely social call," Cassie clarified.

"Cassie called Daddy yesterday to chit and chat and try to find out if they were going to be around today, then we drove up and surprised them. They were both in shock."

"How are they?" Theo asked, amazed his sisters would have done this.

"Fine," said Cassie. "Daddy looked wonderful. Very chipper."

"*Very* chipper," Thalia repeated.

"In spite of having fallen this week," Cassie rolled her eyes.

"In the woods," said Thalia. "Apparently Rosy has told him he's not to go in the woods alone, but you know Daddy. "

"He was hunting for arbutus. Can you believe that?"

"She says it doesn't even bloom for a couple more weeks."

"He fell over a log and hurt his knee. He was barking a lot about that, but the doctor said he didn't break anything."

"He could have broken his hip," Thalia added.

"He's very lucky."

"So," Theo said, handing them their drinks. "Everybody…got along?"

"If you're talking about Rosy," said Cassie, "Yes. It was a bit cool at first."

"That's putting it mildly," said Thalia.

"I don't blame her," retorted Cassie. "I told you that in the car, Thalia. We haven't been…easy, but I'll also tell you that I'm trying to look at this from a new perspective. She does dote on him, I'll grant her that," she told Theo. "And she's sincere, I think. I mean, it wasn't all a show for our benefit. By afternoon I thought we were getting along quite well, Thalia."

"Oh, we were. They took us to the Inn for an early supper, and afterward she even invited us to come back."

"My," said Theo.

"And invited us to spend the night next time."

"I don't dislike her," explained Cassie.

"Well," said Theo. "This is very nice."

"It's a start."

"A very good start," amended Thalia. "And where is our new niece?"

"She went home today. Susan's back."

"I told Bradley Junior and Martha about her. Bradley Junior wanted to know how you accomplished the 'transfer of sperm.' "

"Thalia, really," said Cassie.

"Martha proceeded to explain the process to him as she read about it on the Internet, and I left the room."

"I talked to Daddy, Theo," Cassie said.

"*We* talked to Daddy," said Thalia.

"About finances and things," continued Cassie. "He gave me a piece of his mind."

"*That's* putting it mildly."

Cassie frowned. "He explained to me the way it will be."

"I told him that the insurance was an obscene amount of money to give Rosy," Thalia interrupted, "And he told me he didn't give a shit what I thought."

"He told me to mind my own business."

"Not quite," corrected Thalia. "We changed the subject."

"You're getting the lake house, just like you said."

"And we have no problem with that, Theo."

"Either of us."

The doorbell rang.

"Thalia, come," said Cassie. "We're going. Theo has company."

"It's the pizza man."

"Oh, sure," said Thalia.

"Thalia, put that drink down. Pick up your coat."

"It's just the pizza man," said Theo.

"We only came to drop off Daddy's present."

"And have an adult cocktail beverage," added Thalia, gulping from her glass.

"Really. You don't have to go. Have some pizza."

"We ate."

"At the Inn. We don't drink in front of Daddy," said Thalia, snatching up her coat.

"He's not allowed to drink," explained Cassie in the stairwell.

"Enjoy your pizza!" he heard Thalia call from the first floor as he descended behind them. "Or whatever!"

Below him he heard the laundry room door open and Cassie scold, "Thalia, honestly! You are incorrigible sometimes."

"What did *I* say?"

The laundry room door closed.

Theo went to the front door.

"Hey, doc," said the pizza delivery man. "I thought you'd be Sam."

"He's out."

"I wondered why you only ordered one. Fourteen-fifty. Say, listen," he grinned. "Tell Sam when you see him, 'she's not.'"

" 'She's not...?' "

"She thought she was, but she's not. He'll know what I mean."

The box had been wrapped with care, strap-taped in many places with "fragile" in his father's even print. There was an envelope taped to the packing materials inside. He lay this aside and folded back many sheets of bubble wrap.

"Oh, no," Theo whispered over the elegant instrument. It was his father's telescope—his most prized possession. Used over many years of nights, its metal tubes and tripod legs had on them not a spot of corrosion or an apparent fingerprint. His father must have packed this wearing gloves.

Dear Theo,

Since it seems from your recent letter to us that you have begun to look up and my own vision these days is becoming rather more pedestrian than astral, I want you to have the pleasure of this marvelous device.

As for the other, no. We have spent no time fussing over how you were raised, only a bit over the issue of why it might have taken you so long to tell us about these very important aspects of your life. We didn't know about our granddaughter, of course, but it was quite apparent to us both from fairly early on that your interest in women was, shall we say, academic?

No matter to us. We love the Theo we know.

However, if you do not bring that grandchild up to meet us very soon, there will be hell to pay.

Love,
Dad

When he called while Theo was attempting to fold the pizza box such that it would fit into the kitchen trash container, he said only that he would like to drop by. "Would that be all right?"

"Sure," Theo said.

"Twenty minutes?" Sam asked.

"Sure," Theo said.

During the 20 minutes before Sam was to arrive, Theo had several crises: of clothing (did he look all right, appealing in khakis and a polo shirt?); of neatness (the beds were not made, breakfast dishes still lay in the sink); and of agenda (was Sam just coming to pick up possessions or would they talk?).

He made the beds. He put the dishes in the dishwasher and

284

sponged the sink dry and while performing these tasks prepared himself for any eventuality. Even begging.

Should Sam find him, say, in his den working? Or in the living room watching something cultural on television? As it happened, Theo was struggling into his third shirt selection when he heard Sam call out on the second floor: "Theo?"

"Hi!" he called back. He mopped his forehead with a corner of their bedspread, tucked in his tails, hurried down the hall, then made what he considered a blasé descent of the stairs.

Sam stood, arms crossed, shoulder to the kitchen door frame, deliciously casual in what he had always called "dress-down cowboy drag:" the boots, worn jeans, a thousand-times-washed flannel shirt. The sight of Sam made Theo ache for what he believed to be lost times.

"Hi."

"Hi."

"How're you doing?"

"Fine. You?"

"Fine."

Sam did not move from the doorway.

"I was just...working," Theo said.

"I just thought it was time to call an end to the moratorium."

"That'd be good," Theo said.

"I thought we might talk."

"That'd be good. You want to sit down or something?" asked Theo, waving his arms about.

"No. I was thinking we could go to neutral territory. Take a walk, maybe."

"Sure," Theo said. "Where to?"

"It doesn't matter. Just out."

"I'll get a jacket," Theo said, moving toward the doorway in which Sam stood.

As Theo was about to pass, Sam reached out and plucked

something from his shirt.

"What," Theo said.

Sam read a paper tag. "It says, 'Every attempt has been made to repair this damaged garment.' "

"Huh?"

Sam turned Theo by his shoulders.

"It's the back of your shirt. A lot of it's missing."

"Oh," Theo said, feeling about. There was a gaping space back there. His cheeks flushed. "I'll change."

"Just grab a jacket."

They walked down 26th toward Spruce past the homes of neighbors, few of whom they knew, past homes which had been severely modernized and others which, like their own, retained the original statements of their architects.

Trellises leaned, plant stakes listed within the dark, fenced community gardens across the street. Sam's metal-studded toe tips tapped the sidewalk; Theo's right loafer squeaked. His bomber jacket also squeaked.

"I've missed you. Very much," Sam said after a time as they walked and looked ahead toward their unknown destination.

"Me too," Theo said. "I missed you."

"And I've been thinking about a lot of things all week."

"Me too."

"I made up a sort of manifesto for your consideration."

"I didn't do that. I sort of see myself, you know, as the aggrieving party in this."

"That's true. But it's also true that I bring a lot of this on myself. The house. Things I get myself too caught up in. Not very important things, it seems like. I forget you have a life beyond me."

"Maybe I'm too much into work."

"Maybe. Maybe not."

"But I can't stop that, loving what I do."

"I don't expect you to. I was thinking about this for my manifesto. A sort of trial balloon. You ready?"

"Sure."

"When I talk to you from now on, could you pay attention?"

"OK."

"Like really listen?"

"I haven't done that very well, but I'm catching on...What else?"

"That we set aside time that's ours and nobody else's."

"I'd like that."

"A couple times a week is enough for me, if it's good time."

"We can. That can be."

"Did you hear that part? Good time? When we really communicate, and you don't withhold important things."

"I don't always know what's important to you."

"Theo."

"I do always know. I just don't know."

"And we need some specific rules."

They were walking now so that their steps had slowed and were more in unison, left foot taps simultaneous with left foot squeaks.

"Like what?"

"If you can't be home by 7, 7:15, you call me. I worry, Theo. Not just about this city not being so brotherly-loving anymore but driving. And things that happen. I see them come in my ER doors. Awful things. I worry about you when I don't know."

"I will. I'll do that."

"Tell me about Natalia."

"What about her?"

"What are your plans around her?"

"I don't think I have any."

"That isn't true. Don't withhold, Theo. I hate when you do that."

"I know. There I go…She's going to be very important to me, Sam. A part of my life."

"I don't want to be a parent."

"You don't have to be."

"By default or any other way. She comes to our house; if you have to leave, I'm the parent. I won't do that."

"But I have to leave sometimes. If I get called?"

"I don't mind being a caretaker. An adult in residence. The nice, caring man left in charge. But about the important decisions, you have to be the parent."

"I don't understand."

"Theo, except for the practice of medicine, *every*thing in your life is totally amorphous. Me. Your friendships. Your family. Even your daughter. It's as if you gave us all permission to hang on you like ornaments. And when we begin to annoy you, you shake us all off."

"Do I?"

"Do you?"

"Yeah."

"I was expecting a battle. I can't believe this compliance."

"I'm a desperate man…This week was horrible. Work was horrible. I missed you. And Natalia was horrible. Until a few days ago, then we started to talk some. And we did things together. Little things. We made snow angels the other night. Back there on the tennis court. Fifty of 'em. Each."

"You?"

"We went to the Franklin Institute. We went downtown shopping together. We went to the zoo. She completely changed from this awful creature to this sweet little kid."

"You gave her your attention," said Sam to the sidewalk. "We're exactly the same as her. All of us. All your ornaments."

"I didn't think I was that bad."

"You're not bad, Theo. Just oblivious sometimes."

"OK. I am a lot of the time. But don't expect me to change overnight." Theo sighed. "This takes work, I'm figuring out. But I can live with your terms, Sam."

"You haven't heard them all."

"What else?"

"Pizza."

"Pizza."

"You can't order it in more than once a month when I'm home."

"I don't know. Can I have a little time on that one?...What else?"

"Sex," Sam said.

"Sex."

"Three times a day."

"Why three? Why not two? Or four?"

"All right. Four."

"Sam, I'm 46 years old."

"Two then."

"How about if we see what happens? I've got a lot of surgeries coming up."

"How about if we just say 'more often?' "

"I can do that. When would you like to start?"

"What time is it now?"

Theo rolled toward Sam's side of the bed.

"Sam?"

"Theo, I've *got* to get some sleep."

"The pizza guy says 'she's not.' "

"She's not what?"

"He said you'd know."

" 'She's not'...Oh, right. I get it."

"Hey, Sam?"

"What."

"I'm gonna be the next chief of surgery."

"That's…that's wonderful, Theo. Proud of you."

"Steinhower gave Garlington a blow job. Right in her office."

"I'm glad. Good for Steinhower."

"Micari caught them."

"Sam? Sam?"

"Jesus, Theo. What."

"I can't sleep. I'm wide awake…I love having you back here. In this bed."

"Me too, Theo."

"Natalia wanted to know when you were coming back. She asked me when we went out to dinner. I didn't know what to say. I didn't know if you were coming back. The worst part was when you didn't return my calls…. I thought, 'OK, I've ruined this. I didn't pay attention to balances and he's finally decided to jump off the scale—gone. For good.' I hated that feeling…But somehow it helped having her here. I thought, 'At least here is a clean blackboard. At least here is a person I can sort of start fresh with.' I mean, God, we were stuck together. We had no choice. It was either learn to talk or draw a line down the middle of the house.

"Or chew each other up. She bit me one night. I couldn't believe it. You know what I did, Sam? I bit her back. Right on her bum. There I was, a grown-up adult plastic surgeon holding down a five-year-old, biting her bum. I felt really terrible, you know?…Sam? Sam?"